Bury Me A G

Tranay Adams

Lock Down Publications
Presents
Bury Me A G
A Novel by *Tranay Adams*

Tranay Adams

Lock Down Publications
Email: tranayadams@gmail.com
Facebook: Tranay Adams
Like our page on Facebook: Lock Down Publications
@www.facebook.com/lockdownpublications.ldp

Cover design and layout by: Dynasty's Cover Me
Book interior design by: Shawn Walker
Edited by: Shawn Walker

Acknowledgements

I would like to thank everyone that has purchased my novels, reviewed, and suggested them to a friend and/ or has given me a shout out. I greatly appreciate it. There are too many of you to name so I hope this will suffice. Thank you a trillion timez for your support. I fuckz with chu the long way.

Shouts out to my turf, South Central Los Angeles. I stay putting on for our city. I hope to make my brethren proud. Salute!

Salutationz to all of my label mates.

Big upz to my editor, Shawn Walker, the best in the business. That'z on mommaz.

LRB if they don't know they don't need to know.
Hookah, I hope we stay friendz forever, I love you to death.
Netta, what'z understood doesn't have to be said.
Tiaz, I just made you immortal. Lol #MyGuyTy

Ain't No Friendz In Dis Shit! It'z All Business, Nuttin' Personal. If I close my eyez after this one, just know that I gave this game my all. I tried to kill it every single time I put dat pen to dat pad, I swear to God. I waz tryna be the best there ever waz or ever will be. Hopefully I gave you a classic outta deez four bookz 'cause I for damn sho' tried. #DaLiezICantTell #RealLife

The Saddest Thing In Life Is Wasted Talent-Alonzo *A Bronx Tale*

Tranay Adams

Chapter 1

The sun went into hiding bringing forth the night and allowing the white marble known as the moon to reign over the City of Angels. Its glow stood out in the dark sky and dimly illuminated all that was beneath it.

A black on black '94 Chevrolet Caprice with pitch black tinted windows and chrome twenty-two inch rims pulled into an oil stained driveway. The loud music playing within its confines could be heard faintly as it caused the vehicle to vibrate. Once the engine of the ghetto classic was executed, its Carolina blue headlights died along with it. The driver's side door swung open and Chevy stepped out carrying a purse and lunch bag, making her way to her white stucco home.

Chevy was a slim, high-yellow chick with a dimple in her chin. She stood five feet seven inches and had long jet-black hair that reached her heart shaped ass. But the highlights of her features were her soft brown eyes and full lips.

She had just left from her job at Platinum Protection Security. She was a $12.34 an hour security guard for the company. The pay wasn't all that grand, but combined with the money she had stashed it helped to keep the bills paid and a roof over her and her son's heads.

The gig was pretty much easy. All she had to do was play watch dog to an under construction apartment building. The tenement was downtown on Skid Row, so most of the time she was chasing off homeless people looking for some place to crash for the night, or scrap metal and copper to steal and sell. When she wasn't doing that, she was scribbling down chapters that would eventually be her first urban lit novel *I Got Your Back*. Since she was a little girl she fantasized about being a published author, mentioned beside the likes of Donald Goines, Ice Berg Slim, Claude Brown and the rest of the greats. So for now, she was on her grind. Writing, working and stacking dough aside that she'd need to publish her book.

When Chevy entered through the door of her home she found her ten year old son, Te'Qui, and her younger brother, Savon, sitting on the couch playing the PS4.

"Hey, momma." Te'Qui greeted his mother without taking his eyes off of the flat-screen. He was an intelligent but very impressionable kid that rocked his hair in five cornrows and wore glasses.

"Hey, baby," Chevy responded, hanging up her hefty jacket and lunch bag. She kissed Te'Qui on top of his head before heading into the kitchen.

"What are y'all playing?" She took a Heineken from the refrigerator and leaned against the doorway of the kitchen.

"Madden," Te'Qui answered.

"Yep, and I'm beating the brakes off of him, too." Savon chimed in.

Savon was fair skin, much like most of the members of his family, compliments of his Puerto Rican heritage. He sported his hair in a close fade that swirled into 360° waves. His right eyebrow had an old scar over it that stretched over onto his eyelid.

Savon was making a pretty good living peddling crack about four years ago, until two jack boys crashed his trap and left him with two in his chest. That was the day he turned his back on the game.

Not long after he left the hospital, he gave his remaining products to his lieutenant and took what money he had to start his own business, *Cleanliness Is Next To Godliness*. It was during his recovery when he decided his life wasn't worth the cost of the hustle, so he didn't mind backing out and going legit. At least after he handled all unfinished business.

About two weeks after he returned home, the cats that robbed him were found in the basement of an abandoned house hog tied with the back of their skulls blown out. After paying his debt to the game and tying up loose ends, Savon cleaned his hands and strictly operated his cleaning service business.

"Te'Qui, did we get any mail?" Chevy asked after feeling inside the letter holder and finding it empty.

"Uh huh." Te'Qui answered, chewing his tongue and working the controller. His eyes hadn't left the flatscreen.

"Well, where did you put it?" Chevy grew impatient with his vague response.

"Umm, it's on the nightstand in your room. What're you looking for? A letter from your jailbird boyfriend?"

"Te'Qui!" Chevy shouted and stomped her foot angrily. "What did I tell you about putting my business out in the street? You want me to come over there and smack you into next week?"

"Ah, decisions, decisions." Te'Qui flippantly spoke before Savon punched him. "Ouch!" He rubbed his arm and looked at his uncle like he was crazy. Savon was wearing a scowl like a young Ice Cube in his N.W.A. days. "Whatchu hit me for?"

"For talking back to your mother. Now get cho ass in your room! I'll be in there to talk to you in a minute." Savon's eyes followed Te'Qui as he didn't hesitate to head into his bedroom, frowning and rubbing his arm. He got to his feet and turned off the flatscreen and the PS4. Savon treated Te'Qui more like he was his son. He, his sister, and his nephew were closely knit. He loved them to death.

"What's up with chu, Chevy? You can't find one of them white collar brothas to square up with? After Faison I thought chu would have had enough of these thug ass niggaz." He popped the cap off of the Heineken he'd just gotten out of the refrigerator.

Faison was Chevy's ex-boyfriend and Te'Qui's father. They'd been together since high school and had plans to get married down the line.

Faison was heavy in the streets, trapping like his life depended on it. But he would definitely put his money where his heart was. He copped the house Chevy and their son lived in and the car she drove. He'd even set aside the dough Chevy needed and still has set aside for her book to be published. Everything was running as smoothly as a well-oiled machine and their relationship seemed to be picture perfect, that was until Chevy came home one day and found Faison dicking down the next bitch.

At first Chevy just stood in the cracked opened door silently crying, but then something within her mind snapped. Her face twisted with anger and she barged into the bedroom. She located the gun she had stashed inside of the closet. Faison was trying to give her an explanation for his infidelity, but she wasn't trying to hear none of that shit. She turned around spewing vulgarities and letting her ratchet buck. Faison and his fuck-buddy had escaped outside in the nick of time. The girl had managed to flee with her life, but he had caught one in the shoulder and went stumbling to the sidewalk. Chevy stood over him with her cannon pointed down at his face ready to blow him away.

"I loved you. I fucking loved you!" She roared like a lioness with hot tears streaking her cheeks as her chest rose and fell. She whimpered and her bottom lip quivered. She wiped her tears away with one hand but quickly placed it back on her weapon, double clutching it.

"Baby, please!" Faison winced and pleaded, lifting his hand.

"Don't 'baby please' me! You got caught fucking another woman in my bed. In my bed? Really, Faison? In my mothafucking bed?" Her brows furrowed and her jaws squared, "Kiss your black ass goodbye, nigga!"

She was about to pull the trigger when Savon snatched the pistol from her grasp.

"Fuck are you doing?" Savon spat, snapping her back to reality. She blinked her eyes as if she were in a dream and looked down at Faison. He was groaning in agony and his blood was sprinkled over the cracked sidewalk. "Get Te'Qui and take 'em in the house and lock the doors."

Chevy looked to Savon's car and Te'Qui was inside with his face and hands pressed against the glass, he'd seen the whole scene unfold before his eyes. She didn't question him. She just got her son and they ran into the house, slamming the door shut and locking all of the locks as her brother ordered.

Savon tucked the pistol on his waistline and got Faison to his feet. He planted him into the passenger seat of his Camero and drove off. He wiped the pistol clean of Chevy's prints and tossed it into the gutter.

"Listen up, I don't know why my sister shot you. In fact, I don't even give a shit." Savon explained as he maneuvered his Camero through traffic. "Knowing what kind of person she is, I'm sure she had good merit. But should any harm come to her over this you may as well grab a shovel and start digging a fucking hole for yourself 'cause you sure as hell gonna be a dead man. You hear me?" His scowling face snapped from the windshield to Faison.

"Arghhh." Faison grumbled in agony grimacing as he held his bleeding shoulder, his blood seeping between his fingers. He was too consumed with his wound to refute what had been said. So he just lay there wrinkling his forehead and gritting his teeth, writhing. "Errrrgh."

That was a year ago. Since then Faison would send his men over faithfully every weekend to pick Te'Qui up so they could spend time together. He'd stop coming by once they'd fallen out about her seeing this local hustler by the name of Azule.

Faison hated the ground he walked on. He was what you would call one of those old swagger jacking ass niggaz. He walked, talked, and even acted like Faison. As if that wasn't enough. The nigga wore his hair and dressed exactly like him, too. Now he was laying the pipe to his bitch. *Goddamn!* Faison couldn't wait until the day came when he came across that ass because he was going to do him something bad.

The cold part about it was Chevy wasn't even messing with dude anymore. He sold her a dream, got the pussy a few times, and disappeared. The nigga changed his number and even moved. It was like he'd went into the witness protection program.

Chevy folded her arms to her chest. "Last time I checked, you were a thug, too."

"Ex-thug, sweetheart, I'ma business man now. Cleanliness Is Next To Godliness." Savon held up the logo of his company which was emblazoned on his denim Dickie shirt.

"Well, painting stripes on a hippo doesn't exactly make it a zebra, now does it?"

"Whatever, Chevy. I'm through with the streets." Savon lied. He wasn't slinging crack, but he was selling ounces of exotic weed on the side. It wasn't because he needed the money. He just loved the thrill of the hustle. He tried to step back but it kept calling him. So with little fight, he was back in the mix that held him hostage.

Chevy knew all about Savon keeping one foot in the game and the other in the square world because she knew her baby brother was full of shit. She gave him the *yeah right* expression, waved him off and took a swig of her Heineken.

"Look, I'm worried about chu, that's all. You're my big sister and I love you. I don't wanna see you get mixed up in some shit behind some dude, feel me?"

"Aww, that's sweet of you, but you don't have to worry about me. I can handle myself. Trust." Chevy smiled and pecked her brother on the cheek before leaving the living room, taking the remainder of her beer to the head before tossing it in the nearby trash.

Chevy entered her bedroom closing and locking the door behind her. She removed her nightstick and her Glock. After storing them away, she peeled off her uniform and tossed it into the clothes hamper. Throwing on a gown, she sat down on the bed and shuffled through the mail that lay upon her nightstand. Finding the letter she was looking for, she slid under the covers and ripped open the envelope. She unfolded the letter that was inside and began to read it.

What's up, Love?

How are you doing? I hope well. As for me, I'm alright. As good as alright can be when you're living under these circumstances. I'll make it though, niggaz like me are bred to survive anything. I've missed you, which is funny considering I just saw you two days ago. Those two days seem like a century, crazy right? I'm not trying to game you or nothing. I'm just telling you how I feel, keeping that shit one hunnit, like I always do. I can't wait 'til your next visit when I can see that beautiful face, admire that breathtaking smile of yours, smell the scent of that sweet perfume you wear and feel your body pressed against mine when we hug. Damn, you gotta nigga thinking about breaking up outta this bitch to come and see you. It would be worth the extra time I'd get. Anyway, I can't wait to see you again.Take care of yourself and lil' man. Peace.

Love always,
Tiaz

Chevy held the letter to her chest and fell back in bed, a smile curling her lips. She then flipped over and buried her face in the pillow screaming. "Oh, my God. I'm like so in love with him," She moved her legs like she was underwater trying to swim.

She rolled back over, glancing at the letter and kissing it. She exhaled and stared up at the ceiling, thoughts of him going throughout her mind. She then folded the letter up and placed it back inside of the envelope, sitting it inside of the nightstand drawer.

After pushing the drawer closed, she turned off the lamp light and snuggled under the covers. The smile transcended to a grin as thoughts of Tiaz carried her off to sleep.

Chevy had never been the one for online dating, but one day while she was getting her hair done at the salon she heard this lady talking about how she'd met the love of her life on Penpals.com. Initially, she turned her nose up at the idea, feeling as though she was too good to go looking for her soul mate on the net. But one lonely night she decided to to make a profile and go browsing.

She was hesitant at first but she went ahead and contacted Tiaz. They went back and forth messaging one another until he had to go. They talked about anything and everything under the sun. She felt like she knew him inside and out. It was like they didn't have any secrets between each other. He was real easy to talk to and understanding. He didn't judge her for anything, nor did she judge him. They got along great. Their souls were the perfect marriage.

***

"What I'm tryna say is since your father isn't here, you're the man of the house now. And it's your job to love, respect and protect your mother, man. All y'all have now is each other." Savon lectured his nephew as he sat beside him on his bed.

"What about you?" Te'Qui looked up to him.

"You'll always have me. Your unc ain't going anywhere." Savon threw his arm over Te'Qui's shoulders, pulled him close and then kissed the top of his head. He then glanced at the calculator watch around his wrist. "Let me get up outta here. I gotta be at work in the next couple of hours." He rose to his feet and headed for the bedroom door. He pulled it open and was about to step through it when his nephew called him back. "What's up?" He threw his head back.

"I love you. No homo," Te'Qui stated.

Savon chuckled, "I love you too, neph'." He closed the door behind him as he left, locking up the house.

Te'Qui locked his bedroom door behind his uncle and dashed over to his dresser. He pulled open the drawer and reached under his folded undershirts. He grabbed a red bandana and a pair of black sunglasses. He tied the bandana around his head Tupac style and slid on the sunglasses. The dips of his forehead deepened and his nose scrunched up as he struck gangster poses in the full body mirror, throwing up the set he was destined to be from.

"Yeahhh," he spoke, feeling like an official G as he took in his reflection. He wanted to be the hardest, grimest nigga living from the Bloods and he wouldn't stop until he'd gotten that glory.

Chapter 2

Tiaz sat on the commode taking a shit and flipping through the pages of Smooth magazine as his cellie laid across his bunk. A sheet hung along a line that separated them and as soon as he dropped a turd, he'd flush it. This was done out of respect for his cellmate and so he wouldn't funk up their living space.

Tiaz' cellmate was his partner in crime and closest friend, Cameron or Threat as he was called in the streets. He was lying on the top bunk with his hands clasped behind his head. The prison was on lockdown over a riot between the brothers and the Mexicans so they were holed up in their cell together.

"When was the last time you heard from her?" Threat asked after listening to his road dawg tell his story.

"'Bout six months now." Tiaz answered as he flipped through the tattered magazine.

"Six months?" Threat raised an eyebrow. He couldn't believe that long of a time had passed since his then right-hand man talked to his main squeeze.

When Tiaz was out in the streets, he and Ta'shauna hadn't spent so much as a day apart. Back in the day, if Tiaz wasn't off scheming on another dollar, he was with Ta'shauna booed up.

"Yep, six months." Tiaz rose to his feet wiping his behind. He dropped the toilet paper into the commode and flushed it down. Once he pulled up his boxers, he carried his six foot muscular frame over to the sink and washed his hands under the flowing faucet water. "I called her house and the number was disconnected. I called her mom's house and she claimed to have not heard or seen her, but that's bullshit! I tried to hit her up the next day and a recording came on the line saying the subscriber didn't accept phone calls from correctional facilities. What do you think is going on? You think she's creeping out on me?" He stared at his reflection in the mirror watching the water that he'd splashed upon his face run and drip from off of his chin.

Tiaz rocked a fade and a 5 o'clock shadow. His body was covered in muscles. His form looked chiseled and as solid as steel, like if you'd knock on it a sound would echo. His complexion teetered between pecan brown and bronze depending on the season and the weather.

Since the age of fourteen, he'd been in and out of correctional facilities. He was a man that preferred to solve his problems from behind the barrel of a gun. He and Threat had been as thick as thieves since elementary school. The pair was almost the exact replica of one another personality wise but physically, they were drastically different.

Whereas Tiaz was a tall and muscular cat, his partner in crime was short and skinny, with skin as black as ash. He sported a thin mustache and a fade rippled with deep waves.Having the Napoleon complex he was quick to violence, making sure his bite was feared more than his bark.

Threat didn't know if he should tell his closest friend what he really thought. He knew Tiaz was in love with Ta'shauna and if he'd gotten the idea in his head that she'd been fucking around on him, it would kill him. Although he was known as a straight up killer in the streets, when he was with Ta'shauna he was as harmless as a bunny rabbit. He worshiped the ground she walked on and treated her like she was the queen of Egypt. There wasn't anything he wouldn't do for her. He loved her unconditionally. Hell, his sole reason for being locked up was behind her.

One day while Ta'shauna was coming out of China Town Express over on Florence and Vermont. A knucklehead, wanting to pull a jack move, punched her in the eye and yanked the gold Rolex chain Tiaz had gotten her for her birthday from around her neck. He took her bracelet and all of the rings on her fingers. He also took the food she'd purchased. She was mortified and went home with a swollen black eye that silently told her man what had occurred.

"Fuck happened to your face?" Tiaz held her about the chin as he examined her eye.

"I got robbed coming outta the Chinese food place off of Florence."

"By who?"

"I don't know who the nigga was." She admitted teary eyed, a bit shaken up by what had transpired with her hands trembling.

"Chill, babe, it's okay." He embraced her lovingly. "I'ma take care of this nigga for you, that's on everything. Now can you remember anything that I can use to identify this fool by? A scar, a tattoo, or something?"

He watched as she thought about it.

"He had a tattoo of a pit bull on his neck."

"Was it fading?" he asked.

She nodded yes. "Do you know him?"

"Mothafucka!" He looked to the floor with his hands on his waistline.

"Bae, you know who did this to me?"

"Know 'em? I'm about to give the nigga his eulogy. Go get my shit."

While Ta'shauna went to get his Glock, Tiaz got dressed for the funeral. A black Dickie suit, Chuck Taylors and black sunglasses was his attire. This was his murder gear.

Click Clack!

He chambered a round into his head bussa and tucked it at the small of his back. After kissing his lady hard and passionately, he headed out of the house to go on his mission. He knew exactly who the cat was that got at his boo. He knew him from around the way. He was a young hoodlum that went by the name Tim-Dog.

Tiaz knew exactly where to find him. He rode through the Hoovers and just like he suspected, he spotted him posted up at a Jack in the Box on Manchester and Figueroa. He was chopping it up with some big booty broad. Too distracted to see death creeping up on his bitch ass.

"Alright, what is it?" Tim-Dog asked, looking down at his cell's screen ready to punch in old girl's number.

"323-759—"

Bloc! Bloc! Bloc! Bloc!

A succession of gunshots ripped through the night's air cutting the conversation short. Tim-Dog's legs burst with blood looking *like busted ketchup packets. He hit the ground in the parking lot hard, dropping his cell phone. The chick he was macking ran off as fast as she could, after kicking off her high heel pumps, screaming at the top of her lungs.*

"Ahhh! Ahhh! Ahhh!" she hollered.

"Shut up, bitch! Keep pushing 'fore I blast on yo ass too!" Tiaz' voice boomed. Setting his sights back on Tim-Dog, he advanced on him, banger pointed at his face.

"Ahhh, shit, man! My mothafucking legs!" Tim-Dog looked down at his bloody lower half in hysterics as he clutched them. His excruciation was plastered across his face. "Sssssss, Ah, damn!"

"Your legs are about to be the least of your fucking problems!" Tiaz stomped his legs twice.

"Arghhh, arghh!" Tim-Dog grimaced before looking up and seeing the gun trained on him. His eyes widened like a deer caught in head lights when he saw his deviant lifestyle flash before his eyes.

Tiaz snatched Ta'shauna's Rolex chain from around his prey's neck and relieved him of the two bands he had in his pockets.

"It's time to pay The Piper, homes." He pointed that steel back up at his face.

Tim-Dog squeezed his eyelids closed and clenched his jaws, waiting to feel the hotness sizzle his brain when God smiled upon his black ass in the form of a police cruiser.

Urrrp! Urrrp!

Tiaz reactively darted out in the middle of the street, attempting to flee the scene and got hit by a speeding car. He went over the length of the vehicle and crashed to the asphalt on his back squirming and grimacing. When he peeled his eyelids open two police officers were standing over him with their guns pointed in his face.

"Shit!" Tiaz groaned. His body was in pain and now he was fucked.

He took a plea deal for five years and got sent out of state. It was there he ended up cellmates with Threat who was doing a bid for robbery.

"Talk to your nigga. Let me know what's real. Keep that shit one hunnit, too." Tiaz told Threat as he lay back in his bed staring up at the bottom of his bunk. He poked the bottom of his comrade's bunk trying to get his attention once he didn't answer him right off.

"Come on, Threat. You know how we do, give it to me straight, no chaser."

Threat closed his eyes and exhaled summoning up the nerve it would take to give his friend the truth. "If you haven't heard from Ta'shauna in six months, I think it's safe to say she's living foul."

"What chu saying? That she's fucking around?" Tiaz sat up in bed, he already knew what his homeboy meant but he was hoping he'd heard him wrong. Threat's silence was enough for him. He knew what it was now. He brought his hand down his head and over his face, exhaling.

He shut his eyes and got mental flashes of Ta'shauna being sexed by another dude. He envisioned closeups of her face as she enjoyed nearing an orgasm. He could hear her cries of passion echoing inside of his head, and it was driving him insane. His face twisted into a mask of rage with veins sprouting out of his forehead and neck. As he balled his hand into a fist tightly, he saw the dude that was busting his lady down get up from between her legs and approach him with a smug grin, saying, *"I'm her daddy now."* Tiaz' eyelids snapped open and with a growl, he stood up and punched the solid concrete wall. There was a crunch and crackling sound and then excruciating pain engulfed his hand like the flames of a fire.

"Arghhhhh! Shit!" He gritted in agony, cradling his broken hand. Threat jumped down from the top bunk and went to his homeboy's aide.

"Fuck." Threat frowned as he examined his hand.

"Argh! I think I broke my hand!" Tiaz grimaced.

Threat rushed to the bars calling out for the correctional officer. "C.O! C.O!"

The C.O came hustling down the tier as fast as he could.

"What happened?" He asked as he unlocked the cell.

"I don't know. He broke his hand somehow."

"Shit." The officer examined Tiaz' hand. "You're gonna have to go to the infirmary."

"No shit." Tiaz winced as he got to his feet, cradling his hand. Escorted by the officer, he went to go get his fractured hand checked out at the prison's medical facility.

A few days later…

Tiaz stood in line with the rest of the convicts impatiently waiting to use the telephone. He couldn't wait to get on the jack to try to reach Ta'shauna again. He'd convinced himself he'd dialed the wrong number before when first trying to reach her. Anything was better than believing she truly washed her hands of him.

Tiaz was one person behind from using the telephone. He blew hard and rolled his eyes, having to listening to homeboy plead with his girl to put money on his books. He shook his head and massaged the bridge of his nose. It was quite sad. Once old boy in front of him wrapped up the conversation with his broad and hung up the telephone, he was right behind him picking the receiver back up. He punched in his number and placed the phone to his ear. He tapped his fingers in a rhythm on the wall while tapping his foot and listening to the phone ring.

When someone picked up, he stood erect ready to talk but it was a recording that came on.

We're sorry, but the number you've reached has been disconnected, or is no longer in service…

He hung up the phone and dialed the number again and received the same recording. He dialed the number once more, but this time he pressed the numbered buttons slowly thinking maybe he'd accidently pressed the wrong buttons by accident when he first called. Again, he received the same recorded message.

Tiaz couldn't believe Ta'shauna had changed her number on him. He could feel his rage building inside each time he dialed the number and received the same result. He had ended up dialing her number fifteen times before he'd known it. Unbeknownst to him the convicts behind him were getting antsy. Many of them were talking shit under their breaths and whispering to one another, but one cat in particular had the balls to step to him.

"Damn, homie! How many numbers you gon' dial? There are other niggaz waiting to use the jack!" The man known as Bishop barked.

Tiaz looked him up and down with twisted lips like *Nigga, you best raise the fuck up out of my face.* He then focused his attention back on the ringing telephone, paying Bishop's ass no never mind. When someone finally picked up, he spoke into the receiver. "Auntie, have you heard from—" Before he could finish getting out what he was trying to ask, the dial tone had sounded off in his ear.

He looked up and Bishop was removing his hand from the lever. Rage exploded in his chest and he went into beast-mode right on the spot. He whipped around on that nigga and cracked him in the face with his casted hand, breaking his nose and causing blood to spray from his nostrils. Homie cupped his spurting nose and staggered back. Tiaz was on that ass, though. He cracked him upside the head with his cast twice, slumping him against the wall in a daze. The rest of the convicts gathered around as he kicked and stomped dude out, giving him that work.

Bishop's head deflected off of the wall. He was barely conscious. His eyes were rolled to their whites. All he could do was sit there as he took a crucial ass beating. The convicts cheered and egged him on. The C.Os then rushed in. Tiaz was able to knock a couple of them out but eventually he was slammed to the floor. The correctional officers mashed the side of his face into the cold dirty floor and battered his back with their nightsticks.

Crack! Whack! Wop! Bop!

Tiaz' forehead wrinkled and he clenched his teeth as his back was assaulted by the black steel rods.

"Ahhhh! Fuck you! Fuck you!" He bellowed over and over until a sharp blow to the back of the dome put his hostile black ass out cold.

***

Threat was out on the yard watching two convicts in a heated verbal exchange. They were freestyle battle rapping while a hefty dude provided the beatbox by cupping his meaty hands together and spewing unique noises with his lips. The two rappers had drawn a sizable crowd. They were going at it for a big carton of Camel cigarettes so they were giving it their all.

Threat was enjoying the show and seemed to be impressed with the lyrics the two men were spitting. He thought it was too bad that they were lifers because they sure enough had the talent to be signed to a major record label.

A short peanut head man with black bags under his eyes and a beanie pulled low over his brows strolled over to Threat. He tapped him on his arm and motioned for him to lean closer so he'd hear what he had to say.

"What's up, Roach?" Threat asked.

"They just tossed your boy into the hole." Roach informed.

Threat's forehead wrinkled. "For what?"

"Got into it with that nigga Bishop over the jack. Broke homeboy off something real proper like, too."

"Good looking out, my nigga." Threat dapped him up.

"No problem, folks," Roach replied, before wandering off through the crowd of prisoners.

Chapter 3

Tiaz spent the next few weeks in segregation exercising, pacing the floor, and thinking about Ta'shauna. He'd been locked up for nearly five years and everything seemed to be going smoothly between them. For a time, they'd kept in contact with one another regularly through letters, telephone calls and visits. In fact, the last time she'd come to visit him she seemed to have been her usual radiant self. She didn't show any signs of being upset with him, so he couldn't understand why she'd gone AWOL. Tiaz began to think that Threat was right. Maybe she had hooked up with someone else and had forgotten all about him. He didn't want to believe it but there was a strong possibility it was true.

If she did that to me, then that's fucked up. After all the shit I've done for her. Out here hustling in the streets, throwing stones at the penitentiary. I put a roof over her head, clothes on her back, food on the fucking table, copped her new whip. Helped her raise her son, treated the lil' nigga like he was mine. I know that bitch ain't gon' try to play me like that! Shit, she the reason why I'm locked up inside this shithole! Tiaz thought to himself.

His face twisted with anger and rage stirred inside of him. He cocked his good fist back as he was about to punch the solid cement wall again, but at the last second he caught himself. Having looked to his casted hand, he remembered what happened the last time he'd punched the wall. Tiaz lowered his fist and allowed the rage he'd built up to slowly die. He lay back on the hard one inch, state issued mattress and tried to calm down. His imagination had gotten the best of him. He was jumping to conclusions. He didn't have any proof that Ta'shauna was stepping out on him, but yet in his head he'd already played her judge, jury and executioner.

Tiaz rested his arm behind his head and stared up at the ceiling in deep thought. The only way he could find out if his lady was creeping or not would have to be through Threat. His homeboy would be going before the parole board sometime next week. If he got paroled, he would have him do some investigating and find out why Ta'shauna had run off like she had.

Finding his eyelids growing heavier by the second, Tiaz eventually closed his eyes and drifted off to sleep.

One week later...

Tiaz stood in his cell shadow boxing. His body lightly sweated causing his wife beater to cling to him like latex. His forehead was wrinkled and his eyes held the concentration of a man attempting to defuse a bomb. His fists were swift and calculated, moving like flashes of lightning. His breaths were quick and measured, with each of his fluid movements.

Fuck Ta'shauna, the thought of his lover came across his mental once again. *If she shitted on me, she ain't gon' live long enough to regret it. That's on my pop's grave. Play me? Nah, never that, bitch just made it easier for me to move on. I'ma just take this as a sign from God. He blessed me with Chevy and put me in this situation to see that my old piece ain't shit. Good looking out G.O.D. A nigga see the light now.* He lifted the crucifix from off of his chest and kissed it, looking up into the sky. *Thank you, Lord,* he mouthed to The Man upstairs.

Moments later...

"I made parole! I'm going home!" Threat appeared at the cell wearing a jovial expression across his face. He picked Tiaz up and spun him around. He was excited, real excited. Finally, after three and a half years he was going home. He sat his comrade down and they embraced, manly like.

"I'm going home, baby. Home!"

"Congrats, my nigga." Tiaz chuckled, genuinely happy to see his man free. He gave him a complex handshake and snapped his fingers. He patted him on his back as he retrieved his store sheet of goods, looking over it.

"Yo man, I got plenty of shit on here that you can have. I mean, it isn't like I'm going to need it now that I'm going home." He turned around with the sheet. His forehead crinkled when he saw the worry written across Tiaz' face. "What's up, T? What's happening, homie?" He dropped the sheet at his side.

"Ain't nothing." He exhaled and sat down on the bottom bunk. He steepled his hands under his chin and let his thoughts take him away.

"How long you been my nigga?" He leaned against the sink, folding his arms across his chest.

"Since third grade." He looked up at him.

"Exactly, I've known you long enough to know when something is on your mind." He tapped his finger against his temple.

Tiaz blew hard and brought his hands down his face. "It's this shit with Ta'shauna. It's eating me alive not knowing. I gotta know, fam. I can't sleep until I know what's up with her."

Threat looked away nodding, understanding his friend's position. If he was in his shoes he'd want to know too.

"Look, once I get outta here I can ask around if you want. See exactly what's going on with ol' girl."

"You would do that for me?"

"I would do that for my brother," he nodded.

Tiaz shot up from the bed. "Aw, thanks, Crim. Thank you so much." He gave him a brotherly hug. "Shit means a lot to me. It's killing me behind these walls not being in the know."

"I got chu. Don't even worry about it."

"I can't thank you enough." Tiaz looked into his eyes, clutching his shoulder.

Tiaz felt a little better knowing that he had a set of eyes and ears in the streets to find out what he couldn't from the inside. He was sure that Threat would find out everything that he needed and wanted to know. Now all there was left to do was wait. He didn't know what was going to kill him first: the anticipation or the news.

A few weeks later…

Tiaz sat on his bunk staring at the contraband cell phone he'd G-checked one of the convict's for waiting for it to ring. He'd touched bases with Threat a couple of weeks prior and he assured him that he was closer to finding out what Ta'shauna had been up to for the past six months. He hadn't heard from his right-hand since then. And every day since then he found himself checking the cell phone, anxiously awaiting his call.

Tiaz' chest had tightened and his stomach fluttered. He was driving himself crazy waiting to hear from his best friend. His forehead was wet with perspiration and his palms had sweated so much that he found himself wiping them off on his pants every so often.

Tiaz nearly jumped out of his skin seeing the cell phone's screen light up and vibrate in his palm. Familiar with the number on the display, he pressed answer and brought the cell to his ear. He gave a cautious scan up and down the tier before he began talking.

"What's up, Crim?" Tiaz spoke into the cell. Readying himself for the devastating news his crime partner was sure to deliver.

"I'm shacked up with three other dicks right now. I'ma get up outta there, though, just as soon as I come upon another lick. I mean I can't do it my nigga. I'm used to having my own crib and shit. That fool Don Juan talking about letting me work a block for 'em, but I told 'em I'll think about it 'cause I ain't never really been too big on slinging, especially for someone else." He took the time to cough before continuing with his story. "It is a check, though. I might fuck with it until I find a score that'll put a nigga back on his feet."

Tiaz nodded his head. "That's what's up, but when are you gonna quit stalling and tell me what's good with Ta'shauna?"

All was silent for a minute as Threat thought to himself before answering.

"It's just like I figured, she's fucking around."

Tiaz blinked his eyes as if he'd gotten something in them and began hyperventilating. He placed a hand to his chest and tried to calm his breathing. *Damn, love hurts.*

"Yo, T? T? Are you alright, man?"

Tiaz huffed and puffed, struggling to regain control of his erratic breathing. He closed his eyelids and peeled them back open, taking two deep breaths.

"T, are you still there?"

"Yeah, I'm still here."

Tiaz had already suspected what Threat had told him but it was different thinking it then having it confirmed. Still holding the cell to his ear, he lay back on his bunk. He felt stinging in his eyes and knew tears wouldn't be too far behind but his pride wouldn't allow them to fall. Instead, his eyes became glassy and what most would have considered an expression of anger was really one of hurt. He was heartbroken. He cleared his throat. "Who is he?"

"Man, you don't even wanna know."

"Who.The. Fuck. Is. He?"

"That nigga, Orlando."

"Her fucking baby daddy?" he asked heatedly. He couldn't believe it. "She got back with that bum ass nigga? Dude left her and Jaden out in the cold to fend for themselves, and she goes running back to him?"

"That's not all either," Threat said. "They're getting married tomorrow."

When Tiaz heard that he felt like he'd been shot in the heart with an arrow.

"I'm sorry, T." Threat could sense his brother's hurt.

"How did you find all of this out?"

"I broke into her mother's house and bugged all of the telephones. For the past couple of weeks old girl would call rambling about the typical shit that broads do. Then one day they started talking about the upcoming wedding, and this cat named Orlando. I remembered we ran into him at Universal City Walk that time and you pointed him out as her baby's daddy."

The line went silent as Tiaz was milling over the heart aching discovery.

Threat picked right up on it. His friend was hurting.

"I'm sorry, Crim."

"Nah, nah, don't be sorry, Threat. Ain't cho fault, homie. It is what it is." Tiaz thought about how his homeboy had always been down for him no matter what. He knew that loyal people were few and far between and he appreciated those that he came across. "You're a good friend, Threat, a real good friend. You always held your mans down, so I hate to trouble you for another favor but it's one I have to ask."

"Name it."

"I want chu to throw Ta'shauna a going home party."

"You sure you want me to do that? I mean maybe you should take some time to chill and think it over." Threat was skeptical of Tiaz irrational request.

"Nah, I want chu to go ahead and throw her one. Let her see that I'm not even tripping off of her leaving a nigga in here on stuck. She's moving on and I'm moving on. Ain't no hard feelings, feel me?"

"Alright then, I'll start making the arrangements."

"My nigga."

Tiaz disconnected the call and slid the cell under his pillow, laying his head back against it. He closed his eyes, remembering how Threat had always held him down.

He recalled one night, many years ago when they'd rode their bikes out into the wrong side of town to these sisters' house that they bumped at the Baldwin Hills shopping plaza. They were young niggaz then, so when it came to risking their wellbeing over pussy, it was a no brainer.

But things took a turn for the worse when they entered the girls' yard. Right when they reached the first step, the shadows began to come alive giving birth to a hungry pack of wolves, thirsty for blood and reputations. Tiaz and Threat managed to make it out of the yard but not before losing the knives they'd brought along and the shirts off of their backs.

They hadn't been on foreign soil ten minutes before they had a mob chasing after them.

Haa! Haa! Haa! Haa!

A younger Tiaz and Threat breathed heavily as they sprinted down the dark alley. Their faces were shiny and masked with perspiration. Their chests heaved up and down and their lungs felt hot. Their legs were aching having ran so long but they dared not stop because if they did that would have been their asses.

Threat looked to Tiaz as he lagged beside him. He was tired as shit and looked like he was about to collapse. However, the echoes of a thunderous crowd caused his head to snap over his shoulder. Those angry niggaz were hollering and yelling insults as they drew closer.

"Come on, T, keep up." Threat yelled over his shoulder to Tiaz.

"Ahhh!" Tiaz fell to the ground, looking as if he was about to faint. He was so exhausted. "Haa! Haa! Haa! Haa!" He panted out of breath as he looked up at Threat trying to pull him up, all the while checking to see if their nemesis were still on them, they were.

"Get up, man! We've gotta get outta here!" Threat struggled to get him on his feet and moving again.

"Gon', Threat, I'm through! I can't hack it no more." Tiaz waved him along. "I'm done, go on without me."

"Nah, fuck that!" Threat pulled his comrade up to his feet and leaned him up against the brick wall inside of the alley. He looked ahead and their adversaries were still charging after them, their numbers swallowing up the dark path. They wanted blood, their blood.

Threat's head darted all around the alley trying to find something they could defend themselves with. He spotted an empty clear glass bottle of Captain Morgan on the ground beside a trash bin. Snatching it up, he shattered the end of it, creating a jagged edge and a lethal weapon. He tossed the broken bottle over to Tiaz, and he tested it out, jabbing it at an imaginary body and head. When Threat looked up he saw a 2 X 4 sticking out of the same trash bin. He pulled it out and practiced swinging it as if it were a baseball bat.

"Here they come!" Tiaz alerted Threat before springing into action.

Sniktttt!

"Gaaaahhh!"

One of them staggered back grabbing his face with both hands after meeting the jagged edge of Tiaz' broken glass bottle.

Sniktttt!

"Arghh!" Another one grabbed his cheek, the meat hung and blood slicked his fingers.

Crack! Whackk! Bwhackkk!

The 2 x 4 broke in half and sent splinters and debris everywhere. Threat had lifted the last of the men off of his feet. He came flying down on his back, legs going up in the air and eventually falling back down. They fought on courageously and were holding their own until a loud noise stopped them all.

Bop! Bop!

The report from the handgun froze everyone in their tracks. They looked up to find a skinny light skinned nigga with a Mariner's S tattooed between his eyes. He sported his long hair in pigtails and a barely visible goatee framed his mouth.

"You two niggaz don't move, cuz!" Pigtails moved his gun between Tiaz and Threat. His homeboys pulled their wounded to their feet and ushered them off to the sidelines. "Drop the bottle." He ordered Tiaz and he obeyed. He and Threat stood there with their chests swelling and deflating as they breathed hard from the rumble. "Now y'all gon' stand there while my Locs beat ya'll asses or I'ma leave you in here stinking, feel me?" Although he didn't receive a response, he knew the young hoodlums understood him. He gave his Locs the nod and they swarmed their prey.

"Ooof!" Tiaz dropped to his hands and knees from a gut punch.

"Ahhh!" Threat was slammed against the trash bin from a forceful punch to the face. Then he was slung to the ground beside his partner in crime. All they could do was ball up into fetal positions as they were kicked, stomped, and punched. Once they

were handed down their ass whoopings, Pigtails tucked his banger on his waistline and approached them, unzipping his Dickies.

He smiled fiendishly as his swept his limp dick between Tiaz and Threat pissing on their faces and bodies. After he was done, he stashed his meat and zipped up.

"Marks." He kicked Threat hard but Tiaz even harder. He threw up his set and motioned for his gang to follow him as he walked off down the alley, leaving both men unconscious.

An hour later Threat was groaning as he was rubbing the back of his head. His eyelids peeled apart and the sky was a murky blue with the sun beginning to rise. He looked to his hand and it was slicked red. He looked to Tiaz and found him wincing and moaning as well. He scrambled over to him.

"Yo, Tiaz, are you alright, man?" He hunched over him trying to shake him conscious.

Tiaz eyelids slowly peeled open and he looked up at Threat. He then looked all around trying to figure where the hell he was.

"Nah, I'm fucked up. I think my fucking ribs are broken."

"Come on, we gotta get chu to a hospital." Threat pulled Tiaz up to his feet and threw his thick muscular arm over his shoulders. Holding him about the wrist and waist, he walked with him down the alley.

"You didn't leave me, Threat. You coulda bounced on a nigga but chu didn't. That's love."

"You're my brother; I'm always down for you. Like you're down for me, right?"

"Right. Til the death of us."

That moment in their history would go down as the day they'd proven themselves willing to risk their lives for one another. Love, Loyalty, Honor, Trust and Respect would be what held their friendship together and they wouldn't have it any other way.

Later that day…

"Tiaz Petty!" His government was called during mail call.

He retrieved his letters and headed back to his cell. He lay back in bed with his head propped against a pillow facing the bars.

He shuffled through the letters. There were some from his auntie, homeboys, and the women who he'd met and communicated with through Penpals.com, a website where male and female convicts could possibly find their significant other.

He received at least fifty letters a day from women all across the world. At first he just looked at the women as something to help make the time fly and keep his mind off of Ta'shauna, but one ended up catching his attention. Her name was Chevy and he'd spent quite some time talking with her in particular.

They'd chop it up over the phone and through letters. Every now and again she'd catch a bus out to the prison to come see him. Light skin had his undivided attention and he didn't see it wavering any time soon, especially since he'd found out about Ta'shauna's infidelity.

Tiaz picked Chevy's letter out of the bunch and sat the rest of them aside. Chevy's envelope was beautifully designed with flowers and butterflies. He removed the letter from out of the envelope and inhaled, taking in Chevy's perfume and the sweet smell of her pussy. The last five letters she sent had the scent of her Vajayjay and the Chanel #5 perfume she wore. That had let him know she felt they'd grown closer to one another. A smile emerged on his face and he looked to her picture, which was on the wall beside him. He closed his eyes for a moment and imagined her in his cell, lying in bed beside him. He peeled his eyelids open and began reading her letter.

What's up, boo?

I read your letter, and I must say you really know how to make a girl feel special. I hope those words are just for me and you're not using them to have your other lady friends smitten.

You say you're keeping it one hunnit, well, I am too when I tell you I've fallen for you. When I'm up I'm thinking about you, when I'm sleeping I'm dreaming about you. It's like that song Usher sung back in the day "You Got It Bad". Well, I have it bad. I got it bad for you. I love me some you. I can't wait to see you again, too.

XOXO

Chevy

Tiaz folded up the letter and placed it back into the envelope. He picked up a pen and writing tablet and began penning a response letter to Chevy.

Chapter 4

Chevy lay in her canopy bed fast asleep. The morning had brought forth the rays of the ember sun whose rays shined through the openings of the blinds, illuminating her face and stinging her eyelids like bees. Her face twitched with irritation causing her to turn over and cover her face with a pillow. Then the alarm clock went off and she covered her head with a second pillow to block its blaring siren. She tried to go back to sleep, but the noisy clock wouldn't allow it. She removed the pillows from her face and peeled her eyelids open. Staring at the clock on her nightstand, it took a moment for her sight to adjust but when it did, she read the time clearly: 6:40 A.M.

Fifteen mo' minutes then I'll get up, Chevy told herself before turning off the alarm clock. She turned back over and closed her eyes for the few valuable minutes and that's when the telephone rang. She allowed it to ring the first and second time, but on the third she figured it may be an emergency so she answered it.

"Hello?" she said groggily and with attitude, letting the caller know they'd put her in a bad way by fucking with her sleep.

"You still fucking with that nigga Azule?"

Hearing Faison's voice Chevy's eyes shot open and she sat up in bed.

"And if I was?" she said with attitude, moving her neck like black girl's in the ghetto do when they're heated.

"I'm not playing witcho high-yellow ass, Chevy."

"I ain't playing either, nigga." Veins ran up her neck as she talked that shit. "Ain't none of yo' mothafucking business who I got up in my house."

"You better watch cho mouth and remember who you're talking to."

She took the time to spark up a cigarette and blew out a cloud of smoke.

"Oh, I do, boo boo, my faggot ass baby daddy, Faison."

"I ain't gon' be too many more faggots, ya hear?"

"Alright, trick!" She disconnected the call and sat the telephone on the nightstand, running her hand down her face. The telephone rang again and she looked up at it. She stared at it as it rang for a time before picking it up. "Goddamn, nigga, get cho life!" She barked into the receiver. "We're through so get off my bumper, please, Jesus!" Once she'd quieted down, she heard labored breathing. He was pissed the fuck off.

"I'ma drive over there and bust you in them big ass lips!" Faison growled.

"Come and try it, bitch!" Chevy barked into the phone heatedly. "You remember what happened the last time? You bring your ass in here and they'll be carrying you out! I got my shit cocked, locked, and ready to go. Let me know it's real and wobble your fat ass over here!" she said, sitting up in bed. Then there were knocks at her door and she knew that it was Te'Qui. Every morning she'd get him up for school so he could get dressed while she made him breakfast. Chevy held the phone to her chest and called out to her son. "I'll be out in a minute, baby. Go ahead and brush your teeth." She waited until she thought he had left and pressed the phone back to her ear. Faison had been ranting the entire time, but now she was just in time to catch the last of his verbal assault.

"...I swear on everything I love, bitch, I bet not ever catch you in the streets on some solo shit. You better have a couple of them boys with badges with chu 'cause I'ma knock you smooth the fuck out for disrespecting me! You must of slipped, fell, and bumped yo mothafucking head this morning."

"You just remember one thing, sweetheart. You gotta bring ass to get some. On that note, I'll be hanging up. I gotta go cook my son some breakfast and send him off to school, so I can then suck and fuck my man. Deuces!" She hung up the phone and journeyed into the kitchen. She whipped up Te'Qui's breakfast: French toast, scrambled eggs, bacon and a glass of Simply orange juice. While little man went to work on his meal, she dipped off to the bedroom. She wrapped her head up in a scarf, slipped on one of Faison's T-shirts, sweatpants and lady Air Maxes. She grabbed her car keys from off the nightstand and made her way back inside of the kitchen.

"You ready?" she asked Te'Qui.

He held up a finger while he gulped down the last of the orange juice.

Belch!

He sat the glass down and stood up, grabbing his backpack. "Ready."

Chevy cracked a grin as she ruffled her baby boy's head and kissed the top of it.

"Come on." She headed for the door with her son on her heels. She pulled it open and was about to step through it when she thought to herself. She headed back into her bedroom where she lifted the mattress, revealing a Taurus .9mm. She checked the magazine for a full clip and smacked it back inside, chambering one in the head. She tucked the banger into the waistline of her sweatpants and made a beeline out of the bedroom.

Jumping behind the wheel of her car, she opened the glovebox and stashed her gun inside. She slammed it closed and fired up the engine. Three minutes later, Chevy was pulling up at 28th Street Elementary school and turning down the stereo system.

"Are you staying after school today, or do you want me to pick you up?" she asked.

"I think I'ma stay today and play basketball, if that's okay." Te'Qui replied.

"Yeah, that's fine." She smiled.

"Alright, see you later. Love you." Te'Qui said, opening the door.

"Wait a minute, lil' man, I know you're not hopping outta this car without giving your momma a kiss." Chevy watched as he looked around to make sure no one would see him giving her a goodbye kiss. The coast was clear.

"Alright, one kiss. Make it quick." He hoisted his backpack upon his shoulder.

Chevy leaned forward and Te'Qui gave her a quick peck on the lips before hopping out of the car and running into the yard of his school.

She laughed until he disappeared and shook her head before driving off.

She was about to take it home when she suddenly got a craving for a breakfast from Tam's. For some strange reason she kept picturing cinnamon toast, scrambled eggs, bacon and a bottle of Minute Maid orange juice inside of her head. Just the thought of the hot breakfast made her stomach grumble in hunger. She was so busy cooking up Te'Qui's breakfast and trying to make sure he made it to school on time, she forgot to feed herself.

She made a U-turn and headed back up San Pedro. Peering through her rearview mirror, she spotted a gray '87 Buick Regal with pitch black tints making a U-turn at the exact same time she was. She paid closer attention to see if the car would follow her when she bent the corner on Adams and San Pedro, and it did.

Growing suspicious, she mashed the gas pedal and accelerated the Caprice up to forty miles an hour. She glanced in the rearview and the Buick was right on her ass. Going down Adams she made a swift right on Stanford Avenue causing her Caprice's tires to screech and the vehicle to slightly tip. She stole a peek in the side view mirror and sure enough the Buick had bent the corner behind her going at the same speed.

Chevy's heart was pounding. She thought for sure it would leap from her chest any second. Then she bent a quick left on the corner of 27th street and popped open the glove-box. Keeping her eyes on the street ahead of her, she blindly felt around inside until she found the Taurus .9mm. She was glad she brought the gun along now. Feeling the black plastic handle in her grip put her at ease. She mashed the brake pedal and brought the Caprice to a screeching halt, nearly causing the Buick to slam into the back of her.

She threw the car in park and swung open the door, grabbing her piece from her lap. She whipped around banging three rounds through the windshield and making the Buick back up in a hurry.

The Buick rolled in reverse until it nearly reached the end of 27th street coming into San Pedro, before whipping around and pulling out into traffic. With a heaving chest, she lowered her gun and looked around. The coast was clear so she hopped back into the Caprice and drove off.

***

Chevy ran into the house and slammed the door behind her. She took a quick peek through the curtains to see if she was followed. The coast was clear. She tucked her keys into the pocket of her North Face jacket and walked into the kitchen. She took a glass down from the cupboard and a bottle of Captain Morgan from the refrigerator. Chevy pulled her Taurus from her waistline and sat it down on the table before pouring herself a glass. She took a sip and her cell phone rang. She pulled the cell from her pocket and looked at the screen. Faison's name and picture lit it up. Chevy sat the glass down on the table and pressed *talk*, placing the cell to her ear.

"You may wanna get cha self some professional hitters, play-boy. Them niggaz you sent are novices. A bitch is still breathing," Chevy boasted, taking a sip from her glass and listening for Faison's response.

"Don't get cute, I just sent them boys to scare your ass. You're lucky you're my son's mother 'cause otherwise you'd be dead right now. The next time I send my people they're flat lining everything. I'm talking you and that faggot ass nigga Azule you got lying up in there. I'll just take my son and raise him myself."

Faison disconnected the call. Chevy sat her cell on the table and casually sipped from her glass.

Faison was bluffing. He had no intentions on killing her. In all actuality, he was still very much in love with her. His heart longed for his family. He realized he had fucked it all up because he couldn't keep his dick in his pants, so he understood Chevy being hurt enough to want to kill him. Hell, if he was on the receiving end of the betrayal, he would have murked her and whoever he caught her in bed with.

Faison understood the reason why Chevy shot him, but that didn't stop him from feeling some type of way about it. He hated the way she made him feel and he hated himself for still being in love with her despite it. He felt the only way for him to feel better was to pump fear into her. And in doing so, he hoped she'd come crawling back to him. And if she did, there was no doubt in his mind he'd take her back.

It all went down about four years ago. Faison hadn't quite yet reached Top Dawg status yet, so he was still putting in most of his own work.

The Dickson Brothers had muscled their way on his territory. After repeated warnings to shut down shop were ignored, the young upstart resorted to what he felt was the best solution, murder. Faison went at both of them boys with two chrome 9 double M's. He gave them flatlines, but there was only one problem. Someone had seen him when he laid down his gunplay.

"You may as well go on and live your life, baby, 'cause I'm through. I'm washed up." A defeated Faison spoke into the telephone from behind the Plexiglas of the county jail's visiting room. He was dressed in a blue jumpsuit.

"What?" Chevy frowned, worry lines across her forehead. She looked like hell having been stressed the fuck out about his situation. "How much time are they talking?"

"Life." He told her with a pair of glassy, red webbed eyes. He shook his head and bowed it as he was massaging the bridge of his nose. "My ass is in the fire here and there's only one way I can pull it out."

"How?" She sat up, desperate for his answer.

"How much do you love me?" He locked eyes with her.

"I love you more than any human being can possibly love another." She matched his intensity.

"Good." With that said he hung up the telephone and rose from the stool, walking away. Chevy looked alive, rising to her feet.

"Faison! Faison!" She called after him but he kept his stride.

Later that night…

Bone, one of Faison's hands, made a visit to Chevy. He gave her the rundown on his case and the cat that had become a liability by the name of Sha'Quell. Homeboy had given up Faison's involvement with the three homicides. The crazy part about it was that he wasn't in any real trouble himself. He had been picked up with enough crack for him to pass off as a user instead of possession with intention to sell. But when The Boys applied a little pressure to him he broke like a pregnant lady's water bag.

"Homie's gotta meet with death if Faison wants to see another sunset, ya feel me?" Bone said to Chevy as she held open the door for him.

"He's not just the love of my life, he's the father of child. I'll do whatever I have to do to help him."

Chevy was given a wallet size photo of Sha'Quell and placed on his trail. One morning she found him at IHOP having breakfast with who she believed was a couple of plain clothed cops. She didn't want the police to identify her so she gave his waitress a twenty dollar bill and wrote a kinky message on a napkin with her phony name and telephone number. She finished her coffee and shot him a sexy smile on her way out of the restaurant. They went out a few times until she made him feel comfortable. Then one night when the time was right, The Grim Reaper made his appearance after they'd come back from the movies.

"Alright, baby, good night."

"Good night."

Sha'Quell kissed Chevy sloppily. When they pulled away they both wiped the corners of their mouths, smiling. Suddenly, Chevy's expression morphed into a hateful one and she shoved him backwards, slamming the door in his face. A look of confusion crossed his face as he stumbled back and nearly fell. His face tightened with anger and he was about to charge up the steps until he heard the rustling in the bushes.

His head snapped to the right and a dark figure emerged. It lifted something. Sha'Quell peered closely trying to see who it was but it was already too late. Flickers of fire flashed before his pupils. Hot bullets went through his cheekbone and eye. Horror crossed his face and he toppled over. With the work put in, the gunman fled into the darkness.

Chevy had gotten Sha'Quell to sneak out of the way of police protection. For a week straight he'd dip off with her to a cheap motel to get busy. They sucked and fucked like it was going out of style. Sha'Quell had gotten hooked on her loving and with that came his stupidity. She was finally able to lower him to a knock off house that Faison had gotten a suited up crack head to renovate under a dummy name.

With the witness out of the picture there wasn't anyway to link Faison to the murders. Therefore he was set free. Faison was grateful to Chevy for sacrificing her body and dignity in order for him to be released from jail. With that act, he knew she was down for him and finding someone else worthy to be on his arm was going to be a hard task.

Chapter 5

Threat made his way across Florence Avenue smoking a cigarette. He wore a tan bucket hat pulled down over his brows and cheap liquor store shades over his eyes. His T-shirt was dingy and his cargo pants were a size too small, so he sagged to make them look like they fitted. The homies had blessed him with some paper to get him some new digs since he'd just came home, but he decided to hold that change to get him through the next couple of months until he came upon a lick.

He'd lost a considerable amount of weight since he'd been out these past few weeks, which wasn't surprising since he'd been eating like he was still on lock. Every day he'd eat what jail niggas called a spread, which consisted of noodles, clams, sardines, and mayonnaise. The dish was the bomb when he was locked up, but now that he was out and had caught whiffs of the fine cuisines out in the free world, the spread made him sick to his stomach. He would have to make due for now because his pockets were on tilt and the come ups were few and far in between. He knew that he could easily hit some of the homies up for a couple of dollars until he got right, but begging from another grown ass man wasn't his shtick, he'd rather die of starvation than ask for a hand out. So for now, he'd make it on what he had until he was able to do better.

Crossing the street and heading toward Mount Carmel Park, Threat spotted Don Juan leant up against the grill of his Porsche truck eating a bag of popcorn and spitting at some caramel dipped fox. He figured he must have been saying all of the right things because he had old girl blushing and smiling. By the time he had approached Don Juan the girl had put her phone number into his cell and pecked him on the cheek before leaving. Don Juan smacked her on her ample ass and admired the sway of her apple bottom as she sauntered away, throwing it extra hard as she went along. He smiled and bit down on his bottom lip, shaking his head as he enjoyed the show. He imagined himself burying his black cobra deep inside of her sugar walls. The thought caused his joint to stiffen and jump behind the zipper of his jeans.

"What's cracking?" Threat spoke as he drew near to Don Juan.

Don Juan turned around with his hand near his waistline ready to pull his banger if it was drama. But seeing it was Threat, his face softened and he smiled. "What's cracking, boy?" He slapped hands with Threat and snapped his fingers. Don Juan took in the threads that he was wearing. His clothes said what his mouth didn't have to. He was hungry, and Don Juan was going to throw him a bone. If he acted like he wasn't sure of what he wanted to do again, then he wasn't going ask him anymore. He'd be damned if he was gone beg a nigga to put some money in his pocket. "You ready to get put on and get this money, or what?"

Threat nodded and rubbed his hands together greedily. "Yeah, I'ma get down."

"That's what I'm talking about. Come by the house 'round 9 o'clock tonight. I'ma set chu out and set chu up."

"Cool." Threat nodded and dapped him up. "But look, I gotta lil' something, something I gotta take care of so I'ma need a throwaway."

Don Juan formed his hand into the shape of a gun and he nodded *yes*. "I got chu. You don't need any backup, do you? You know I gotta couple head bustas that are always ready and willing. Sheeiiit, you wouldn't even have to get your hands dirty."

"That's love. I appreciate it, but I gotta handle this dolo. Feel me?"

Don Juan nodded his head. "Alright. Well, come on. I'ma get that hammer for you." He dropped the empty bag of popcorn and smacked the crumbs from his palms before sliding behind the wheel of his truck with Threat in the front passenger seat.

The next day...

The doors of the chapel flew open. The bride and groom came down the steps smiling from ear to ear. Their family and friends followed behind them, applauding and cheering them on. The newlyweds narrowed their eyes into slits and held their arms above their brows as rice and colorful ribbons were thrown at them. The bride's Uncle Bruce, an older cat with a salt and pepper goatee and a shaved head, stood on the side of a Mercedes Benz. He beamed when he saw the couple, smiling and boasting his thirty-two whites. Uncle Bruce tossed the car keys over to the groom and he looked into his palm, the key chain was black and had the Mercedes emblem on it. The groom smiled and embraced his wife's uncle before they hopped into the Mercedes and drove off. *Just married* and *congratulations Ta'shauna and Orlando* was spray painted on the back window. The empty soup cans that were attached to the fender by yarn chattered on the streets as they sped along. The wedding guests ran out into the street happily saying their farewells and waving goodbye.

"Can you believe it? We're actually married." Ta'shauna excitedly held Orlando's hand as he pushed the Benz.

"Yep, Mr. and Mrs. Greene," Orlando gave her a quick smooch. He then held up his wife's hand and kissed it.

His loving expression turned into a bewildered look when a honking horn brought his attention around to the driver side window. He saw an old raggedy sky blue Saab rolling beside him with a smiling driver motioning for him to let his window down.

"What does he want, baby?" Ta'shauna asked.

"Probably some directions," Orlando said, holding down a button and letting the window down. "What's up, chief?" He asked the driver of the Saab.

The driver's smile transformed into a mask of hatred and he pointed a dull black Desert Eagle in Orlando's direction. Orlando's eyes bugged and his mouth dropped open. The barrel of the Desert unleashed triplets, all of which struck its target in the chest. A single bullet entered his temple and blew out his right-eye. Blood splattered onto Ta'shauna's face and she screamed out in horror, hands trembling. Orlando's head hit the steering wheel as he slumped over dead. His foot mashed the gas pedal, speeding up the Benz and sending it barreling toward a light post. She tried to get control of the steering wheel, but it was too late. The Benz crashed into the light post and wrapped itself around it.

Ta'shauna peeled her head from off the dashboard, groaning. There was a nasty gash in her forehead. She was disoriented and her sight went in and out of focus. She looked into the rearview mirror and saw the Saab pulling up behind her. Frantic, she tried to shake Orlando awake, but he wouldn't budge. Realizing Orlando was dead; she opened the door and fell out into the street on her hands and knees. She crawled toward the opposite side of the street, looking over her shoulder. When she saw the driver of the Saab hopping out, she crawled faster and screamed for someone to help her.

The driver wore a blue bandana over his head and one over the lower half of his face. His eyes were hidden behind a pair of black sunglasses. He moved forth in a stroll as if he didn't have a care in the world with his gloved hand wrapped around the handle of his gun.

Ta'shauna made her way across the street to the corner. She tried to pull herself up with the support of the light post, but her right leg refused to cooperate. She looked down and saw that her leg bone was poking out of the side of her leg. She tried to hop along, calling out for help as she went but eerily no one came to her aide.

The driver ran up behind her and tripped her good leg out from under her. She fell and busted her mouth on the sidewalk. She grimaced as she slowly pulled her head up, exposing her red teeth and raining droplets of blood onto the pavement. She moved to get up again and pain shot through her scalp as her head was yanked back by her hair, nearly ripping out the tracks of her weave.

The driver brought his mouth near her ear. "This is for breaking Tiaz' heart, bitch!" He pressed the Desert Eagle into the top of her skull and pulled the trigger. A crimson spray misted the air and Ta'shauna hit the ground like a tackling dummy. Threat surveyed his surroundings and saw people peeking out from behind buildings and parked cars. He tossed the Desert Eagle beside Ta'shauna's body and retreated to the Saab, pulling away from the scene with police sirens blaring from afar.

***

Threat parked the Saab in an alley. He wiped down the steering wheel and everything else he'd touched. He hopped out of the car and hurried down the alley. He jogged across the street, looking over both of his shoulders. Once Threat reached the other side of the street, he flagged down a taxi. He hopped into the backseat of the yellow checkered taxi and gave him his destination.

Without even asking if he could smoke, he pulled out a cigarette and fired it up. As soon as the smoke reached the driver's nostrils, he looked up into the rearview mirror at Threat. The thug locked eyes with him and blew out a cloud of smoke like, *What the fuck are you going to do about it?* The driver shifted his eyes back to the windshield while Threat went about smoking, focusing his eyes outside of the backseat window.

He didn't feel remorse or regret for what he'd done. It was nothing more than doing a favor for an old friend. Tiaz was his brother from another mother and he'd follow him to hell and back if he'd asked.

The cab made a left at the corner of Pico and disappeared into the scenery of Los Angeles' traffic.

Threat had handled the task he'd been given and couldn't wait to report the news to his right-hand.

The day after...

Tiaz was playing cards inside of the day room when a news report came on the television. At first, he wasn't paying the report any mind, but then he heard a familiar name that got his attention altogether. He stopped and turned around in his chair toward the television, listening closely.

"'Sup? Are you gon' finish your hand, or what?" The old head that was playing cards with Tiaz asked. He held up a finger for the seasoned convict to give him a minute.

Orlando Greene, 32, and Ta'shauna Reed, 26, were gunned down yesterday afternoon. The victims were shot several times, leaving the male dead on arrival, but miraculously the female

47

survived. She was admitted into Cedar Sinai hospital and is in critical condition. More news to come.

"Goddamn!" Tiaz cursed and threw down the cards.

An hour later...

Tiaz paced the floor of his cell taking sips of Pruno. Forty five minutes ago he placed a call to Threat to find out exactly what had went wrong on his mission. He promised to hit him back after he drove out to a telephone booth just outside of the city's limits. Now all he was left with was the waiting, which was killing him slower than cancer.

Seeing a flashing light at the corner of his eye, Tiaz whipped around and saw the cell slightly shaking as it was on vibrate. He snatched it up and sat down on his bunk, sitting his jar of Pruno on the floor beside his foot.

"I fucked up. I fucked up good. You don't even have to say it." Threat admitted as soon as he came on the line. "But I'ma make it right, though. If she survives, I'll be right there to finish the job. My word is my bond." He pounded his fist over his heart.

"Did she see your face, tattoos, or anything she could identify you by?"

"Come on now, my nigga. You're not dealing with a novice here. I live and breathe this murder shit. I was masked up. The bitch doesn't know anything that'll link me or you to that dirt." As soon as the lie left his lips, Threat thought back to the day he shot Ta'shauna. He then remembered. *This is for breaking Tiaz' heart, bitch!* Before letting one off in the top of her dome.

"Are you positive?"

"Yes!"

Tiaz brought his hand down his face and exhaled. "Okay, alright." He squeezed his eyelids closed and bit down on his curled finger, shaking his head and hating that his friend had failed the mission he'd sent him out on. He exhaled and continued. "Are you alright out there? You need some paper to get chu by?"

"Nah, everything is copasetic. I ended up bowing down, man. I'ma 'bout to get on Don Juan's payroll. But don't trip 'cause I'ma 'bout to work this inside thang. I'ma peep all of the Top Dawgs copping from 'em and we gon' see about hitting 'em for a fat pay day, ya feel me? As soon as you touch the turf me and you gon' get back to what we do best."

"Okay then my nigga, stay up."

"Sorry about all of this, T. I'ma make it up to you, I promise."

"Don't even wet it, homie. Shit happens." He brushed it off as if it was nothing.

"Alright."

"Peace."

The skin on Tiaz' forehead bunched together and he clenched his jaws, throwing the jar at the wall hard. It exploded and its contents spilled down the wall.

"How could he fuck that up?" He swung on the air a few times, venting his rage. "All he had to do was walk upon the bitch and shoot her dead in the forehead. Bam, she'd be gone. Fuck is so hard?" He threw his hands up frustrated and plopped down on the bunk. He hung his head and clutched it with both hands.

Ta'shauna may have survived the hit but he was going to make sure she didn't make it out of that hospital alive.

***

A medium built man with a round belly and skinny arms looked out of the ceiling to floor windows of his house which overlooked the beach. His hair was done in small twisties. He had light brown eyes and a scar that ran from his top lip to his right nostril. The hair on his face was cut into a design of swirls and diamond shapes within diamond shapes. The chain that hung from his neck was from his great, great, great grandfather who was a slave. Any time twisties found himself facing trying times, he'd touch the chain around his neck. The chain would remind twisties that whatever he was going through at the time was nothing compared to his grandfather's hardships.

The fingers of twisties right-hand, which he wore several unique rose gold diamond rings on, were wrapped around a glass of Cognac. He took casual sips as he watched the dark waters of the ocean crash against the shores of the beach. Over his bare chest he wore a leopard print bathrobe and matching pants. His feet were adorned in a pair of black suede house slippers.

At his back sat Uncle Bruce on a black leather sectional couch. His eyes were bloodshot and his face was stained with tears. He wiped his eyes with tissues as he went along talking to twisties.

"The doctors successfully removed the bullet from out of her head. She's in a coma now, but if she does wake up she'll most likely be blind for the rest of her life." Uncle Bruce told him. "As soon as Ta'shauna comes outta that coma, I want to try and get a description from her of the cat that shot her. That way we can give it to the police, so we can see if they can find this mothafucka." He waited for his nephew's response, but he didn't receive one. "Junior, you hear me talking to you, man?"

Twisties stood looking out of the window a moment longer before turning around to his uncle, swirling the Cognac around in his glass. "I heard you, Unc, but there will be no police. I don't do Five-O. When Ta'shauna comes outta that coma and gives up the cat that shot her and Orlando, I'll handle it. She is my sister, I got this. Her shooter will answer to me." His sipped the Cognac and his uncle nodded his head in approval.

Twisties hadn't spoken to his kid sister in eight years. They had a fallen out behind her then boyfriend, Orlando. Twisties knew Orlando from the streets. He was a conniving conman with the gift of gab. His game had broken many naïve women and sent them packing for the poor house. Twisties tried to warn his sister about the shyster, but she turned a deaf ear to him. When he made her pick between he and Orlando, she chose the ladder. Once Ta'shauna had chosen sides, she was as good as dead to him. He refused to attend any family functions she was at and he wouldn't accept any of her phone calls. He didn't even go to the hospital after she had Jaden. If it weren't for his mother showing him baby pictures of her son, twisties wouldn't even know who he resembled.

"Alright." Uncle Bruce slapped the applejack back on his head and rose from the couch. He then embraced his nephew. "Go by the hospital and see your baby sister." Twisties nodded without a second thought. Uncle Bruce opened the door and looked back at him. "I'm serious. You need to put that beef behind you. Besides, you never know what may come of this. You don't want that shit on your conscience, nephew."

"I will. I promise." Faison swore, taking a sip of Cognac.

Tranay Adams

Chapter 6

Don Juan knocked on the front door of one of many of his trap houses in a rhythmic code. He glanced back at Threat who was standing behind him, but turned back to the door once he heard shuffling around and the locks being undone. The door pulled open and standing before them was a Hershey brown skinned nigga with a Mohawk. His eyes shifted from Don Juan and Threat before stepping aside so they could enter.

"What up, Don? What it do, Threat?" Jaquez greeted the twosome as they stepped through the door.

"What's cracking, Jaquez?" Threat threw his head back as he passed him.

"Where's Boxy?" Don Juan dapped him up.

"He's in the kitchen." Jaquez nodded over his shoulder.

Don Juan and Threat walked into the kitchen and found Boxy standing at the microwave cooking crack. Seeing the men in his peripherals, he turned around to them. He greeted Don Juan and slapped hands with him, and sized Threat up, looking him up and down with a scowl. Picking this up, Don Juan decided to make the introductions. "Threat, this is my nigga, Boxy. Boxy, I'm sure you know Threat."

"Yeah, I've heard of him." Boxy said, unimpressed. He was familiar with the shorter man and how he gave it up in the streets. He'd heard many stories about him, but he wasn't impressed. He may have been somebody in his day, but this was the era of the 90's baby and he'd have to show him something now, if he wanted his respect.

"Check this out, crimey," Don Juan began. "From now on I'ma have you rocking the spot on 79th and the homie's gonna handle this one." He tapped Threat.

Angry, Boxy folded his arms across his chest. "Fuck you mean? You're switching shit up to accommodate this mothafucka? Fuck that, I got seniority." He jabbed himself in the chest with his finger.

"Nigga, come outta your feelings," Don Juan told him. "I need you over there. You know Hump and Woogie don't be on their shit, fucking up the paper."

"Why don't chu drop them two bum ass niggaz then?"

"Now, you know that's wifey's brother and cousin, they're family. I just can't cut 'em off like that. You know you gotta take care of your own. Besides, if I put chu over there, I know them boys gon' do right 'cause they know you don't play. You can hold it down over there and make sure everything is everything, and Threat will make sure everything's Gucci here." Don Juan knew exactly what to say to the youngster to get him to go along with what he had planned.

Boxy massaged his shaved chin as he thought on it for a moment. "Alright, if it's for the good of the team, then I'm with it." He slapped hands with Don Juan and snapped his fingers.

"Show this nigga how to cook and how we run things around here." Don Juan gripped his shoulder.

Boxy opened up the microwave and motioned Threat over. Threat studied the husky man as he went about his business. Seeing that everything was good, Don Juan patted his new recruit on the back and headed for the door.

***

Chevy stood beside the mailbox smoking a cigarette and impatiently tapping her foot as she waited for her mail to be delivered. It had been a few days since she'd written Tiaz and she couldn't wait to get his letter to see what he had to say. Casually taking pulls from her square, she watched Te'Qui play football in the street with the neighborhood kids. The youngsters were playing pretty rough and she thought about making him come in the house, but she'd hate to be the one to damper all of the fun he was having. Not to mention, she couldn't handle him with kid gloves, like she would with a little girl. He was a boy, so she had to take a different approach in raising him. After all, she didn't want her baby boy growing up to be some soft ass nigga. She was trying to raise a man. The world could be a cruel, cold place and Te'Qui would have to be tough if he was going to stand a chance in it.

Chevy looked as if she could barely control herself when she saw the mailman approaching. He was an older cat so he moved at a snail's pace. She wanted so badly to run upon him and snatch his bag and rummage through it herself until she found her boo's letter. When he made his stop at her house, the mailman went through his blue bag looking for the mail he had for Chevy. Once he came up with her mail for the day, he handed it over.

"Here you go." He forked over Chevy's mail.

"Thank you." She then shuffled through the envelopes until she found the one she was looking for. Seeing the envelope with Tiaz' name on it caused a smile to emerge across her face, but the smile turned into a smug look when she looked up and saw one of the kids pulling Te'Qui up to his feet after he'd been tackled to the grass on the sidewalk. "Te'Qui, I want chu in the house by seven for dinner!" She wanted him inside just then, but she reminded herself he was a boy.

"Alright!" He yelled back as he continued playing the game with his friends.

Chevy damn near skipped inside, holding the letter close to her heart. Once she was inside, she started a spaghetti sauce from scratch and then she poured herself a glass of Moscato and casually sipped it while she read over Tiaz' letter.

What's up, Love?

You looked so fine the last time you came to see me. It took all I had to stop from jumping over that table and eating you up. You really had me going. I don't have to tell you what I did once I got back to my cell *wink*. Anyway, as you already know I'll be making my exit from this shithole in the next two weeks. That's right! Your boy will be a free man. I'm looking forward to finally being out on the streets. I got a second chance at life and I'm not gonna fuck that up. I'm going to get myself a job, work real hard and hopefully save up enough dough to open up my own auto body *shop. I know it's not going to be an easy task transitioning from the streets and squaring up, but I'm going to give it a real shot.*

I know I can't be surrounded by the same people, or be in the hood no more. I got to distance myself from negativity if I'm truly going to make a change for the better. I was hoping to crash at your place for a while until I can get back upon my feet. I hope I'm not doing too much. If you say no, don't trip, we're still good. Anyway, I'll call once I think you've received this to get my answer. Just remember whether your answer is yes or no, it won't change anything. I'll talk to you soon.

Love,
Tiaz

Chevy put the letter back into the envelope. She took a sip of her wine, then placed the glass on the table. She turned the fire from underneath the spaghetti noodles and dropped the meatballs into the sauce. She removed the garlic bread from out of the oven and took the Caesar salad out of the refrigerator. She sat the Caesar salad on the table and made two plates, one for herself and the other for Te'Qui.

"I was just about to come get you," Chevy said to Te'Qui as he came through the door. He had pulled out his chair and was about to sit down until she protested. "I know your trifling behind is not about to sit down and eat with those filthy hands?"

"Why not? They're my hands and my food that I'ma 'bout to eat with."

"Boy, go in there and wash your hands." She smacked his butt with a dishtowel.

"Ah, man." He complained.

"*Ah, man.*" She mocked him and laughed.

When he came back from washing his hands, he and his mother sat at the kitchen table. She gave him the honor of saying grace.

They held hands and he blessed the food.

"Amen." Mother and son said in unison.

Te'Qui tore into his meal like a starved caveman. Chevy shook her head and smiled. "Slow down, boy. You're going to end up choking."

Chevy ate half of her food and picked over the rest. She spent the remainder of the dinner sipping Moscato and watching Te'Qui eat his meal. He finished his food, drank some juice and then belched.

"That was the bomb, momma." He complimented his mother.

"Thank you, son," She put a cigarette in between her thick lips and lit it.

Smoking a square was something she did after dinner and sex. She knew it was a nasty habit but she just couldn't shake it. She expelled smoke and fanned it away with her hand.

"Te'Qui, how do you feel about momma having a friend to come stay with us for a while?"

"You mean, Auntie Kantrell?"

"Not exactly, one of my other friends."

"Who?"

Chevy cleared her throat as she tapped the end of her cigarette, dropping ashes onto her dinner plate. "You, um, you, uh, don't know him, baby. He's momma's new friend."

Te'Qui frowned. He already knew who his mother was talking about and he wasn't feeling it in the slightest bit. "You're talking about the jailbird, aren't chu? They finally set him free? Why does he have to come here?"

"Well, baby, he's trying to turn his life around, and he feels that the only way he can do that is by distancing himself from certain friends and his old neighborhood."

"What about dad?"

"What about your father?"

"If you guys are trying to work things out, do you really think he's gonna like that you have some dude staying here with us?"

"Te'Qui, me and your father getting back together isn't likely. It's been a year now, and we've grown a part. We both moved on."

"Are you saying you don't love him anymore?" His eyes welled with tears.

"No, baby, no. I love him; I'm just not *in* love with him, not anymore." She grabbed his hand.

"What?" Te'Qui snatched his hand away, staring at her eerily. "You're just gonna say fuck dad? And let some other nigga slide into his slot?" Hot tears rolled down his cheeks and he quickly wiped them away with the back of his hand.

"Te'Qui! You watch how you talk to me! I am your mother goddamn it, and you will show me the proper respect!" Chevy shot to her feet.

"You want me to show you respect? How can I when you're tearing our family apart? Can't you see that? You're gonna kill whatever chance there was of us reconciling!"

"Te'Qui," she reached for him.

He moved back and away from her. "Man, fuck this!" He then stormed off inside of his bedroom and slammed the door behind him.

Tears welled up in Chevy's eyes. She picked up the bottle of Moscato and headed over to the couch. She sat the bottle down on the coffee table and continued to smoke her cigarette, while she flipped through the cable channels. Landing on Fresh Prince of Bell Air, she mashed her cigarette out into the ashtray and took the bottle to the head. She cried and drunk herself into a stupor.

Chevy's eyes flickered open as she lay on the couch. She sat up looking at the space where she'd laid her head and saw a dark spot where she'd drooled. She wiped the slobber from her lips and looked around as if she didn't know where she was. She picked up the bottle of Moscato from the floor and turned it upside down once she placed it to her lips, but it was empty.

Chevy sat the bottle on the coffee table and called out for Te'Qui. When he didn't answer, she got up and headed for the door. She knocked on the door and called out his name again. She waited, but she didn't receive an answer. "Te'Qui, open up this door." Still no answer, so she knocked again. "Te'Qui, I know you hear me!" When he didn't answer, she threw her shoulder into the lock of the door until the door broke open and sent a spray of splinters everywhere. She looked around Te'Qui's bedroom. He was gone. His bedroom window was open, and the cold breeze that blew inside ruffled the curtains hanging over it.

"Oh, my God!" She ran out of his bedroom.

Chevy called the police and her baby brother, Savon.

***

Savon drove Chevy to the police station to help with finding her boy, but the police told her that she couldn't file a missing person's report until Te'Qui was missing for forty-eight hours. With that said, Savon and Chevy drove around looking for Te'Qui all through the night.

"We've gotta find 'em, Savon. We've just gotta." Chevy stared out of the front passenger side window, scanning the streets as they drove past them. Her face was streaked with tears. "That's my lil' man, my heart beat, the air I breathe."

"Don't worry, sis. We're gonna find 'em." He grasped her hand affectionately. "If I gotta turn this whole mothafucking city on its head looking for him, we're gon' find my nephew, you hear me?" She nodded *yes* and placed her other hand on top of his, her wandering eyes still searching the streets for her baby boy.

Savon agreed to continue the search for his nephew only if Chevy stayed behind. If he was going to be out wandering the streets looking for Te'Qui, then he was definitely going to be packing. It was in the wee hours of the morning and all of the wolves would be out looking for a come up or stripes. Savon didn't want his sister to get caught up in a situation, so he made her stay home while he went on the mission.

When he pulled into the driveway of her house, she hopped out of the car.Chevy pulled off her jacket and hung it on the coat stand as soon as she came into the house. She turned on the flat-screen TV to see if there were any news reports on that may involve Te'Qui. So far, nothing. So, she picked up the cordless telephone and plopped down on the couch. She looked from the screen to the buttons on the telephone as she punched in the digits.

It would be the first of many calls she would place to the hospitals and precincts.

Hours later...

The sun had begun to rise over the horizon, making the sky convert from pitch black to a golden orange.

"No, thanks anyway." Chevy's shoulders slumped feeling defeated. She disconnected the call and sat the phone down on the coffee table. That was the hundredth call she'd placed in search of her son. She stared ahead, looking at nothing but thinking of all of the horrible predicaments her son could be in. Realizing if he was in some kind of danger that there wasn't anything she could do about it. Her eyes welled up with fresh tears. Her vision blurred and they fell down her cheeks. Right then and there she got down on her knees at the coffee table, hands together in prayer, looking up at the ceiling.

"God, please, oh please, bring my baby home to me." She whimpered and sniffled, nose running. She closed her eyes as she tried to regain her composure before continuing. She could feel herself about to go to pieces. "Please, please, I need my baby. I need..." she trailed off and snorted back snot, wiping her eyes with her arm. "I need my son back. You bring him back to me and I'll serve at your feet for all eternity."

Hearing a car speeding up the block, Chevy jumped to her feet and ran to the window. She pulled the curtain back and peered outside. She saw Savon's black Camero with the silver racing stripes on the side pulling out in front of her house. She looked alive in hopes that her baby boy was with him.

"Te'Qui? Te'Qui?" Chevy came bursting out of the house and running down the steps. She damn near tripped and fell trying to get to her brother's car.

She narrowed her eyes trying to peer through the tinted windows of the sport's car, but she couldn't see a thing. The engine of the vehicle died and Savon hopped out, putting his keys into his pocket. He and Chevy locked eyes, and it was at the moment she knew he hadn't found her son.

Chevy dropped down to her knees and hung her head low, tears falling from her eyes at rapid pace. They splashed when they hit the concrete, turning parts of the ground darker. Moments later, an approaching vehicle grabbed her attention. She wiped her eyes and looked up to see a Mercedes Benz truck pulling up.

Faison hopped out of the SUV and came around to the other side. He opened the door and Te'Qui hopped out wearing a backpack. Chevy broke down crying even harder and ran over to him.

"Oh, thank you, God." She looked up into the sky, hands together in prayer. "Thank you so much, Father. My baby." She ran over to Te'Qui and wrapped her arms around him, squeezing him lovingly. She kissed him all over his face and then held him by it, looking into his eyes.

"Don't chu ever run off like that again, do you hear me?" He nodded his understanding. "Where have you been?"

"My house," Faison interjected.

"Thank you for bringing him back home."

Faison nodded then spoke. "We need to talk."

"I'll take Te'Qui inside," Savon said. He led Te'Qui inside of the house and posted up on the porch. He folded his arms across his chest and watched Chevy and Faison like a guard dog.

Chevy folded her arms to her chest and shifted her weight to her other leg. "So, what's up, Faison?"

"That's what I'm trying to see." Te'Qui said. "There's no chance of us reconciling and becoming a family again. Is that true? You said that?"

"True story, we're done. We had our run, and it has come to an end."

"Tell me what I gotta do to make this right. Whatever it is, I'll do it. Matter of fact, it's done."

Chevy shook her head. "There is nothing you could ever do, Faison. We're over. I don't have those feelings for you anymore. You stepped and stomped on my heart too many times. You broke it into a million pieces. You blatantly fucked around in my face. You weren't even trying to hide the shit. I mean damn, how much do you want a bitch to take? You had to have known I'd have a breaking point."

"I'll admit that I fucked up. I broke your heart and I feel like shit every time I think about it. But it isn't like you didn't get some getback behind it." He pulled the collar of his shirt down and exposed the healed gunshot wound in his shoulder. "I use this as a daily reminder of how I slighted the most important woman in my life. Shit, sometimes I wish Savon wouldn't have stopped you from putting one through my dome. It wouldn't have been like I didn't deserve it. At least then I wouldn't have to keeping feeling the pain I feel knowing that I hurt chu."

Chevy stared into Faison's face with tearful eyes and a scowling mug as he went on talking. She tapped her foot on the cracked sidewalk listening intently. Once he finished saying what he had to say, she spoke. "Why would you say some shit like that, Faison? Then Te'Qui wouldn't have a father."

"I know. But it still doesn't change the fact. I miss y'all. I'm dying without my family. I know I fucked up, Chevy, but all I am asking is that chu give me just one more chance." He clasped his hands together. "Just one more chance and I swear on my life I'ma do right by you, baby."

Chevy shook her head and wiped the tears that spilled down her cheeks. "No. We're just gonna go back to you doing the same old shit. Just as soon as you get comfortable, it's back to you sticking your dick in every ratchet that glances in your direction. I'm tired of going through this bullshit with you, Faison."

"What do you want a nigga to do, beg? Fuck it. I'll beg. What's pride to a man in love?" Faison got down on his knees with his hands together looking up into Chevy's eyes. "Please, take me back, Chevy. I love you, I love our son, and I want to come home."

Chevy stared down at Faison in deep thought as tears continued to trickle down her face. She wanted so badly to take him back and give him another chance. She wanted to give Te'Qui a shot at being raised in a two parent household. She wanted him to have a family. She wanted for her and Faison to get married and live happily ever after. Chevy wanted all of these things, but she'd never get it from Faison. He would never change. She'd caught him fucking around more times than she could count on both hands. He'd give her a lecture on how he was going to change and she'd take him back. But not this time, she was tired of the bullshit.

"I'm sorry, Faison, but we're done." Chevy pulled her engagement ring from her finger, placed it into his palm, and closed it. He watched as she turned her back and headed for the house. He was in awe. He knew he'd lost her for good this time. With each step she took toward the house, the crack in his heart opened further down the middle until it was split in two.

Faison felt like a fool having put himself out there like that with Chevy and being shot down. He always abided by the three *F*s when dealing with the opposite sex: find them, fuck them, then flee them. But now he was experiencing the pain he'd caused all of the women he dealt with and the consequence of not following his rule. It was in that moment, he understood why people referred to karma being a bitch.

Faison's face twisted in anger and he rose to his feet, throwing the expensive diamond platinum engagement ring aside. "You want us to be through? Fine! But you bet not bring another nigga into the house that I paid for. I better not catch wind of 'nan nigga laying up in mine. You keep that fucking jailbird away from my son or else!"

"Or else what?" Chevy turned around from where she stood on the porch. "You're gonna send a hit squad to kill me and whoever I bring up in here? How would your son feel growing up knowing that his punk ass daddy was so in his feelings he had his mother whacked in the same space he lays his head? He'll grow up to hate cho black hearted ass, Faison. Then he'll probably kill you, himself. Matter of fact, nigga, you know what?" She raced down the steps toward Faison, getting in his face. "You may as well kill me, right now," tears rimmed her eyes and came to spill over. "Shoot me dead, mothafucka, 'cause I'm bringing me a man into my house, whether you like it or not. I'm not finna grow old and alone running behind your ass. I'ma get me someone that loves and appreciates everything I have to offer."

"Over my dead body you are!" His nostrils pulsated like an angry bull.

"Let's just hope it doesn't lead to that." She went to turn around and he grabbed her arm, jerking her around violently.

"Don't chu turn your back on me!" He grumbled, madness dancing in his eyes.

"Take your hands off me!" She tried to snatch her arm away but he held fast.

"Nah, yo ass is gon' stay right here and listen to me!" He wagged a chubby finger in her face.

"Let me go!" She steadily tried to yank her arm back.

"What I tell you, homeboy?" Savon came running from off of the porch, darting toward Faison and pulling his sagging jeans upon his skinny ass.

The husky man let go of Chevy and squared up with her brother. They locked ass like a couple of Rottweilers throwing those thangs.

Crack! Bwap!

With no hesitation, Savon gave him a two piece to the face and jumped back, strategizing his next move. "Uh huh, what's up with it, Blood?"

Wop!

Savon jabbed him in the eye but when he went to stick him again, Faison weaved and gave him some act right. A three punch combination dropped him on his ass. Faison went to rush him, but Savon kicked him in the balls. He staggered back holding his precious jewels, eyes bulged and lips twisted. Seeing Savon hurrying to his feet and reaching for the small of his back, he forgot the lingering pain in his crotch and drew his steel too. Chevy's little brother was right behind him, drawing a gun of his own. They stood there with their bangers pointed at each other.

"Stop!" Chevy looked from up the block to the two warring parties. "The police are rolling."

"Fuck Binem this nigga 'bout to get his issue, on the set." Savon swore.

"Savon, don't be stupid this will be your third strike if you get caught out here dirty." She reasoned, eyes looking from the approaching police car and then to them. "Put the gun down."

He held his gun on Faison for a minute longer before tucking it at the small of his back. Faison tucked his on his waistline and drew his shirt over it. The police cruiser then coasted by. The officer in the front passenger seat chewed gum and eye fucked everybody. The cruiser then sped up and made a left at the end of the block.

Faison and Savon mad dogged one another for what seemed like forever. Finally, the husky man broke eye contact and trekked back to his truck. He climbed behind the wheel and fired it up. He looked out of the front passenger side window and locked eyes with Chevy. He then focused his attention through the windshield and pulled off.

"Are you alright?" Savon asked Chevy as he approached her. She closed her eyes and tears ran down her face as she slowly shook her head. Her shoulders shuddered as she made an ugly face, bottom lip quivering. She opened her arms and he embraced her. He kissed her forehead and ran his hand up and down her back soothingly.

"Ahh, haa! Haa! Haa! Haa!" Her entire body trembled as he held her in his arms, tightening his arms around her. She bawled long and hard. When Savon saw his nephew looking out of the window at them, he motioned him out. The front door swung open and he leaped down to the last step, running over. He collided with them and threw his arms around them both. Savon rubbed his head and kissed the top of it. La familia.

***

Chevy lay in bed on her side snuggled under the covers. She wasn't asleep, but her eyes were closed. She was thinking about what happened earlier that morning with Faison and what would become of her relationship with Tiaz once he moved in. She was jolted out of her thoughts, opening her eyes when she heard the knob of her bedroom door click as it was being turned. The door opened and a light cut through the darkness of the bedroom. She picked her head up from the pillow and looked to the doorway. She found Te'Qui standing before her in his pajamas.

"Momma, I'm sorry. I don't want chu to cry anymore. If your new boyfriend wants to come live with us, then I'll try to get along with him. Okay?"

Chevy smirked. "Come here. Come lay in the bed with me." She patted the empty space beside her. Te'Qui closed the door and hopped in bed beside his mother. She pulled the covers back and draped them over her son, snuggling up next to him. She put her arm around him and kissed the top of his head. She closed her eyes and exhaled, relieved.

Thank you, Father. Thank you for allowing my baby to accept my man. And please, God, let this union go as I have always imagined it.

They both closed their eyes and waited for their dreams.

Chapter 7
That night

The elevator doors parted and Faison stepped out, holding a bouquet of flowers. He rounded the corner and journeyed down the corridor, glancing in each room as he went along. He wasn't quite sure where the room was that his sister was staying in, so he approached the nurses' station. He spoke with the clerk. After memorizing the information he was given, he headed toward his destination. Reaching the room number he was provided, he stepped through the door. Faison's heart dropped when he saw his baby sister lying in the cast iron bed in ICU. He could feel his eyes beginning to tear up. Feeling his knees buckle, he quickly grabbed the bed railing to keep himself from collapsing.

Faison took in Ta'shauna's appearance. Her head was wrapped in bandages. Her right leg was concealed in a cast. She was hooked up to machines with tubes running in and out of her petite frame. He couldn't believe it was his baby sister lying before him. It always tripped him out how someone could be so full of life one minute and be on the brink of death in the next. It was right then that he understood there was a thin line between life and death.

Faison sat down in a chair beside her bed. He lay back in his chair and watched her chest rise and fall as the breathing tube pushed oxygen into her lungs. Tears rolled down his face as he thought about what had been done to his sister. He didn't know who it was that shot her and for their sake they'd better hope he never did because if he ever caught wind of who the shooter was they would be on their knees begging for a quick death.

Faison had vowed to take care of his little sister but this time he wasn't around to help her, and it ate away at his conscience.

***

Faison was kneeled on the ground shooting dice amongst a host of kids his age and older. In one fist, he clutched a few dollars while the other fist rattled the dotted cubes. He chewed his tongue, determined to roll out a seven or an eleven on the come out. He threw his hand forward, letting the cubes roll off of his ashy palm. The craps danced on the asphalt. The first one stopped on a one while the other kept spinning.

The boy's faces frowned and they whispered under their breaths what they wanted it to land on. The dice slowly stopped turning, stopping on two. A look of disappointment washed over his face and his shoulders slumped. "Fuck!" He cursed, kicking over the empty Pepsi can.

He was about to catch the fade of the next shooter when he heard his sister over his shoulder.

"Faison, Faison!" A nine year old Ta'shauna came running as fast as she could, tears spilling from her eyes and flowing through the wind. Faison turned around with a scrunched forehead wondering what was wrong with his sister.

"What's wrong, Shauna?" He gripped her shoulder as he asked out of concern.

"Those boys..." She paused as she was out of breath. Her heart thumped fast under the crack of her emotions as she rubbed her eyes, lips trembling. "Those boys—they—they..."

"Calm down, Shauna," Faison leveled his eyes with hers. "Take a deep breath, now tell me what happened."

Ta'shauna took a deep breath and exhaled, calming herself down. She wiped her eyes and told her big brother what happened.

"The Dickson Brothers took—took my doll."

"Where they at?" Faison asked, ready to get into some niggaz asses for fucking with his little sister.

Ta'shauna pointed across the street to two boys, one brown and the other fair skinned. They were posted up outside of a liquor store, passing a joint between them. The brown one was holding the Raggedy Anne doll, playing in its stringy red hair. He blew smoke out into the air, eye fucking Faison from where he stood. He tapped his brother and pointed at him and his sister. The Dickson Brothers laughed loud and hardily.

Faison rolled up the sleeves of his sweatshirt and jogged across the street, his little sister on his heels. When he stepped upon the curb, the brown skinned Dickson boy dropped the half of joint he had left on the sidewalk and mashed it out under his All Star Chuck Taylor Converse.

"Give my sister her doll back." Faison demanded of the brown skinned brother.

He twisted his lips, looking him up and down. "I ain't giving her shit back, nigga. You betta beat the street 'fore you catch a bad one out here."

"I said, give my sister her doll back." Faison fumed, clenching his fists tightly.

"I ain't gon' tell yo fat ass again, kick rocks." Brown skinned ordered, stepping forth, scowling.

"Arghhh!" Brown skinned doubled over and dropped the Raggedy Anne doll, having been kicked in his balls. When he went to grab his pained testicles, he was cracked across the jaw. He stumbled off to the side and crashed to the sidewalk.

Faison swung on the other brother and he caught him square on the chin, dropping him. Dazed, he crawled toward the doll. He pulled it into him, just as the brothers pounced on him, giving him a good old passionate ass whipping.

He tucked the doll to his chest and balled up into a fetal position and squeezed his eyelids closed as the Dickson's wreaked havoc on his body. Faison winced as they brutally assaulted his form with all they had. Blood ran from his ears and nose, and his lips were busted.

"Stop! Stop! Stop it!" Young Ta'shauna screamed at the top of her lungs, veins running up her neck and tears spilling down her cheeks.

"Shut up, you lil' bitch!" The oldest of the Dickson brothers hollered at her, spit jumping from his lips. She rushed him screaming and swinging, clocking him in the balls. He doubled over in pain with his eyes bulged and his teeth clenched. He swatted her like a fly and she went flying back, tumbling a short distance.

Stump! Stump!

"Punk ass mothafucka, damn near broke my jaw." The young-est of the brothers shifted his bottom jaw back and forth after stomping on Faison. He then spat blood on the ground and nudged his sibling. Together they made their way up the block laughing at what they'd done to young Faison.

Ta'shauna scrambled to her feet and ran over to her brother. He grimaced as she pushed him over on his side.

"Faison, are you okay?" She questioned concerned, forehead running with lines.

"He—here," he said through swollen lips, holding up the Raggedy Anne doll. A smile christened her innocent face and she took the doll. She clutched it to her chest and closed her eyes, savoring the moment.

"Oh, thank you, Faison, thank you. You're the best brother in the entire world." She hugged and kissed him on the cheek as he rose from the ground.

"You welcome." He spoke like it hurt to do so. Seeing him limp along and almost falling, Ta'shauna threw his arm over her shoulder for support. They walked beside each other, looking at all of the kids standing around watching them.

"Are you alright, Faison." She looked up at his wrinkled face and him holding his side.

"I'll make it."

"I can't believe you did that for me."

"Well, believe it. I'm your brother. I always got cha back."

"Always?" She smiled.

"Always."

***

Faison reached over and grasped Ta'shauna's hand, gently stroking it as he spoke. "The streets ain't talking, T. Nobody seems to know who it was that popped you and Orlando. Look, sis, I'ma get that nigga for you, though. All I need is for you to come outta this coma. I need you to come out and tell me who did this to you. Gimmie something to go on, anything. And I'll find this batty boy and splatter his ass. I swear on everything I love." He kissed her hand and rose from his chair. He walked to the door, stopped and turned around. He closed his eyes and said a quick prayer for her before continuing out of the door.

Faison came out of his sister's room and made a beeline down the hall where he spotted his mother. The moment she saw him, a weak smile formed on her face and she hurried over to him, wrapping her arms around him. She embraced him lovingly.

"Oh, Junior, I'm so glad you came." Faison's mother's voice cracked under her emotions. "Have you been to see your sister yet?" He nodded *yes*. "Come here, everyone is inside the waiting room." She took him by the hand and led him into the waiting room. He was hesitant but he went along to appease his mother. He hugged and kissed his aunts and female cousins, and slapped hands with the men of his family. He made sure he greeted everyone except his father, Faison Reed Sr.

Faison Sr. and his son had been beefing since he was fifteen. Faison Sr. had found an ounce of weed in his son's sneaker and kicked him out of the house, even after his wife begged him not to. After spending a couple months out on the streets, Faison Jr. tried to return home but his father wouldn't let him. He cried and pleaded with his father, but the old man wouldn't budge. He'd warned the boy twice before in the past about bringing drugs into his house, and the stunt he pulled was the straw that broke the camel's back.

In turn, he told his father he was dead to him before returning back to the streets he now called home because she was the only one that would accept him with all of his flaws and imperfections. Like a mother she'd fed, nurtured, and raised him, and eventually brought him into the man he was today. Ever since then Faison Jr. loathed his father with an undying hatred.

His father had sent him out into the cold world alone. A place no child should have to face without the proper tutelage, tutelage that could only be passed down from a father to his son. Faison Sr. was supposed to have been the man to groom him for it, but instead he discarded him like a piece of trash.

Faison kissed his mother goodbye and made a beeline for the door. Seeing his son headed in his direction, Faison Sr. rose to his feet and removed his fedora, holding it with both hands as he watched his son approach. His forehead wrinkled with surprise when his son walked right past him and headed toward the door. He'd almost made it through the door when his mother, Gloria, grabbed him by the sleeve of his trench coat.

"Junior, aren't chu gonna say hello to your father?" her brows furrowed, as she looked at her son as if he was burning up with a fever.

"Who? This nigga?" Faison pointed to his father. "This mothafucka ain't my father, my pops been dead since I was fifteen." He looked his father up and down with a glare, then said, "Fuck him!"

Faison Sr. stepped into his son's face. "Let's get this under-stood, boy! I am your father, and you will show me the proper respect!"

Faison looked at his father like *Who in the fuck do you think you are?* "You got life fucked up, old man. I'm not a kid anymore, I'ma grown ass man, so miss me with that respect shit. You ceased to have that the day you threw your baby boy out on his ass!"

"Is that what this is all about? Some shit that happened fifteen years ago? You brought that on yourself! I'm the father, you're the son! My house, my rules, you abide by them. You didn't, so I tossed your ass out. And if I could go back, I wouldn't change a goddamn thing, I'd do it all over again." He rained spittle in Faison's face as he wagged his finger.

Fasion's anger got the best of him and he smacked his father's hand from out of his face. His father responded by punching him in the jaw. The blow whipped his head around. Faison countered by cracking his father across the chin. The punch spun him around and left him on the floor, knocked out cold.

Gloria rushed to her husband's aide. She looked up at her first born as if he was the devil himself when she saw him unconscious. She couldn't believe he had the gall to put hands on his own father. What she didn't know was her baby boy wasn't the kid that left home fifteen years ago. He was a grown man scarred by hard living and corrupted by the ills of his environment. He was a ghetto bastard.

The next day...

"One more week and I'ma free man, baby." A smile curled Tiaz' lips as he thought of his freedom.

"Yeah. I know." The jovial expression melted from Chevy's face as she looked down then back up again into his eyes. His eyebrows lowered and he angled his head, seeing the uncertainty etched across her face.

"Babe, what's wrong?" He inquired, his thumbs caressing her hands as he held them.

She took a deep breath and began. "I want chu to promise me something."

"Anything, Love." He stared into the depth of her eyes, sincerity lingering in his.

She took a deep breath. "Promise me you won't go changing on me as soon as these people give you yo walking papers."

"Of course not, baby. I already told you, it's me and you."

"I know. But you know how a lot of these guys are once they are from behind the wall. They promise single, broken, naive women the world to get what they want and then once they are outside they switch up."

"Oh, so I guess you're just gon' toss me into a bag with the rest of these niggaz up in here, huh?" His eyes took a quick scan of the convicts sitting at the tables and moving about.

"I'm just scared of getting hurt again, is all." Her eyes pooled with tears and ran down her face. Seeing her like this tugged at his hearts strings. He wanted so badly to cleanse her of all of the hurt and pain she felt. And he knew that he could too. It was just going to take some time.

"Don't cry, Queen, 'cause you hurting me right now." He brought his hand to her cheek, sweeping his thumb back and forth across the side of her face. "My heart bleeds when I see you like this. Hear me when I say this, I'm nothing like any of the niggaz that you've ever dealt with. I'm gon' leave such an imprint on your heart that anyone you entertain after me will have to know me in order to understand you, you hear me?"

She nodded *yes* and held his hand to her face, closing her eyes and brushing her cheek up against it lovingly.

Her heart had been poisoned by tainted love and his touch was the antidote. The more he talked the more she wept. She silently prayed to God that he was the one for her. The one she needed in her life.

"I know its gon' take some time but I'm gon' make you a believer." He swore, holding her gaze and meaning those words with every cell of his being. "I'ma give you a love that's only been heard about in fairy tales. Trust and believe in me." His eyes were glassy and swimming with honesty. "I'ma give you the love you need, the love you want, the love you deserve. All I ask in return is for one thing." He held up a finger. Her eyelids peeled open. They were pink and running wet.

"What?" Her voice cracked and she sniffled.

"That thing beating behind your left breast plate." He pointed and she looked down, touching her bosom. "That's right, your heart. That's all I want. That's all I need from you. You give me that and I promise with my right hand before God I'll make you the happiest woman on the face of this earth."

"You mean it?" She wiped her eyes and licked her lips.

"You're damn right I do." He swore up and down. "I've never been as sincere as I've been about anything in my life until this very moment."

"Okay." She nodded rapidly.

"Okay?" He questioned with a grin.

"Yes." She grinned, still nodding and gripping his hands.

"I promise you won't regret it." He brought her hands to his lips, kissing them affectionately. He then rose to his feet and embraced her lovingly, squeezing her tight in his strong arms.

Later that night…

"What's up with chu, Boxy? I'm feeling a lotta heat radiating from off that stool." Jaquez said hunched over a glass of Hennessy.

"Just been thinking, is all." Boxy said, mad dogging no one in particular as he stared ahead.

"Thinking about what? Spit it out. You look like you just found out that your bestfriend's been fucking your baby momma or something. And I know I ain't touch 'nan part of Shan's big ass. She could beg me to suck my dick and I wouldn't let her do it." He laughed and nudged Boxy, looking to get a witty comeback which on any other occasion he would have gotten from him. Boxy cracked a halfhearted smile, but Jaquez could tell that whatever was on his mind had a strong hold on him. "Damn, am I gonna have to beat it outta ya? Talk to your nigga. What is it?"

"This shit with Don Juan, man, bringing this new nigga in." Boxy confessed. "You see how he ran that game with me? Like I'm stupid and just don't know any better? I studied dude long enough to know how he gets down. He can't just tell me anything. I'm not one of these duck ass hoes he be fucking with. I was just playing the role."

"Why didn't chu call 'em out on it, Box? You let a nigga pull the shade over your eyes once and he's sho'nuff gon' try it again."

"Nah, I'm not tripping." Boxy rubbed on his shaved chin. "I know how to play the backseat until the driver gets to where he's going."

Jaquez's forehead wrinkled. He didn't know what the hell Boxy was talking about. "What're you getting at? It's like your speaking in riddles, nigga. Use layman's terms." He snapped his fingers.

"Don Juan.The nigga walks around with his ass on his shoulders, like his shit don't stink. Here we are making all of the moves and all of the money. All he does is cop the dope and set it out. We're the soldiers." He jabbed his finger into the bar top for emphasis. "We cook, bag, and sling the shit and our guns are going off when niggaz are getting outta line. We're putting in all of the work. All this nigga doing is sitting up in the big house getting fat off the sweat off our backs and the blood we shed. He's not even setting us out."

"What chu mean, bro? We eating." Jaquez corrected him.

"Yeah, we eating, but not like we're supposed to. Remember this, my nigga. And I call you my nigga 'cause I fucks with chu the long way. Can't nobody pay you how you gon' pay yourself. It's time we stepped our game up and become the bosses we supposed to be, feel me?"

"That's what I'm talking 'bout. Well, shit, let's tell Don Juan we stepping back to do our own thang. I'm sure he'll front us, or at least cut us a deal on some work."

"Do you hear yourself? Once we venture out to do our own thang, he's not gon' do anything to help us. We gon' end up being the competition. Therefore, he'll be looking to knock us over so he can keep the whole pie for himself."

"So, what chu suggesting we do?" Jaquez asked. Boxy gave him a knowing look and a sinister smile spread across his face.

The scandalous mothafucka was talking about robbing Don Juan and killing him. A man that had shown him nothing but love since he'd touched American soil.

Boxy and Jaquez ran as fast as they could down the street, occasionally glancing over their shoulders at the angered mob behind them. Their faces were hot and coated in sweat. They huffed and puffed, sneakers pounding the pavement as they broke up the block. Boxy tripped on his loose shoe strings and fell, bumping his head on the ground, grimacing. Jaquez pulled him to his feet, taking the time to gander at their rear.

"Come on, Box, they're on us!" Jaquez warned him. Once he'd gotten his friend back on his feet, they kept running, their feet smacking against the cracked sidewalk. They dipped off into the alley being swallowed in the darkness. The stray cat that shot past their line of vision was nothing more than a blur it was moving so fast. The hostile voices of the brown faces at their backs increased their stamina. They knew that if the men got a hold of them that

there wouldn't be enough of them left for either of their families to identify them.

Boxy and Jaquez's hearts dropped when they reached the other side of the alley and found a dead end. Hearing the stampeding feet behind them slow to a trot and eventually stopping, they whipped around. Their heads moved from left to right taking in the scowling faces of the Mexicans that literally had their backs against the wall.

The Mexican spear heading the mob wore his long dark hair slicked to the back and had a mustache that curled over his top lip. He smiled wickedly as his malevolent eyes looked over his intended victims. He drew a knife from his waistline—Snikt—once his knife had been drawn, the ones of his homies came out one by one. Snikt! Snikt! Snikt! Snikt! It was as if they were pulling them out of the air.

Boxy and Jaquez swallowed hard seeing the knives being brandished. Their eyes took in the harden faces of their aggressors, they could tell they wouldn't be satisfied until they lay twisted and bloodied at their feet.

"You mayates are dead, homes." Slick licked his thin lips and moved to carve Boxy and Jaquez up like a Thanksgiving turkey when a door swung open at his back, stealing every ones attention. The loud music from the pool hall came spilling out into the alley along with a drunk and staggering Don Juan who was fiddling around with the zipper of his jeans.

"Fools holding the bathroom hostage and shit, and a nigga gotta piss like a motha...." He cut himself short seeing something at the corner of his eye. When he turned around his forehead ran with lines. He looked at the knife wielding Mexicans to Boxy and Jaquez at the end of the alley, wondering what the fuck was going on. "Poncho, what's up?" he asked the leader of the pack. Although he sold poison to his people he didn't like the idea of another race butchering his own kind.

"These fuckers stole from my father's store." Poncho swayed his knife from Boxy and Jaquez, but kept his eyes on Don Juan.

"You mean, robbed it?"

"They came in like they were gon' buy a couple of sandwiches and ran off with 'em. Its okay 'cause it's judgment night, you feel me, homie?" He turned his frightening eyes on the pair. They weren't afraid though. They looked like they were ready to go down fighting if they had to.

"You're good, Don, gon' and bounce, homes. I don't want chu catching the heat in case the policia turns out."

Don Juan's head snapped from the Mexicans to Boxy and Jaquez, trying to make a quick decision before the little homies met their doom.

"Hold up." Don Juan spoke up, halting Poncho and his crew of degenerates.

"What? You know these mothafuckaz or something?"

Don Juan locked eyes with Boxy, holding his gaze as he tried to make his final decision.

"Yeah, these are my lil' cousins." He looked to Poncho with a straight face. The Mexican narrowed his eyes and angled his head as if he was trying to figure out if he believed him or not.

Poncho looked to Boxy and Jaquez then back to Don Juan. *"Cousins, huh?"*

"Yeah, man, those are my peoples, straight up."

"So what, Poncho, fuck that!" One of the degenerates spoke into Poncho's ear. *"Let's do these fools, they stole from yo familia, ese."*

Poncho stared into Don Juan's eyes as he weighed his options. He could say fuck it and leave his cousins bleeding like a couple of stuck pigs in the alley, but then he thought about he and his father's business relationship.

See, Don Juan supplied his father with the drugs he sold on the low out of his store. That's how his family ate. The last thing he wanted to do was fall out of favor with him.

Poncho exhaled and tucked away his knife. He kept his eyes on Don Juan when he said, *"They're free to go."* The statement brought the disappointment and remarks of his crew. He quickly whipped around to them. *"Shut the fuck up, I'm running this outfit."* He silenced them and marched over to Boxy and Jaquez.

"And you two..." he motioned a finger between the two young men. *"...if I ever see you so much as spit in the direction of my father's store I'll have your heads."* His hateful eyes looked between them as his nostrils flared. With that said he headed out of the alley with his crew bringing up his rear. He stopped by Don Juan. *"You owe me, Don."* Don nodded in agreement then dapped him up. Once the Mexicans left Boxy and Jaquez approached him.

"Thanks," Jaquez showed his appreciation.

"Good looking out." Boxy dapped him up. *"Not to sound ungrateful or nothing. But why'd you step in?"*

"We're an endangered species, black man, we've gotta look out for one another." He stated seriously, getting both of their head nods. *"What are y'all doing stealing sandwiches and shit? Y'all niggaz hungry, fam?"* He pulled a thick ass wad of dead presidents from his pocket and peeled off two hundred dollar bills. *"Here."* He went to pass it to Jaquez but Boxy grabbed his friend's arm. He looked to him and shook his head. *"Problem?"* Don Juan raised an eyebrow.

"Yeah, fam, we don't accept any handouts. We'll work for ours."

Don Juan cracked a smirk. *"Pride? I respect that. That's what makes men, men."* He shoved the money back into his pocket. *"I've gotta job for y'all, we'll chop it up over dinner."* He motioned for them to follow him with a wave of his jeweled hand, walking off down the alley.

Boxy and Jaquez exchanged glances trying to figure out what they should do. Don Juan stopped and turned around. *"Y'all coming or what?"* Boxy tapped Jaquez and followed his destiny, his road dawg right on his heels.

Don Juan took the boys to In & Out Burgers where they sat outside at a table beneath an umbrella. He smoked on a blunt as he watched the young men devour their double cheese burgers and French fries with the Thousand Island dressing on them.

Once they'd wiped out their food, they sipped their strawberry shakes. Boxy gave Don Juan the rundown on his life. He was sent to America to stay with his aunt and uncle after killing a man back *home in Nigeria that tried to molest him. He was unaware of their addiction to crack since moving to the states.*

They spent every nickel his family sent with him and pawned all of his most prized possessions to fund their habits. When he bucked against their mistreatment of him they kicked him out of the house. He met Jaquez while he was running a card hustle and the two had been stuck together ever since doing whatever they could to survive in South Central Los Scandalous.

"I'ma give y'all lil' niggaz a shot at getting money with me." Boxy and Jaquez exchanged smiling glances. "But you gotta do what I say when I say it. No questions asked."

"Whatever you need we'll do, long as you feed us." Boxy spoke up.

"You." Don Juan pointed at Jaquez.

"I'm down." He nodded.

"That's what I'm talking about. Now for the payment of y'all meal." He pushed forth the In & Out Burgers bag, taking a cautious look around.

Boxy's brows furrowed seeing him act so suspiciously. None-theless, he opened the bag and looked inside. Its contents were a blue steel Bulldog revolver with tape around its handle. He looked back up at the man that had saved his life earlier that night. The boys were going to have to kill someone for him in order for him to trust them.

That very night they stole the life of a nigga with loose lips by the name of Steven, earning a spot in Don Juan's budding organization and landing in his good graces. From then on out he treated the youngsters like they shared the same bloodline.

A light bulb came on inside of Jaquez's head. He'd just caught on to what Boxy was trying to relay to him. "Ohhh, now I see where you coming from. You know if you're with it then I'm with it."

"Then let's get it." Boxy touched glasses with Jaquez in a toast, then they sipped their drinks. And capped their night off talking about how they were going to nod Don Juan and make off with all that he had. *Cold world.*

Tranay Adams

Chapter 8
The next day

That was some wild shit that happened the other day, Blood. I thought cha pops was gon' put hands on your mom's and shit. I grabbed my strap. I thought I was gon' have to buck pops down." Baby Wicked relayed to Te'Qui from where he sat perched on a Huffy. The young hoodlum had a hand in every crime you could name. He was a young knucklehead looking to gain hood stardom, and he was looking forward to bringing his homeboy along on his journey. Two years prior he'd gotten his officials and was now claiming Eastside Outlaws Rolling 20's Bloods Gang.The same set his big brother had pledged allegiance to.

"Man, chill with all of that murdering my dad shit. That's my pops." Te'Qui continued eating from his bag of chili cheese Fritos and drinking his Arizona ice tea.

"I know. No disrespect. I'm just saying your mom's cool people, Blood. I'd lay something down behind her. She treats me like I'm her second son and shit." He spat on the ground.

"I feel you. I'm just saying, though. That's my momma and my dad. I don't want anything to happen to either one of them."

Baby Wicked nodded his understanding. Though he was only three years Te'Qui's senior, he had a great deal of respect for the youngster. They'd done some crimes together and it was through those illicit acts that he'd grown to respect him as a down ass little nigga.

"My fault," the YG slapped hands with Te'Qui.

When he pulled back his hand, the sun's rays bounced off of something on his waistline causing it to gleam and blind Te'Qui. The youngster blinked but once his eyes came into focus he saw that it was a pistol on his homeboy's hip.

"What's that?" He nodded to the strap.

He knew what he was referring to immediately. "Oh, that's a .38 special. It was one of my brother's pieces, but he let me have it before he got locked up."

"Let me see it."

"Alright," Baby Wicked looked around to make sure no one was spying on him before brandishing the revolver.

Te'Qui wiped the crumbs from the chips on his jeans before reaching for it. He'd held his mother's Taurus .9mm before. He even taught himself how to shoot it, but the little revolver was foreign to him, though. He'd seen the pistol on TV, but he'd never held one in real life. He tested the weight of it and looked through its sights. "This mothafucka beefy."

"It's alright." Baby Wicked begged to differ. "It's cool to use to patrol the hood and all. But if I ever really wanna cause some damage, I'd get that pump or that choppa my bro got hidden in the back of the closet. If a nigga get hit with one of them, one of the two are gon' happen: one, limbs gettin' torn off, or your ass is gon' be flat out dead." He held an imaginary choppa and swept it across, pretending to shoot up the enemies of his set.

Te'Qui passed the ratchet back to his homeboy and he tucked it, while making sure no one was watching him. "You wanna bust on some crabs with it."

"Hell yeah, I'm with it." Te'Qui rubbed his hands together mischievously, ready to do some dirt.

Zoooooom!

Day Day zipped down the block on his mini motorcycle stealing the youths' attention. Their eyes followed him as he shot right back and did donuts in the middle of the block, smoke trailing him.

"What's up, y'all?" He called out to the young niggaz.

"What's up, Day?" Te'Qui replied.

"What that shit two?" Baby Wicked responded.

The youngsters wore smiles across their faces as they watched the skinny nigga on his miniature bike clown.

"Let me ride that mothafucka, D!" Te'Qui called out.

"Alright." Day Day stopped the mini motorbike and sat the kickstand in place, waving the boys over.

Day Day was a young nigga who stayed in the streets. If he wasn't running to the store for the D-boys or stealing cars, then he was telling other niggaz' business for a couple of dollars. That's how he made the bulk of his money—snitching. If people needed to know who was fucking with whose baby momma or who got locked up or shot, then he was the cat they needed to see. Day Day was playing with fire running around the hood telling every ones comings and goings but ironically that's what kept him alive. See, niggaz wouldn't dare kill him because what he knew always came in handy. Now if it wasn't for that, the little dude would sure enough be lying six feet under in someone's cemetery.

The boys ran over to Day Day and his mini motorcycle. They took turns on the bike racing back and forth down the block, enjoying themselves.

Suddenly, the front door flew open and his mother stepped out onto the porch.

"Te'Qui!" Chevy called out, looking paranoid.

***

The ringing of the telephone brought Chevy out of her sleep. She had sprung up from where she laid gasping for breath and pointing her gun around the bedroom. Her face glistened with perspiration and her chest heaved. She'd been jumpy ever since the confrontation with Faison from the day before. She was paranoid and didn't know what he would pull next, if anything. Chevy lowered her gun and wiped the sweat from her forehead with the back of her hand. She leaned against the headboard and blew a sigh of relief. She looked to the ringing telephone and answered it.

"Hello." Her eyes shifted as she waited to hear a response but there was only silence on the other end of the line. "I see we're back to this bullshit again, huh? Get a life." She hung up the phone and closed her eyes. Soon as she drifted back into a peaceful slumber, her telephone rang again. Her eyes angrily popped open. "Look, nigga, if you keep on playing with me, I'ma pack up our shit and get ghost. And you'll never see your son again, so keep fucking with me if you want to!"

"Chevy, it's me, Kantrell." The woman on the other end of the phone laughed. "I was just playing with you, girl, hahahahahaha-ha."

Chevy blew hard and brushed her hair out of her face, pulling it behind her ear. "Bitch, you play too much. I really thought you were him. That mothafucka is driving me up the wall."

"Why don't chu have Savon and his goons take care of him? Hang him up in an abandoned warehouse somewhere and go to work on 'em with a powerdrill and an electric saw. I bet that'll straighten him out."

"Girl, are you crazy? He's still Te'Qui's father. And I still have love for 'em. Besides, I'm not tryna have my baby brother down in Central cased up on the account of my bullshit. I'll figure things out, I just need a minute." Chevy stood up, slipped her feet into a pair of house slippers and headed out of the door. With her shoulder pressing the cordless phone to her ear, she journeyed into the kitchen where she went about the task of making herself a cup of coffee.

"So, what's up with baby daddy number two?" Kantrell asked.

Chevy had to laugh at that one. "Girl, please, you're fast forwarding ahead. We got to get to know each other. Feel one another out, first. Besides, the next man I have a baby by will have to slip a ring onto my finger."

"I'm not mad at chu, sis. Are you and nephew all right over there, though?"

"Yeah, we're good. I got my nine and my Glock. If Faison send some niggaz over here, they're gonna be in for a rude awakening. Best believe that. 'Cause this high-yellow bitch don't play." She sat her cup of coffee down on the table and plugged her laptop's charger into the wall.

"So, Prince Charming is coming home in a minute, huh?"

"Yep," Chevy smiled. "I got butterflies and shit. I haven't felt this giddy since Faison asked me out in ninth grade. Girl, this nigga got me open like a can of paint."

"I'm pulling for you, Chev'. I'ma keep my fingers crossed. You deserve to be happy, ma."

"Thanks, baby momma."

"You know I got chu. Well, look, let me get back on this clock. I'll call you once I get off of work. Smooches."

It's too quiet in here, where is this boy? Chevy peeked out of her bedroom door looking for Te'Qui.

"Chevy, did you hear me?"

"Oh," she suddenly realized she was on the telephone. "Yeah, yeah, smooches. We'll chat later." She disconnected the call.

"Te'Quiiii?" Chevy called out to her son. When he didn't respond, she checked the bathroom and his bedroom. "Hmmm."

Her forehead wrinkled when she didn't see him. Hearing Te'Qui and Baby Wicked outside, she wandered into the living room. Something between the openings of the curtains caught her eye.

She spotted a black Lincoln Town car up the block. The door opened and a man in an expensive suit and tie stepped out, wearing black sunglasses. He adjusted his tie, reached into the backseat, and removed a box of long stemmed roses. Chevy wasn't buying his get up, though. The man looked menacing. The long scar that traveled along the side of his face made him appear rough, nothing like a friendly flower delivery man.

There was something off about the man and Chevy could feel it in her gut. Some shit was about to go down and she didn't want her son and his friend to get caught up.

Chevy threw open the front door and stepped out onto the porch.

"Te'Qui!" Chevy called out, looking paranoid.

"Hey, Chevy." Day Day gave a wave. She didn't even notice him. She was too focused on the car across the street.

"Momma, did you hear Day Day talking to you?" Te'Qui inquired, sitting on the miniature motorcycle.

"Y'all come into the house!" she ordered, eyes stuck on the car.

"Ma, we were just…"

"Now goddamn it!" She barked with authority. With that command, the boys darted into the house like they had hot coal up their assholes. "Te'Qui, take them into your bedroom and lock the door, don't come out until I tell you to."

Chevy recovered her .9mm from her bedroom and headed back up front. She was just in time to see the flower delivery guy knocking at the front door. She undid the locks, removed the chain, and opened the door. The delivery man was just about to open his mouth to say something when she grabbed him by his tie and pressed her gun under his chin. The delivery man dropped the box of flowers. His legs buckled and he looked scared.

"What the fuck is this?" He stammered, eyes lit with fright.

"You tell me." She patted him down for a weapon, but came up with nothing. "Did Faison send you here for me? If so, he done fucked up 'cause I'ma 'bout to send yo' ass back in a bag."

"Oh, God, I don't know any Faison." The delivery man swore nervously. "I'm just a flower delivery man." He trembled with fear.

Chevy reached into his suit and pulling out a business card, she read over it: Jerry's Floral Arrangements. She then removed her gun from under the delivery man's chin and told him to kick rocks. The delivery man ran off of the porch. He stumbled and nearly fell but kept on going.

Chevy picked up the flowers and removed the card attached to it. She opened it up and Ruben Studdard's *I'm Sorry* played. The inside of it was signed *Faison*. She took the card and flowers and dumped them into a trashcan out on the curb. She gave the Buick Regal one last look before heading back up the steps into the house.

***

Faison sat in the backseat of the Buick Regal watching the whole scene play out. He was crushed when he saw Chevy dump the flowers he'd delivered to her in the trashcan.

"Boss man, did you peep that?" Bird asked from the front passenger seat. He was a dark skinned cat with beady eyes and a hairstyle that put you in the mind of Coolio in his Gangster's Paradise music video.

"I saw." Faison replied as he casually sipped Cognac from a plastic cup.

"Lil' momma a G behind hers, you're engaged to a rider, fa'sho'." Bone declared from behind the wheel of the Buick Regal. He was a muscular dude with a deep voice and a shaved head. He was the oldest between him and Bird and had put in the most work. Faison nodded his head. Bone looked into the rearview mirror and saw Faison's glassy eyes. He could tell he was hurting. "Yo', fam, you want us to snatch baby momma up?"

Faison was quiet for a time before he replied, "Nah, fuck her."

Chapter 9
Five days later

Chevy stood beside her Caprice with her arms folded across her chest. Her eyes were hidden behind burgundy tinted Chanel shades that covered most of her face. Her long and normally jet-black hair was now blonde. She had gotten it dyed the week before after Tiaz told her how beautiful she'd look with it. She hadn't dreamed of changing her hair color, but since he thought it would make her more enticing she decided to give it a shot. When her hair dresser unveiled her new style, she was floored. She fell in love with her new look.

Chevy chewed on gum as she checked her appearance in the sideview mirror for the umpteenth time, fixing her hair. She twisted the cap off of her M.A.C lipgloss and smoothed some over her luscious lips. Hearing a buzzer at her rear, she hurriedly put the cap back on her lipgloss and tossed it into her purse. She turned around just in time to see the gate of the prison rolling back. She spat out her gum and straightened out her D&G salmon colored dress. When the gate had rolled all of the way back, her man stood out in full view. He was in a charcoal gray short sleeve Dickie shirt, which he wore buttoned at the neck with matching pants and dark shades sat at the top of his head, making him resemble a black Cholo.

Chevy's eyes became glassy when she saw her man. A smile stretched across her face and she folded her lips inward. She fanned her misting eyes and pounced up and down. She was overwhelmed. It was like she was in a desert and he was a mirage. It couldn't be him standing there, live and in the flesh. She cupped her hands over her nose and mouth, tears flooding her cheeks now.

Tiaz was smiling like a mothafucka while feasting his eyes on his boo. She was even more beautiful than she was in her pictures. It still hadn't hit him that he was free, so seeing her really had him fucked up in the head. He wanted to pinch himself to make sure he wasn't dreaming. Chevy took off running toward her man, and he took off right behind her. She leapt up into the air and he caught her. She wrapped her arms around his neck and her legs around his waist.

They kissed long, hard, and passionately, like the world was falling apart around them and it would be their last time doing so.

Tiaz carried her over to the Caprice and laid her down on the hood. She cupped his face as their heads bobbed from their kissing. His hand slid up her dress and he moved to slip off her white cotton panties, but she grabbed him by the wrist. She pulled her head back and looked into his eyes smiling, still in disbelief that he was right there with her right now.

"Easy tiger, we've got plenty of time for that." She slid off the hood of the car.

"Mind if I drive? It's been a minute since I've sat behind the wheel."

"Hey, knock yourself out." She gently punched him in the chin. He ran over to the driver's side and she tossed him the carkeys. He resurrected the engine and she slid in on the passenger side. He turned the key in the ignition and resurrected the vehicle, driving off.

Tiaz gunned down the freeway doing eight-five miles an hour. Chevy stuck her head out of the window and allowed the wind to blow through her hair causing it to waft like a lone T-shirt on a clothes line. She smiled as she climbed out and sat down on the windowsill. She shouted like a drunken white girl as she held her fists in the air. Today was a beautiful day. She was young, she was alive, and her man had come home.

A smile emerged on Tiaz' face hearing Chevy make all of those crazy noises. He looked into the rearview mirror and saw a police cruiser far off in the distance. "Aye, get back in, The Ones are coming up."

She ducked back inside and rolled up the window. She took her pack of Newports from out of the ashtray and pulled a square from out of the box. She lit up the square and blew out a gust of smoke.

"I went out and got chu a few things to wear out on job interviews." Chevy grabbed a Macy's shopping bag from the backseat and sat it on her lap. She went through the items inside with her free hand while the other held her smoldering cigarette. She pulled out a button down shirt, laid it against her chest along with its matching tie. "What chu think?" She asked of the two items. Tiaz spared the items a glance.

"That's what's up." He refocused his attention back to the road.

"I got chu some shoes, too. They're Mauri's Italian leathers." Chevy removed a lid off the shoebox and pulled out a lone black leather alligator skin shoe. The shoe was so clean they had a polish to them like a buffed floor.

"Yeah, those are fly," Tiaz declared. "I can fuck with them."

"I gotchu a few other things, they're back there in the bags.I don't know your style, so I bought you an assortment of things. I kept the receipt, so if you don't like them you can take them back."

"I'm sure I'll love them, babe." He leaned closer and gave her a peck on the lips.

"Where are we headed?"

"Inglewood Cemetery," Tiaz answered. "I haven't visited my father in five years. Are you down?" He held out his fist.

"I'm down."She dapped him up. The rest of the ride to the cemetery, she leaned her head against his muscular arm and closed her eyes, a grin forming on her face.

***

Tiaz pulled the Caprice to a stop at the top of the hill that overlooked his father's gravesite. He reached into the backseat and grabbed a bouquet of flowers he'd gotten on the way over. Opening the door, he turned around to Chevy. "I'll be right back," kissing her on the lips before hopping out of the car. He made his way down the rich green grassy hill, en route to his old man's resting place, occasionally glancing at the various headstones surrounding him. Once he reached the one he was looking for, he kneeled down and laid the flowers down. He stuck his hands inside of his pockets and stared down at the black marble with *Melvin Eugene Petty* engraved in it.

Tiaz mother had passed away while giving birth to him, which left him in his father's care. His old man was okay. He wasn't big on showing affection, though. He pretty much let him do as he pleased just as long as he knew what time he was coming in and he maintained at least a C average.

Melvin Petty wasn't anyone's fool. He worked two jobs. He worked security at the Staple Center and drove a cab at night. He was at home just long enough to take a shower and grab a bite to eat on his way back out of the door. With him working constantly, he knew his boy would have a lot of free time on his hands. Free time that he knew he'd most likely use to get into mischief. That's why he was given a list of chores and a set of rules that he'd have to abide by just as long as he was living under his roof.

Father and son were getting along quite well. Everything seemed to be alright until the old man lost his job. He couldn't maintain his living expenses working as a cab driver alone, so he turned to the streets. Picking up a gun, he robbed every trap house, D-boy, and corner hustler he came across. When things got too hot for him to handle alone he took his only son on as a partner. Together they took the underworld by storm leaving every Top Dawg in the game shook.

That was until karma came knocking and they found themselves before the barrel of the gun instead of behind it. Tiaz closed his eyes and took a deep breath. Exhaling, he thought back to the night that his father had been murdered in cold blood.

"Goddamn you, Cordell, don't chu kill my boy! Don't chu touch 'em!" Melvin shouted from the chair he was bounded to, spittle flying from his lips and his nostrils flaring. His hands were nailed to the armrests of the chair and his ankles were duct-taped to its legs. His face was bloody and bruised. His left eye was swollen shut while the right was narrowed from swelling. His broken nose was double in size and his busted lips caused him to talk funny. He and his son had spent the past hour being beaten by

Cordell's henchmen. It was a setup. They had gotten a bogus lead that led them straight into a trap.

Cordell held a silver .357 Magnum revolver against a young Tiaz' head causing it to bend at an angle. The boy had gotten his issue just as his old man had. His injuries mirrored his own. The blood that had ran from his face and down his neck had stained the collar of his wife beater pink. His eyes were staring out of their corners and his lips were a straight line.

He knew the risk of the deadly game he and his old man were playing, but he was still scared to die. His pop's made sure he was well aware of the graveyard risks they were taking and he agreed to go along with them.

With that in mind, Tiaz decided he wasn't about to tuck his nuts in the face of death. Nah, fuck that, he was going to let them hang.

Cordell looked from Tiaz to Melvin wearing a devilish grin as he held that steel to the side of his melon. He got a kick out of watching the older man beg for the life of his son.

"Now why wouldn't I kill this lil' mothafucka, huh? Tell me why?" His lips peeled back into a sneer. "Gimmie one good goddamn reason. And maybe, just maybe I'll let 'em walk."

Melvin was quiet for a time as he looked away trying to conjure up a good enough reason to have his son exonerated.

"Welp." Cordell shrugged. "I guess this is goodbye, junior." He cocked the hammer of his revolver with his thumb and moved to squeeze the trigger.

"No! No! No! Wait!" Melvin shouted, seeing his son's brain about to get splattered.

"You better start doing a whole lotta talking real fast." Cordell's eyebrows arched and his nose scrunched as he gritted his teeth. Tiaz squeezed his eyelids closed tightly, waiting to be delivered to heaven or hell, whichever came first for people who'd done the dirt he'd done.

"The money, all of the money we've stole since we've been kickin' in does." Melvin spoke fast, hoping to change the course of his baby boy's fate.

"Money, huh? How much are we talking here?"

"Half—half a million dollars."

"Five hundred big ones, huh? I hear ya talking, but chu gon' have to show me something." He put the hammer back into its rightful place and took the gun away from Tiaz' temple causing him to sigh and relax. "I want that money right here and right now. So where is it?"

Melvin closed his eyes and swallowed, taking a deep breath, thanking the Lord for sparing his offspring. When he peeled his eyelids back open, he started rattling off the address where the money was hidden and were he'd stashed it.

Cordell sent his men after the loot. An hour later they returned with a Puma duffle bag. He ordered them to unzip the duffle bag and hold it open. When they did as instructed, his eyes were pleased by the contents inside. One of the henchmen zipped the duffle bag back up and dropped it at Cordell's feet.

"Now your end of the bargain." Melvin nodded to his boy, keeping his eyes on his abductor.

"Right. I am a man of my word." Cordell turned to one of his men. "Release the boy."

The henchman worked the nail back and forth with the hammer causing Tiaz to frown and clench his teeth, blood splattered on the scratched up hardwood floor creating a small pool.

Snikt! Thump! Snikt! Thump!

The nails made their noise as they dropped to the floor, stained with blood. The henchman kneeled to the floor, sitting the hammer down and unsheathing a knife. He sliced the duct-tape around the boy's ankles and snatched it loose.

Tiaz rose to his feet wincing as he looked at his wounded hands. He quickly forgot about them when he realized his father hadn't been set free, yet. He ran toward him but Cordell stepped in his path. He stared up at him like, Get the fuck out of my way or get your ass bowled over.

"Give us a minute, please." Melvin asked of Cordell and he moved from the young man's path. "Come here, son." He winced, aching from the injuries to his hands and face. His boy stepped before him. "Get outta here, son."

"Pop, I'm not leaving here without you. Fuck these niggaz." He mad dogged all of the opposing men in the room, then he looked back to his father.

"Listen, you've gotta get outta here now. If you don't, we're both dead. Please."

There was silence as father and son stared into one another's faces. Their eyes saying what their mouths hadn't the courage to mention. Melvin hadn't been too big on affection with his first born, so he let his actions show him what he couldn't verbalize.

"I love you, son."

Those words made Tiaz' eyes turn glassy, but he refused to shed a tear in front of the men present. Without saying a word, he wrapped his arms around him firmly. His father kissed him on the cheek and the side of the head.

"Go, son, go! Get outta here." Melvin threw his head toward the door.

"I love you too, pop."

"I know. Now gon' son, get!"

Tiaz headed for the door, glaring at the henchmen as he went along. He stopped at the one that had just opened the door for him, hocking up spit and hawking it into his face. The man closed his eyes and pulled his handkerchief from his breast pocket, wiping his face clean. Tiaz crossed the threshold out of the door.Going down the steps he heard the muffled commotion coming from inside of the house he just left.

"It's time to pay your tides, Mel." He barely heard Cordell say.

"Ol' Melvin Petty has always been good for it. I always pay my debts."

"And that's why I fucks with chu."

"You just remember when it's all said and done, they gon' bury me a G, you hear me? Bury me a mothafucking G! A G! A..."

Bop! Bop! Bop! Bop!

Once the shots went off, Tiaz closed his eyes and tears shot down his cheeks. He never broke his stride as he headed out of the front yard of the trap house, though.

He was sure of one thing at that moment, he wouldn't rest until he avenged his father's murder. And he did too. With the assistance of Threat, he tracked down all parties involved. His execution of them was swift and carried out with extreme preju-dice. It was with this blood pact that he and Threat's brotherhood was sealed.

Tiaz got down on his knees and placed his hands on the sides of the gravestone. He looked at the scars on his hands he'd gotten twelve years ago when Cordell's men had nailed his hands to the armrests of the chair. He couldn't help thinking of how Jesus must have had the same scars that he had when he was nailed to a cross. He had been crucified by his own while he was being crucified by the streets.

Tiaz touched his forehead to the cold marble of the gravestone and closed his eyes. He held it there for a time before kissing it and getting to his feet, smacking dirt from his hands.

"Later, pop." He headed back to the car.

***

"Who house is this?" Chevy asked Tiaz as she stared out of the window at the white and green house they'd just pulled up to.

"This is my dude Threat's spot. He's supposed to let me hold something until I get back on my feet. I'll be right back." Tiaz pecked Chevy on the lips and hopped out the Caprice. He bailed into the yard and up the steps, knocking on the door. A moment later, Threat pulled open the door dressed in a wife beater and boxer briefs, smoking on a smoldering blunt. His eyes lit up when he saw his brethren and he embraced him with a manly hug.

"I thought chu said you weren't getting out until tomorrow, old lying ass nigga?" He threw phantom punches at his brother from another.

"I wanted to surprise you. Let me hit that." Tiaz held out his hand for the blunt. Threat let him have it and he took a few puffs.

Threat looked over Tiaz' shoulder into the Caprice where he saw Chevy sitting shotgun. She smirked and waved at the shorter thug and he waved back. "Come in, fool." He patted Tiaz on the back and he lumbered his bulky frame inside.

"That's yo girl, Chevy, sitting in the Caprice?" Threat asked. Tiaz nodded *yes*. "She's a bad one, Crim."

"Penpals.com, huh?"

"Yep." Tiaz responded journeying down the hallway.

"Man, they got bitches that look like that on there? I should have made me an account," Threat said, leading the way down the corridor. "Have a seat in the living room, I'll be right back." He ducked off into his bedroom, purposely leaving the door open so his righthand could see inside. Lying in the bed fast asleep under silk bed sheets was a thick ass Dominican chick with golden skin and long reddish brown hair. She was a big woman with a really pretty face that reminded most men of the porn star Angie Love.

Tiaz stole a glance of her. The Latin vixen looked scrumptious. Her exposed golden thigh caused the serpent in his Dickies to stir awake. It had been a minute since he had himself a piece and the BBW lying in his friend's bed would have been a treat.

Tiaz sat at the living room table waiting for his road dawg to return. When Threat re-emerged he was in a pair of starched Levi's 501 jeans and canvas All-Star Chuck Taylor Converse with fatlaces. The fingers of his righthand were clamped around two bricks of money that were as thick as two telephone books. He sat down at the table across from Tiaz and smacked the bricks of money down before him. He then leaned back in his chair, massaging his chin.

"Tell me how you love that?"

Tiaz looked up from the bricks of money and into his comrade's face, pointing a finger to his own chest. "This is all me?" Threat nodded *yes*. "Well, good looking. I see working for Don Juan is what it's cracked up to be?"

"Yeah, there's some cool money in this crack shit, but it's too much work, Crimey. Those stacks I just laid on you took a couple weeks to make. When we were out there pulling capers we saw that kind of paper and then some in one day. Shit is peanuts, but like I said this hustle is a means to an end. I'm getting better thangs lined up for me and you, my nigga, feel me?"

"Better thangs like what?" Tiaz leaned closer, giving him his undivided attention.

"In this business I done came across a few niggaz that aren't particularly happy about how their bosses have been treating them. You know, disgruntled employees and narcissistic side bitches. I know of some cats that we can hit that's doing their thang. We can hit 'em all for a payday. I'm talking about a free lunch, Crim."

"Really?"

"When have you known your nigga to fuck around when it comes to getting that paper?" Threat asked.

"Never."

"Alright then."

"What's up with the boy, Don?"

"What chu mean?"

"Shit, is he ripe for the picking?"

"Nah," Threat shook his head. "That's peoples. You know I can't touch homie."

"Alright, I'm just tryna see where you're at with it."

He and Don Juan were alright. They'd say what's up to one another in passing but they weren't homies. Don Juan was Threat's boy, which was the only reason he hadn't become another statistic to a two-eleven. Otherwise, his tall pretty ass would have been food for the vultures.

"I hear you, but Don is off limits. I could never bite the hand that feeds me." Threat told him like it was. "Anyway, fool, where are you holing up at?"

"With homegirl," Tiaz answered. "I gave her this whole line about me going straight, but that was some bullshit. I just need somewhere to lay my head for a minute. She may not feel how

I'ma be getting it in the beginning, so I'ma have to treat her like a virgin."

"How is that?"

"Ease it in, inch by inch."

"You're a fool." Threat chuckled.

"Let me hold something." Tiaz exercised his triggerfinger and Threat picked up on exactly what he was getting at. He nodded, left the table, and returned with a small black box. He sat it on the table, opened it, and revealed a .9mm Beretta with two fully loaded magazines. Tiaz whistled when he saw the gun. He pulled the box closer and looked its contents over. "This bitch clean?" He inquired of the weapon having any murders on it.

"As the board of health," Threat assured.

Once he'd finished inspecting the Beretta, Tiaz put it back inside of the box and closed it. He picked it up from the table and slapped hands with his main man. "What chu about to get into?"

"Some Spanish pussy, you want some?" Threat offered up the thick Latina.

"Nah, you know I'm with lil' momma now."

"Well, if you ever change your mind, you know my number." Threat made his hand into a phone and brought it to his ear.

"I just gotta cell, I'ma text you my number. You let me know when you ready to make that move." Tiaz stated seriously, staring Threat dead in his eyes. He couldn't wait to get back on the scene on his stickup shit. It wasn't just the money; it was the thrills he got from pulling jobs.

"We on, my nigga, they done fucked up and let the dogs loose." Threat slapped hands with Tiaz and embraced him.

The muscle headed goon grabbed his bricks of money and fled the house.

On the way to Chevy's house, Tiaz made a quick pit stop to pick up something he felt would get him in her son's good graces.

***

When Tiaz pulled up in front of Chevy's house, Savon was out on the porch smoking a blunt and staring up at the twinkling stars sprinkled throughout the sky. Tiaz executed the engine and looked out of his window at Savon.

"Who's that?" Tiaz asked.

Chevy looked out of the window then back to Tiaz. "That's Savon, my lil' brother. He watches my son for me sometimes. Come on, I'll introduce you." They grabbed the shopping bags and made toward the house. "Where's Te'Qui?"

"He's in house watching TV."

"Thanks for watching him."

"No problem." He took a pull from his blunt.

"This is my friend I was telling you about. Savon meet Tiaz.Tiazmeet Savon." Chevy made the introductions.

"What's up, homie?" Tiaz dapped up Savon.

"'Sup with it?" Savon threw his head back a little. "I need to holla at chu for a minute, my nigga." Tiaz handed the bags to Chevy and kissed her on the cheek.

"Savon." Chevy shot him a warning expression with a raised eyebrow.

"Don't trip I just wanna holla at my man and see where he's at with it." He assured her with a smirk.

"What's cracking?" Tiaz asked Savon once Chevy had left.

Savon took a few puffs of the loud and passed it off to Tiaz. He took pulls as he listened to what Chevy's brother had to say. "You're fresh out, huh? What were you in for?"

"I shot the fool that beat up my old lady and robbed her." Tiaz said as if it were nothing.

"What happened with cha lady? Does my sister know about her?"

"My girl broke up with me while I was on lock, and yes, your sister does know about her."

Savon nodded in understanding. "So, uh, where are you from, homie?"

"Hoovers…Seven Foe."

"I'ma Outlaw. Eastside Rolling 20s," Savon threw up the B. "It's all love, though. Since you're gonna be fucking my sister that practically makes us family. Check this out, though, fam. My sister and my lil' nephew in there are my mothafucking heart," he smacked his hand over his left breast. "Besides my business and my goons, they're all I have. I don't have to tell you what would happen if a nigga was to play with my loved ones, feel me?" Tiaz nodded. "Alright, dawg, I'm outta here." Savon tucked his hands into his jacket's pockets and stepped off of the porch, heading for his car. Tiaz finished the L he left behind and headed into the house.

***

When Tiaz stepped inside he saw Te'Qui sitting on the couch watching TV. He hung up his jacket at the coat stand and approached him. "What's up, lil' homie?" He held out his fist. Te'Qui laughed at something that happened on screen, completely ignoring him. "What chu watching, man?" Tiaz tried a different approached. Again, the little nigga ignored him and kept his eyes on the screen.

Seeing what the youngster was doing, Chevy came out of the kitchen where she was preparing dinner, picked up the remote control, and turned off the TV.

Te'Qui sucked his teeth and turned around on the couch toward his mother. "What chu doing?" he asked.

"We have a guest, why don't chu try being hospitable." Chevy said.

"Who? This nigga?" Te'Qui pointed a thumb over his shoulder at Tiaz.

"His name is Tiaz. He is an adult and you *will* show him respect."

Tiaz held out his fist for the young nigga to give him dap. Te'Qui looked at his fist and then up at him, shooting him a funny look.

"Te'Qui, what did you tell me the other night? What did you promise me, huh?" Chevy asked. He exhaled and dapped up Tiaz.

Tiaz sat on the couch. He was a bit uncomfortable because it was plain Te'Qui didn't want him around. Annoyance was written across the child's face. After minutes of tension filled silence,

Te'Qui abruptly stood to his feet. "Boy, am I beat, I'm finna lay it down." He rose to his feet and headed for the hallway.

"You sure you can't stay up for a few ticks? I thought maybe we'd play Call of Duty Advance Warfare." Tiaz said.

"Call of Duty Advance Warfare?"

"Yep," Tiaz pulled the video game from a Game Stop bag.

"You tryna buy me?" Te'Qui shot the thug a dirty look and tilted his head.

"Nope, I was hoping to rent. Come on, grab a controller." Tiaz patted the empty space on the couch next to him. He then loaded the video game into the PS4. For a time Te'Qui just stood there with his arms folded across his chest thinking to himself. Tiaz closed the PS4, grabbed a controller for himself and Te'Qui, and sat back on the couch. "Are you tryna play, or what?"

"Alright, but I'm only playing one game," he said, grabbing the joy stick.

Tiaz and Te'Qui ended up staying up all night playing Call of Duty Advance Warfare. They laughed and shot the shit like a couple of old college buddies. Although Te'Qui had to go to school the next day, Chevy didn't have the heart to stop him. She liked the fact that her new man and her son were getting along. Standing in the doorway looking at the men of her life fooling around and having a good time, brought a smile to her face. She hoped things would continue to run smoothly between two of the most important men in her life. She was looking forward to having the family she'd always dreamt about.

Tiaz realized he was kicking Te'Qui's ass in Call of Duty. The game had been pretty much one sided with the youngster handing down the beating, so he knew something was up. He looked to his right and found him with his head leaned back and his mouth wide open, snoring. Tiaz smiled. He turned off the PS4, pulled off Te'Qui's sneakers and draped a blanket over him before heading off into Chevy's bedroom.

Chapter 10

Chevy led Tiaz by the hand inside of the bathroom where she turned the dial of the shower. The showerhead sprayed hot water that slowly began to create a fog that rolled across the floor and engulfed the air. The quarters became warm and comforting, sort of like a sauna.

Tiaz went to pull off his shirt but feeling a hand grasp his arm stopped him. Looking over his shoulder, he found his lady already stripped down to her bra and panties.

"Hold on, King, I got chu." She undone her bra and allowed it to roll down her shoulders before she snatched it off.

She let it drop to the floor and slipped off her panties, leaving them strewn on the linoleum. She then attended to her man, peeling his clothes off of his diamond hard body. His back, arms and legs were all bulging with muscles, looking like they'd been chiseled. He was built like a black Superman. Even his back had muscles. It looked like an upside down pyramid and it lead up to a perfectly sculpted tight, slightly hairy ass.

Chevy took the time to admire her man's physique. The sight of him made her pussy purr. She had to bite down at the corner of her bottom lip.

Down, girl, we've gotta take care of our king right now.

Chevy stuck her hand into the water and tested the temperature. She turned the dial for the cold water a little and felt the water again. It was just right. She helped Tiaz into the tub and grabbed the loofah. She got it soapy with some Dove body wash and motioned her man to turn his back. He did as she commanded, planting his big hands against the tiled walls. He bowed his head and closed his eyes, letting the water coat his form. While he assumed the position, she washed him up, scrubbing every inch of his form admiring every groove, crevasse and indention.

Once she was done she dried him off and led him back inside of the bedroom.

The fresh sent of Coconut Vanilla scented candles teased his nasal passages causing him to close his eyes and grin. The flames of the candles danced on the walls casting shadows. When he peeled his eyes open, Chevy was sitting on the edge of the bed, motioning him over. She was wearing a Kimono and on the nightstand beside her were various oils.

"Lay down on your stomach, baby, I'ma give you a massage." She poured some of the oil into her palm and rubbed her hands together. Once he lay across the bed, she straddled him and massaged him from the top of his shoulders to his lower buttocks. Her hands went over the curve of his ass and dipped down to his muscular legs, working their way down them.

Head rested against the pillow, eyes closed, he smiled.

Baby sho' know how to pamper a nigga, he thought, enjoying the special treatment.

When Chevy was done with his back, she made him turn over. She oiled him from his neck on down, taking her sweet time, making sure he enjoyed every moment of her effort.

Her delicate hands went over his rock hard abs and over his shaved public region. His dick was semi erect, lying partially against his thigh. She grabbed it and stroked it up and down gently, watching his face as she did so. He hummed and licked his lips as his meat grew as hard as steel. The sound of her greasy hands sliding up and down his dick filled his ears. She tugged up and down his member causing it to reach its full potential. She continued to stroke his fuck organ bringing his foreskin over the head of it then down below it.

"You like that, baby?" Chevy cracked a smile as she worked him.

"Mmmmm, yes, baby, I love it." He turned his head and his eyes flickered. "Faster, baby, faster."

"You got it, daddy." She squeezed his meat slightly tighter, stroking it from top to bottom as if she was fucking it with her pussy. She watched as he squirmed and felt his dick pulsate, veins bulging with its head throbbing.

"Yes, baby, don't stop." He stole a peek, seeing her stroke him quicker. "Stroke that mothafucka, stroke 'em. Sssssss, yeah, yeah,

yeah," She squeezed tighter, stroked faster. "Like that, just like that!" His head dropped down into the pillow, sinking in.

"You gon' cum for me, daddy? Huh? You gon' gimmie that nut?"

"Oh, yes, yes, baby, I'ma…" His eyes turned to their whites as the pleasure of her gentle palms choked him up. "I'ma cum. I'ma cum real hard! Ughhh!" He popped like the cork of a bottle of champagne and his children oozed out of his head, slicking over her knuckles. She scooped the warm goo up and used it to keep, tugging up and down his dick.

His body twitched as he released and she worked whatever little bit of baby batter he had left in him.

"Goddamn that shit was fiyah." He watched her wipe her hands off with a washcloth as he pushed and pulled on his dick, getting it back to its hardness.

"Let me gon' get that out chu." He made to get up, still groping his member. He had bent at the waistline when she placed a hand against his chest, slowing his roll.

"I got this." She capped with a crooked smile. "I'ma take care of you now, King. You can take care of yo Queen later, alright?" He nodded. "Smooth."

He lay back in bed and she straddled him. He felt her kisses traveling down his washboard stomach and down toward his southern region. His rod grew harder. She rolled a black condom down onto his meat while playing with her bald pussy, slicking it wet. Standing on her bending knees, she carefully brought her womanhood onto his dick, eloping the two.

"Sssssss." She hissed and closed her eyes, biting down on the corner of her lip.

"Mmmm." Tiaz spoke softly, lying back with his hands clasped behind his head, watching her do her thing.

Chevy licked her lips as she slowly rotated her hips, shifting his love muscle as it remained buried inside of her. She felt a mixture of pleasure and pain as she rode him with both of her manicured hands placed on his muscular chest. After a while, it began to feel blissful. Tiaz could tell she'd found her rhythm once she started showing out. The way she threw it on him caused him to holler out like a little bitch.

"Ahhh, fuck!"

"Uh huh," she threw her head back and kept that thang pumping on him. "Haa! Haa! Haa! Haa!" she breathed heavily, matching his husky draws of breath.

Chevy was working him hard, digging her nails further into his pecks. His endowment massaging her interior felt good, so good that she pulled her fingers back, drawing trickles of blood. "Argghhh." He grunted, with his face balling up and his jaws squaring. The pussy was all of that. He could nearly feel her warmth and moisture through the condom.

"Oooooh, yes, yes, yes," she hollered out in sensual pleasure. "There it go, there that shit go, I can feel it."

Pat ! Pat ! Pat! Pat!

She came down on that thang, her ample ass mashing and forming back, each and everytime it met with his mound. He watched with delight. The sight was hypnotizing. He was in a trance. He couldn't look away. *Goddamn!* Light skin was blowing his mind.

With his dick still inside of her, she turned around so her back would be facing him. She held his ankles and got on bended knees.

The noise of damp flesh slapping together sounded throughout the bedroom as she threw her big yellow ass down onto his mound. He gripped her ass cheeks as she threw it into him, watching the ripple effect that occurred when her butt collided with his pelvis. His face contorted in ecstasy and semen began to build up in his love muscle.

"Arrrr!" His right eye twitched and he bit down on his inner jaw. Feeling himself about to erupt, he squeezed her cheeks tighter, seeing the indentions form around his thick fingers. He grunted, holding Chevy down on his dick and lifting his back from the bed, he released all of his babies inside of the ebony latex. "Ahhhhh, sssssshiiiiiiit! Ssssss, fuck!" He looked like he was turning into a werewolf before an expression of relief crossed his face. Chevy caught her nut right after him.

"Sssssss, goddamn, I could fucking bite chu." She crawled upon him, biting gently on his peck and neck. Her hot wet tongue glided up his neck and she sucked on his throat before sliding over to his earlobe. She nibbled on his earlobe a little before pulling back and lying her head on his chest, his hand sliding up and down his rock hard abs.

She then snuggled up against him, closing her eyes wearing an appeased expression. He held her to him with one arm and stared up at the ceiling. He'd just completed his first mission, and that was busting that *welcome home* nut. Now it was time to get to the main objective: the money. Tiaz closed his eyes and began to think about all of the caked up hustlers he could bring it to for the dough. It wasn't long before he fell asleep wearing a smile on his face.

***

Tiaz' nostrils flared as the aroma of bacon snaked its way into his nostrils. His nose twitched and his eyes fluttered as he began to stir awake from his slumber. His eyelids peeled open and he sat up in bed, rubbing away the crust that had formed in the crevasses of his eyes while he slept. He looked to the side of the bed where Chevy had slept and noticed she was gone. He put on his wife beater and slipped on a pair of sweatpants that lay next to the bed. He stepped inside of the bathroom where he washed his face and brushed his teeth. Once he was done, he carried his hulky body into the kitchen where the scent of a delicious breakfast had brought him. When he entered the kitchen, Chevy was standing over the stove whipping up breakfast: eggs, bacon, potatoes and cinnamon toast. Te'Qui was sitting at the table patiently waiting while playing God of War III on his PSP.

Chevy turned around with a skillet of eggs. Seeing her boo brought a smile to her face. "Good morning."

"Good morning." Tiaz pecked her on the lips then turned to Te'Qui. "What's up, my young nigga? I see you recovered from the butt whooping I gave you last night." He dapped him up and sat down in the chair. Chevy went around the table filling the plates with food.

"What? Momma, you hear this dude?" Te'Qui smirked. "I was chipping you. You may wanna try finding yourself another game 'cause Call of Duty ain't your thang."

"You're right, you got me. I'ma have to go into training for our rematch. But in the meantime, how about that Marvel vs Capcom? I know you can't see me in that."

"That's old school, but it don't matter. I'll still put hands on you."

"Alright. I'ma go see if I can find a copy today, Mr. Get Bad." Tiaz took a bite of cinnamon toast.

Everyone had begun eating. Te'Qui had taken a sip of orange juice and wiped his mouth with a napkin when he noticed the five AK-47 bullets tattooed on Tiaz' forearm. "That tattoo is hard than a mug." Te'Qui openly admired the ink.

"Thanks." Tiaz managed to say with a jaw swollen with food. He'd begun gathering potatoes on his fork when Te'Qui asked.

"Who laced you?"

"This Mexican fool back in prison." Tiaz took a bite of the potatoes.

"Do they mean anything, or are they just bullets?"

"They're five bullets, one for each year I spent in prison."

"What did you do to end up in the pen?"

"Te'Qui, you're asking too many questions, baby. Eat your food." Chevy interjected.

Tiaz held his hand up at Chevy. "Nah, it's cool. I blasted on somebody."

"Why, what did he do? Disrespect you?"

"He hurt something I loved."

"Do you regret shooting him?"

"Yes, but not for the reason you may think."

"Then why?"

Tiaz wiped his mouth with a napkin before answering. "The person that I shot him over wasn't worth the five years I spent in prison. Otherwise, I wouldn't regret pulling those bullets."

"Who was the person you shot someone over?" Te'Qui inquired.

"They're not even worth mentioning." Tiaz went on eating his breakfast.

The telephone rang and Chevy got up to answer it. Seeing who it was on the caller ID, she rolled her eyes and picked up the phone.

"What do you want, Faison?"

"Is that how you speak to the father of your child?"

"Whatever, what do you want?" She looked over her shoulder to see if Tiaz was watching her. He wasn't. He was busy talking with her son.

"Where is my son?"

"He's eating."

"Well, put 'em on the phone."

Chevy had opened her mouth to say something when her son stopped his conversation to ask his mother a question.

"Is that dad?" Te'Qui shouted with a mouthful of food.

She nodded *yes*, and her baby boy's face lit up with excitement. He drank some orange juice to wash down his food, wiped his mouth, and hopped out of his chair. He rushed over to his mother and snatched the phone from her. He then retreated to his bedroom to talk to his father in private.

Chevy was glad to see her son so happy. Even though she despised Faison, she couldn't imagine trying to keep them away from each other.

"That was your son's father, huh?" Tiaz inquired once Chevy sat down at the table. She'd already given him the rundown on their history. He knew exactly who he was dealing with, which is why he'd gotten the banger from Threat. If Faison thought he was gone play those games with him that he was playing with the mother of his child, then he had another thing coming: a barrel full of some hollow tips to be exact.

"Yep, that was him." Chevy took a sip of orange juice.

"Look, Chevy, I'm not up for games, so if homes come over here tryna stunt..." he trailed off. "Well, you know how I get down, baby daddy or not." He warned her and she nodded her understanding.

At that moment a horn was blown, Tiaz walked over to the curtains and peered outside. Through the window he spotted Threat in the driveway. He motioned for his comrade to come outside. Tiaz held up a finger and headed for the bedroom. He stuck his feet into a pair of white Air Force Ones and threw on a hefty leather jacket. He retrieved the banger Threat had given him from the black box and stashed it inside of his jacket.

"Who was that?" Chevy asked him when he returned to the living room.

"Threat. I'll be right back."

Tiaz came out of the house and jogged over to the passenger side of his homeboy's whip. Threat turned down the music when Tiaz leaned down into the window. "What's upper?"

"Hop in." Threat hit the switch that unlocked the door and Tiaz hopped into the front passenger seat. "We're about to take a lil' ride." He backed out into the residential block and pulled off, filling Tiaz in on the caper he'd come up on. "I came upon a pretty sweet lick."

"Who is it? And what're they holding?"

"Majestic," Threat told him.

"So is this cat holding a big bag?"

"From what I gather, he's holding one of the biggest. We're rolling through here to see this cat that put me on to 'em. He knows more than what I do."

Threat pulled into the Slauson Supermall and parked six rows back from the establishment's entrance doors. He looked over to the music installation garage and waved over the man he'd come to see.

Limb sped walked his lanky frame across the parking lot with his head on a swivel as he took pulls from a cigarette. He was dressed in a Niners football jersey and sweatpants. Wire framed glasses accentuated his face and a doo rag covered his head.

Limb hopped into the backseat of Threat's whip and slammed the door closed. "What up, my ninja?" He greeted him with a fist bump. He stole a glance at Tiaz. "Who that up there?"

"Never mind him." Threat replied.

"I'm just saying, fam, my business is with chu. For all I know homie could be The Ones or something." Limb reasoned.

"Fuck is you talking about?" Threat frowned, feeling disrespected, "Anybody I fuck with is official. In fact, I should pop your top for insinuating I'd even share the same air as a rat." He turned around in his seat with his hammer grasped firmly in his mitt. The presence of a banger made Limb raise his boney hands in surrender.

"My bad, my nigga, I'm just tryna cover my ass. You can't blame me with all of these niggaz out here turning fed."

"That's the only reason why I'ma let this shit die." Threat stashed his gun away. "Throw that cigarette out. I just got my shit detailed."

"Oh, my fault," Limb took a quick pull and flicked the cigarette out of the window, embers flying along with it.

"Gimmie the skinny on your man."

"Like I was telling you, the nigga clears like a hundred K a night from all of the traps he got. He sends these two muscle head niggaz along the route to pick it all up. They be in this big ass black truck, I think it's a Suburban or something."

"What kind of hardware are they holding?" Threat inquired.

"Desert Eagles, I think." Limb answered.

"Where do they take the money from there?" Tiaz spoke for the first time.

Limb shrugged. "The hell if I know. I guess to Majestic."

"Who else have you told about this lil'caper?" Threat asked. "Come on now, fam, me and you go back like two flats on a Cadillac. You the only nigga I put on this lick. I'm just looking out for my people."

Threat massaged his chin as he thought on it for a minute. "Alright, Limb. I'ma get up with chu later." He resurrected the engine.

"So, are you gon' go through with it?" Limb asked.

"I said 'I'ma get up with chu, Limb.'" Threat stated firmly, staring into the skinny man's eyes through the rearview mirror.

"Alright then, man." Limb hopped out of the car and jogged over to his Champagne Escalade truck. Threat kept his eyes on him as he drove out of the supermall's parking lot and out into the street.

"So, what chu think?"

"Shit, you hungry?" Tiaz asked.

"Hell yeah."

"Well, let's eat then." He dapped up Threat. "What chu know about this Majestic cat though?

"Is he pussy or what?"

Threat gave him a look like *Are you serious?* He then shook his head. "Nah, T, he's definitely not pussy..." He went on to tell a story about the OG's getdown.

The black pillowcase was snatched from off of his face, his head snapped in every which direction. He realized he was inside of an old warehouse and dangling before a host of masked men. He looked above and saw he was suspended from the ceiling by old rusted chains.

Smelling something familiar in the air, he looked down as his nose twitched. He inhaled and tried to distinguish the overwhelming odor. That's when it dawned on him that it was gasoline he was breathing. His suspicions were confirmed when he saw one of the masked men toss the gas can aside.

"What ya'll think? This shit here scares me?" He looked up at the chains he was hanging from then back at his abductors. *"Fuck death! Gangstaz don't die, we multiply."*

"Is that right, hot shit?" A voice came from within the shadows causing everyone to look in its direction. Right before their very eyes, a snazzily dressed man wearing a fedora peeled himself from the recess of the warehouse, taking deep draws from a Cuban cigar. The men wearing the masks didn't flinch as they recognized their boss. They focused their attention back on their capture while he narrowed his eyes trying to see exactly who it was approaching him.

"Majestic?" His eyelids snapped open and his jaw dropped.

"You guessed right." The tall slender gentleman stepped before him, his face partially hidden by the shade of the shadows.

"What is this all about?" He frowned and shrugged.

"Your blocks, Marcus. I told you to give 'em up, you wouldn't listen. Now here we are." He spread his arms and looked around. *"You ready to die, nigga?"*

"Gon' kill me, it won't stop my legacy from spreading." He told him. *"These lil' niggaz out here hustling on these corners gon' know that Marcus Bristol went out like a boss. My legend gon' infect a hunnit mo' impressionable mothafuckaz and they gon' take to these streets and try to be just like me. You best believe that punk ass, so gon'. Gon' and kill me if you want."* He spat on Majestic's Mauri gator. A nasty yellowish glob spattered on the toe of the Italian leather shoe. The kingpin's head snapped down to his foot then back up at the man that had blatantly disrespected him.

"As you wish." Majestic dropped his cigar into the flammable liquid and a line of fire ripped up the ground toward the opposing man.

His eyes grew as big as saucers. "Oh shit! Oh shit! Oh shit!" He panicked, dancing on the dangling chains looking like a puppet on the end of strings. Blue fire reached the tip of his sneakers and shot up his body, swallowing his entire form. Majestic and his men watched as the man screamed in excruciation, struggling to break free of his restraints.

"Raahhhhhhhhhh!" The man kept screaming and dancing until eventually his throat went raw and hoarse. He started moving sluggishly and then he went slack on the twin chains and his head hung, his chin sitting on his chest. The fire continued its devouring of his carcass, crackling and popping. The smell of cooked flesh invaded the warehouse but the stench didn't seem to bother his audience.

The masked men climbed into their three black H2 Hummers while Majestic slid into the backseat of a limousine. When the limo drove off the the triplets followed behind it.

"Yeah, I hear you, and fuck that nigga," Tiaz said after listening to Threat's story. "He got what we want and we're taking it, straight like that."

"You goddamn right." Threat agreed.

***

By the time Threat pulled back up outside of Chevy's house, the night had already staked its claim over the city.

"Say, man, I appreciate chu doing this favor for me." Tiaz told Threat as he pulled his suit from the backseat which was covered in plastic.

"It ain't 'bout nothing," Threat waved him off. "I'm just looking out for my brother. It's on the love."

"That's what's up." He dapped him up. "Let me get outta here so I can hit the shower and shit, and get ready."

"Alright. I'ma swoop Bianca so that we can get the car." Threat informed. "I'ma slide back through like seven, cool?"

"Bet." Tiaz slammed the door shut and trekked toward the house, with his partner in crime pulling off behind him.

He was about to climb the steps of the house when an ember glow from the side caught his eye. He tried to peer through the darkness but he couldn't make out the figures hidden in the shadows.

Tiaz drew his banger from his waistline and slowly moved in on the figures with his gun extended before him. The closer he got the more the figures began to fill out before his eyes. It was Te'Qui and a taller dark skinned kid who was dressed in a red Cardinals' cap, black Dickie shorts and low-top red All-Star Chuck Taylor Converses.

Tiaz lowered his banger to his side. Te'Qui choked and went into a coughing fit when he saw him. He held the smoldering blunt behind his back and fanned the faint traces of smoke.

"What's up, Tiaz?" Te'Qui asked.

"What's up with it? What are y'all doing over here?" Tiaz frowned.

Te'Qui shook his head side to side. "Nothing, just chopping it up with my homeboy. You haven't met Brice yet, have you?"

"What's up, lil' homie?" Tiaz asked as he sniffed the air. Te'Qui and Baby Wicked exchanged knowing glances. "Y'all back here getting faded?" He snapped his fingers and motioned for him to give him the weed. Reluctantly, Te'Qui passed the blunt to Tiaz. Holding it pinched between his fingers, he sniffed it. "What is this?"

"O.G. Kush." Baby Wicked informed him.

Tiaz took a few pulls from the blunt, holding the smoke hostage in his lungs before blowing it back out.

"Man, you gon' tell my mom's?" Te'Qui asked.

"You can't survive five years on a level four being a snitch. Y'all lil' niggaz do y'all thing." He passed him back the blunt. "I didn't see you and you didn't see me, alright?" He looked between the young men and they nodded. "Alright then, I'm finna take it in." He dapped up the youngsters and made his departure.

Te'Qui and Baby Wicked watched Tiaz' back as he walked away.

"Blood, your mom's new boyfriend cool as a fan." Baby Wicked told Te'Qui as he took the blunt from him.

"Yeah, he is pretty cool." Te'Qui concurred before blowing smoke. A smirk accented his face. He liked Tiaz and wanted to be just like him.

Chapter 11

"He's soooooo fucking amazing." Chevy smiled as she danced around the living room like a ballerina on ice skates. She'd just finished telling her best friend what a dream Tiaz was and she couldn't wait for her to meet him. "I really really think he can be the one."

"Really, girl?" Kantrell beamed.

Kantrell and Chevy had known each other since middle school. They'd gone to Horace Mann Jr. High together. The pair had gotten along famously and carried themselves more like sisters than best friends.

Kantrell's lifestyle was like any other kid's upbringing in the ghetto. Her family struggled to make ends meet just as everyone else's did. It wasn't until her father became the hit man known as Casper that she began to see and experience the finer things that life had to offer.

Jeffery Combs went under the guise of Casper. He'd gotten the name for his skillful kills, being able to strike his targets with expertise and fineness. By the time his intended victims were dispatched, he'd be gone with the wind. It would be like no one was ever there, hence his street moniker.

The blood money was sweet and it kept the family happy. That was until karma came knocking with a warrant for her father's arrest. He was convicted on ten counts of murder and sentenced to death. His execution made Kantrell fatherless and her mother a widow.

These days Kantrell was making her living as a bounty hunter. It was a dangerous occupation but she was prepared.

"Yes! Yes! Yes!" Chevy got down on her knees and took both of her friend's hands. "He makes me feel like—like I'm the most special woman in the world. And when we talk, I feel all giddy inside. It's like high school all over again. Ooooooh," she clenched her fists and looked up at the ceiling at nothing, smiling from ear to ear. "This nigga got me floating on cloud nine. I don't know what this man has done to my head but I like it. Scratch that.

I love it. We're supposed to go out tonight too. I've already got my dress and everything."

"Where are y'all going?"

"I don't know. He wouldn't tell me. All I know is its some fancy five star restaurant."

"Ooooooh, somebody's showing my baby momma the finer thangs."

"Kantrell, I'm so fucking happy I can fucking kiss *you*."

Chevy hopped upon her feet and cupped her best friend's face, planting a big kiss against her lips. She laughed and giggled.

"Damn, bitch! You're far gone." She smirked, wiping her lips with the back of her hand.

"Look at me gloating." She pulled up a chair and sat back down. "I haven't even asked you how things were going with you and yo new boo thang, A."

Kantrell waved her off like *I don't even want to talk about that nigga.*

"What? What's up? Gimmie some tea." She scooted her chair up to the table.

"I'll put it this way I thought I had got me something special when I reeled this nigga in, but boy what a fucking disappointment." She shook her head with regret. "To make a long story short, he ain't nothing like your Tiaz. What I wouldn't do to have someone like that fall into my lap. I tell you, girl, if he's as unique as you say he is, you betta hold on to 'em 'cause this day and age a descent man is hard to find."

Chevy grasped her hand. "I will. I promise I will. And thank you, boo."

Kantrell frowned and coiled her neck. "Thanks for what?"

"For always being such a good friend to me. You've not only been my friend, but my sister. And I've gotta say I love you to the core of my soul." She held her hand to her chest and her eyes became glassy. She was on the verge of crying. She wiped her eyes with a curled finger. "I couldn't—I couldn't..." Her voice cracked. She closed her eyes and pulled herself together, clearing her throat. "I couldn't have asked for a better friend. I really mean that."

Kantrell wiped her dripping eyes with her fingers and thumb. "Chevy, what I've been to you is what you've been to me. Nothing less, I love you more than the air that I breathe." She kissed her sister's hand.

"Awww, gimmie some love." Chevy stood up and spread her arms. She received her sister with a loving embrace. Just as they pulled back and held one another at arm's length, Tiaz was coming through the door.

"Oh, here comes my baby now." Chevy stated, causing Kantrell to look toward the door. She watched as her best friend skipped over to her boo and kissed him in greeting. "Hey, baybee." She sang.

"What's up, Love? Who's your friend?" Tiaz inquired, stealing a glance of Kantrell.

"Hi." She waved and smiled.

"Babe, this is my best friend, Kantrell, she's like a sister to me." Chevy placed her hand on her wrist.

"Oh yeah, I remember her. What's up, Kantrell? I'm Tiaz." He shook Kantrell's hand as he took in her beauty.

Kantrell was a 5'7 number with long brunette hair that she wore flat ironed. She had two palms full of breasts.And from her exotic looks you'd think she was of Brazilian heritage but she was actually the conception of an interracial relationship. Her mother was a full blooded Cherokee Indian and her father was African American.

"Pleasure to meet your acquaintance," Kantrell shook his hand.

Tiaz grinned and nodded. "I'ma go take a shower and get ready." He told Chevy before kissing her and heading into the bedroom.

"So, that's Mr. Wonderful, huh?"

"Yep." Chevy beamed brightly. It felt good to have a man other women found attractive. She knew having a man as good looking as Tiaz would have bitches sniffing around like a hungry dog, and she was well prepared to put hands on a hoe if and when the time came.

Tiaz was eye candy and there were plenty women out there with a sweet tooth.

"Nice looking, man. You betta keep 'em under lock and key 'cause every bitch around the way gon' be tryna suck and fuck on 'em."

"Yeah, I know," Chevy exhaled.

Kantrell watched as Tiaz grabbed a couple of towels out of the hallway closet for his shower. *You're one lucky girl Chevy, one lucky girl,* she thought.

***

Boxy sat slumped behind the wheel of his white '06 Chevy Impala. Jaquez played the front passenger seat. They had four pairs of eyes between them and they all were watching Don Juan who was inside of Fabolous Burgers placing an order.

Through the large glass window they watched as he massaged his chin and stared up at the menu. The plan was simple approach his ass at gun point and make him take them to where he kept them thangz and the money. Once they cleaned him out, they were going to leave him leaking. *Simple enough!*

Boxy checked the magazine of his head bussa to make sure it was fully loaded before smacking it back in and click clacking it. He took a draw from the burning joint Jaquez passed him and expelled the smoke. He mashed out the little that was left and addressed the situation at hand.

"You hop out and hunch down at the front of his truck." Boxy laid down the plan. "When he opens the door you get on his ass, I'ma come from behind him. He won't even expect me. We'll have the drop on 'em. He won't have any choice but to do what we tell 'em or get slumped."

"I got chu faded."

"Matter of fact, they about to give 'em his food, gon' get out." He nudged him hard and fast. They both threw their hoods over their heads and gripped their guns, hopping out of the Chevy. They closed their respective doors and took up their posts.

Jaquez hunched down in front of Don Juan's ride while Boxy stooped low beside his. He held his gun down clutching it with both hands as he took a peek through the driver side window. As soon as he opened the door of his SUV, Jaquez sprung into action, then came Boxy.They both caught their prey by surprise.

"Surprise, surprise." Boxy greeted his boss, cold steel pressed against the back of his dome.

"Shit!" Don Juan cursed, face twisting with anger.

He knew that the young niggaz wanted his stash and his work. And he didn't have a choice but to give it to them if he hoped to live.

Damn! Life is a bitch! He thought as he shook his head.

***

The night was as dark as it had ever been but the moon stood out in contrast against the ebony skyline. It was beautiful, serene even. You could say it was the perfect night, the perfect night for lovers, which was why Tiaz was happy he'd chosen it to take his lady out. A black on black Maybach pulled alongside the curb in front of Chevy's house. The driver's side door opened and Threat hopped out. He was decked the fuck out in a black Brooks Brothers suit with gold cufflinks. The diamonds in his earlobes shined like strobe lights.

The front door of the house swung open, Tiaz and Chevy stepped out looking whipped and dipped. Her hair was feathered out at its ends and her white dress hugged her curvy form. Her full lips were decorated with silver lipstick that glistened with sparkles. An identical belt was around her waist with a big buckle. Her feet were fitted comfortably in a pair of silver high heels, shimmering with glitter.

Chevy looked to her right, admiring all of that muscular man on her arm. If there wasn't anything else in the world she loved more than a thug, it was one that could dress.

Tiaz wasn't anyone's slouch either. He had a keen eye when it came to fashion. Tonight wasn't any different from the other nights he stepped out on the town. Tiaz was in a navy blue suit that hugged his bulging biceps and legs. His tie was a rich chocolate brown and so was his footwear. His feet were in a pair of ostrich and leather lace up shoes, they were shining so hard a chick could fix her makeup in them.

"Is that our ride?" Chevy's eyes lit up when they met the luxury car that her man had rented for the occasion.

"Yep." He smiled proudly, buttoning his suit, "Nothing but the best for my baby."

"Oh, my God, Tiaz." She cupped her hands to her face and jumped up and down excitedly. "I've never ridden in one of those before. I've only seen one on TV."

"Now is as good a time as any. Shall we?" He offered his arm.

"Yes, we shall." She hooked her arm with his and made way for the vehicle.

Once Tiaz and Chevy slid onto the soft leather seats of the nearly half a million dollar car, he popped open a bottle of Belaire. He occasionally glanced over at his lady as he poured up the champagne flutes. He cracked a toothy smile seeing her toying with the umbrella, laughing and giggling.

"You gon' mess around and give us bad luck, Lover, be easy." He warned jokingly.

She set the umbrella aside. "I'm not worried about bad luck 'cause I got my good luck charm right here." She took her flute from his hand and straddled his lap, taking a sip.

"Is that a fact?"

"Uh huh, real life." They set the flutes aside and went at it, their kissing growing hot and heavy, husky breathing between them. He slid his hands beneath her dress exposing her black thong. Still kissing, she started at his belt buckle, ready to get it cracking. It was about to go down when Tiaz peeled his eyelids open and caught Threat watching them through the rearview mirror.

"Hold on, baby.We've gotta fucking peep freak on our hands."
He grinned and nodded up front. Threat casted his eyes away from
the rearview mirror and smiled, diverting his attention back to the
road.

Chevy looked over her shoulder and grinned, sliding off to the
side of her boo. They picked their flutes back up and indulged in
the bubbly, taking the time out to share a quick peck on the lips.

Forty five minutes later, Threat was pulling into the parking
lot of Raphael's, an Italian restaurant out in Hollywood on the
sunset strip. The place was one of the most elegant and exquisite
eating establishments in Los Angeles county. Every one that was
anyone in show business had eaten there from Robert De Niro to
Morgan Freeman.

Chevy was in awe when they walked through its large double
doors. Its interior was like one of a castle with its cream and gold
furniture and fixings. Since Tiaz had made reservations, they were
seated right away and ordered their meals.

Tiaz and Chevy talked about their lives and what they wanted
out of a relationship as they waited.

"I want something real in my life, for once.Ya feel what I'm
saying?" He held her hands within his as he rubbed them with his
thumbs. "A nigga get tired of chasing these ain't shit females out
here and going through the motions. It comes a time in yo life
when you say to yourself enough with the games."

"I feel what chu saying. And I've never been the type to jump
from bed to bed." She spoke from the heart, watching the sincerity
bleed from his eyes. "I'm kind of old fashion. I've always been
content with dealing with one man." He nodded his understanding.

"Chevy, I'm not going to lie to you, I haven't always been
faithfu…"

"Shhh, uh uh," she shook her head. "You don't even have to
say it. I know. Your past is your past. What matters now to me is
the future that we're gonna share. That's all."

"You sure?"

"Positive. You just promise me that from this night forth that
you're a one woman man. I am yours and you are mine."

125

"That's what it is, then."

"Fa'sho." She took a sip of champagne. "Now shall we seal this pact with a kiss?"

"I thought you'd never ask, Lover."

They leaned over the table and their mouths united, marrying into a gentle and loving kiss.

"Oh, you still here?"

A loud feminine voice stole Tiaz and Chevy's attention. Looking over their shoulders they saw a short dark skinned man in a gold turtle neck and a striking cinnamon complexion woman with her dreads pulled back in a bun. The woman was going off on a busty waitress that was holding a bottle of wine.

The woman with the dreads rolled her neck real ghetto like. "I guess you didn't hear me. Chop, chop!" She clapped her hands. "Hurry along now, servant, and fetch us another bottle of wine." She spoke like an 18th century king would to his royal subjects.

"Constance!" The short man said through gritted teeth, slamming his fist down on the table and rattling the dishes. The noise he made snatched the patrons' attention away from what they were doing. Seeing that all eyes were on him, he settled down.

Chevy and Tiaz snickered and turned their attention back to one another. They spent the rest of the night talking, laughing and getting tipsy.

"Anyway," Tiaz shook his head at the spectacle that was made. "I want chu to have something."

"What?" She smiled brightly, excited about what he had.

He held up a finger so she would give him a minute as he reached inside of his suit. When he pulled his hand back he was clutching a small velvet box. Chevy's eyes widen and she cupped her hands to her face.

"Tiaz, I love you but I think—I think you're moving just a little too fast, baby."She spoke with her hand over her left breast.

He laughed. "Nah, Love, it ain't what chu think it is. Check it out." He passed her the velvet box. He took a sip of champagne as he watched her cautiously open it as if it was booby trapped and rigged to explode. She looked up at him as she cracked it open and he gave her a nod like *go ahead*. Chevy opened the box and met with a platinum and diamond key. The lights inside of the restaurant deflected off of it and it shined in her face. A smile graced her lips and she looked up at him. He was smiling as he used the cloth napkin to wipe his mouth.

"It's beautiful baby, but what is it?" She plucked the key from out of the cube and a thin necklace came along with it.

"Here, let me get that for you." He stepped around the table and came to her rear, clamping the necklace around her neck. He then kneeled down to her, taking her hands into his own. "As for what it is, it's a key to my heart." She blushed and looked down at the floor. With a curled finger he tilted her chin up so that she'd be looking at him. "I want chu to know that as long as you have that…" he pinched the key between his fingers and slightly lifted it. "…that chu will forever have the key that unlocks the door where my heart resides. You're the only woman on this planet that I want to have that."

Her eyes misted and rimmed with tears, threatening to roll down her cheeks if she dared to speak. "Tiaz…" Tears jetted down her face and dripped every so often. "Please, please, don't fuck with my heart. I can't take another betrayal by a disloyal man." Thinking about all of the pain she'd been through with Faison had choked her up. She had difficulty forming the words she wanted to speak. Her mouth was moving but there wasn't any sound coming out. "I swear to God I'd die. I'd just writher up like a leaf and die."

"I won't, Chev'. I promise I won't." He held her hands up to his lips and kissed them as he stared up into her eyes. He then rose to his feet picking up a cloth napkin and dabbing the tears from her face. Once he was done, he kissed her lips tenderly and sat back down at the table. The rest of the night they talked and enjoyed their meals as the piano and violins serenaded them.

Two hours later…

Tiaz and Chevy came dancing out of the restaurant hand in hand.The music from the establishment playing inside of their heads. Holding on to her hand, he spun her out like a roll of yarn then she spun back into him. He caught her and bent her over his knee, staring into her eyes wearing a smirk that was a replica of her own. They burst out laughing and he pulled her back up.

"You cold, baby?" he asked, seeing her rubbing her arms. She nodded and he slipped his suit's jacket off, sliding it over her shoulders. "Here, walk on the inside of the sidewalk beside me." They changed places, their fingers interlocked with one another's.

"Let me find out?" She grinned, boasting those beautiful white teeth of hers.

"Find out what?" He tried to contain a smile.

"That you a gentleman."

"I'ma gangsta and a gentleman, sweetheart."

"That's how I like 'em."

"There Threat is." He nodded up ahead, seeing the Maybach pulling out of the parking lot, heading in their direction. Gripping his lady's hand, he jogged over to the luxurious Benz. His man hopped out and rounded the vehicle, pulling the back passenger side door open. He stood aside and allowed the love birds to climb inside, before slamming it back shut.

Chevy snuggled under Tiaz and he threw his arm around her. As they locked lips and the car pulled off, her cell phone rang and the screen lit up. Ms. Helen was on the display along with a picture of a tall slender man with a mole beside his nose. He sported a mop of short curly hair and a thin mustache. Hanging on his arm was a short lady with her hair done in a Chinese bang. She had a pointy nose and a dimpled chin.

Tiaz' forehead creased with lines as he studied the faces of the young couple.

"Is that your mother and father?" he asked.

"Uh huh." She nodded before answering the call.

Chevy and Savon had lost their parents at a very young age. One night after coming home early from work from being laid off, Jewel waltz into his bedroom to find his wife being sexed by his best friend. Without saying a word, he closed the door back as it was and headed out into the garage where he kept his gun stashed.

He trekked back into the house as cool and as calm as he left and returned to his bedroom. Without warning and with an aching heart, he opened fired on his right-hand man and his soul mate. The thunder that had erupted from his revolver drew his children out into the hallway where they found the dead bodies of their mother and their godfather. Eyes spilling his devastation and grievance, Jewel turned to his children and placed his pistol to his temple.

"Daddy loves you, so much," he swore. "And he's sorry, terribly, terribly sorry." He squeezed his eyelids shut and sucked his lips into his mouth. He pulled the trigger and red goo and chunks of brain splattered against the wall beside him. He dropped to the floor like a slinky, leaving his children alone in this sinful world.

"Alright, baby, good night. Mauh." Chevy disconnected the call and tucked the cell into her handbag.

"That was lil' man, huh?"

"Yeah, calling to check on me."

"That's good, him looking out for his mom's and all."

"Yeah, that's my baby." She smirked, thinking of her baby boy.

Chevy interlocked her fingers with his and kissed him on the lips twice. She then laid her head on his shoulder. She drifted off to sleep listening to the sounds of the night's traffic, before dreaming of the wonderful life she'd have with Tiaz.

Tranay Adams

Chapter 12

Threat made his way down the corridor of the west wing of the hospital, trying to be incognito. His disguise was a wig of cornrows and a pair of glasses. He was wearing powder blue scrubs and white sneakers. A forged name badge hang from the breast of his shirt with the name *Derwin Crothers* scrolled across the bottom of it beneath a picture of himself. He'd shelled out a $150 bucks for the badge and believed it was worth every penny since it was the only way he'd be able to sneak his way into the hospital and blend in with its medical staff.

Threat had an unfinished job on his hands and he planned on wrapping it up tonight. He couldn't afford for Ta'shauna to come out of her coma and give Tiaz up to the police. He'd be damned if he'd let his ace go down on the account of his fuck up. Tiaz was what the Italian mobsters would call a *standup guy*. Even if he was arrested and charged for the attempted murder of Ta'shauna and the murder of Orlando, he wouldn't mention Threat's name. Tiaz was a loyal dude and believed in *Death before Dishonor.*

Threat stopped by the nurse's desk and got Ta'shauna's room number. He'd gotten the information with ease being that he looked like one of the members of the medical staff. Now all he had to do was make the proper arrangements for her to meet her maker. He turned the corner at the end of the corridor and made his way down the hall, sliding his hands into latex gloves. He was nearing Ta'shauna's room when Faison emerged through the door. He ducked off into a nearby room and placed his back against the door. He looked over his shoulder and found an elderly white lady in bed, eating a Jell-O fruit cup.

"Excuse me, young man. Do you think I could get a second Jell-O fruit cup?" The elderly white lady held up her tray.

Threat held a finger to his lips signaling for her to be quiet. He poked his head into the doorway and Faison had just walked past. He waited a few moments more, then poked his head out of the door again. Faison was just turning the corner at the end of the hall. Threat came out of the woman's room and entered the room Ta'shauna occupied.

Upon entry, he checked the room to make sure there were no other persons present. The only other person was her roommate who just so happen to be asleep. He drew the curtains over the man's sleeping quarters and approached his prey's bed. She was lying in bed in a peaceful coma. He watched as her chest slowly rose and fell as oxygen was being pumped into her lungs. He stepped into her quarters pulling the curtains closed.

He turned off the heart monitor and approached her bed, smiling sinisterly. He bent Ta'shauna's breathing tube, cutting off her oxygen. "That's it. Don't fight it, sis. Just let it happen, let cha self go," he said in a hushed tone.

Hearing someone entering the room, Threat quickly let go of the oxygen tube. Through the slight opening in the curtains, he spotted Faison approaching. He drew the curtains opened and was surprised when he saw a male nurse there. He had two fingers on the inside of her wrist while he stared at his watch, checking her vitals. Once he was done he scribbled something on a clipboard and looked up at Faison, seemingly startled.

"Oh, hey, how're you? Just checking her out, making sure she's okay." Threat told him, sounding professional than a mothafucka. It was like that nurse's uniform had transformed him from the thug ass nigga he was.

"You her nurse now?" Faison's forehead crinkled as he massaged his chin. "I thought Lakita was."

"Oh, Lakita's out sick." He capped his pen, sliding it into his breast pocket. "I'll be attending to her tonight." He smiled and extended his hand. "I'm Derwin."

"Faison." He shook his hand.

"Well, I'll give you some privacy, don't hesitate to buzz me. I'll be right at the front desk."

"Thanks. I appreciate it."

Faison pulled up a chair to his sister's bed as Threat was disappearing through the door. He placed Ta'shauna's hand in his and gently rubbed it. He frowned seeing a deep crease in her breathing tube. He rose to his feet and examined it further. He could tell that someone had intentionally bent it to stop her from getting oxygen. When he looked beside him he saw that the heart monitor was off.

"Aye, how's she doing?" A jovial female voice came from his rear, startling him. He whipped around to a nurse in purple scrubs.

"Lakita?" The crinkles in his forehead deepened. "I thought you were out sick."

"No. I just got here." The skin on her forehead bunched.

Faison looked from her to the crease in the breathing tube and the black screen of the heart monitor. That's when things came together and made sense. He made a mad dash toward the door, bumping into Lakita on his way out.

"Uhhh!" she winced and fell.

Faison bolted out of the room and into the corridor. He saw Threat bending the corner as he sped walked. He ran after him. Threat looked over his shoulder and saw Faison on his heels, in pursuit. He took off running like he had a pack of wild coyotes snapping at his heels. When Faison made it to the elevators he could see the doors closing together on the elevator that Threat was on board. He watched to see what floor the elevator would stop on. When the letter *P* flashed he hit the staircase running and jumping down to the landings.

Boom!

The door of the first floor of the parking garage flew open when Faison kicked it with all of his might. The door banked off of the wall and Faison spilled out onto the ground. He scanned the parking lot and saw Threat darting toward his car ahead. He pulled his car keys from his pocket and hit the locks on his truck. He raced over to his truck just as Threat was pulling his car out of the parking stall. He opened the door and grabbed his pistol out of the stash spot inside. He saw the back lights of Threat's whip as he checked the magazine of his weapon and smacked it back in. He extended the hand that held his gun over the roof of the car parked beside him and took aim. He was just about to finger fuck the trigger when he heard people approaching him from behind.

"So, what do you want Subway, Chinese, Mexican?" A cop asked his partner as they stepped off the elevator.

"I was thinking a pastrami melt from Tam's." His partner replied.

"Tam's it is then."

Fuck, Faison cursed and lowered his pistol. He tucked it in his waistline as he walked back to the elevators. The cops gave him a nod of acknowledgement but he ignored them. He whipped out his cell phone and punched in a number, placing the cell to his ear.

***

Faison stood at the center of the hospital's waiting room talking to his goons, Bone and Bird. Faison's eyes were webbed red and glassy. He was pissed off and slapping his hand in his palm as he talked for emphasis. He made sure to make eye contact with each of his goons so his point could get across clearly.

"This mothafucka got nuts the size of King Kong to come into a hospital and try to murk my baby sister. Either that or the nigga is crazy. He couldn't have possibly did his research on her 'cause he would've known that I'm her big brother and I ain't the nigga to be fucking with. But I got something for his punk ass just as soon as I get a hold of 'em, believe that. Don't nobody play with my family. There are three things you never fuck with when it comes to a man and that's his money, his pride, and his loved ones. Those are three things that'll fa' sho' 'nuff get cha monkey ass killed. From now on, I want somebody up here at all times watching my sister. I don't ever want her alone, under any circumstances. Nigga pulled this shit, so there's no telling when he's gonna try to do it again. My intuition tells me it's the same cat that popped sis's hubby and put one in her dome. I don't know what she did to have niggaz on her like this, nor do I give a fuck. I want y'all to put cha ears to the streets. Let niggaz know I'm offering twenty large for any information on the shooter that took the hit on my peoples, alright?" Bird and Bone nodded. They rose from where they were perched and slapped hands with Faison before walking off.

***

"I need to get to that bitch, man. But I know they gon' have security out the yin yang now that I was caught up there in her room. Fuck!" Threat pounded the steering wheel with his fist in frustration and leaned his head back against the headrest.

"Don't wet it. You said she doesn't know anything about who hit her or put the hit out on her, right? Well, we'll wait 'til they release her from outta the hospital then we'll do her up real nice. Matter of fact, I'm out now. I'll take care of her. You fall back and let my second nature serve me. I'll make sure that gutter snipe ho catches some eternal Zs."

"I'm saying, my nigga. You entrusted me with that, so it's only right I finish what I started."

"I appreciate that, but it's best that I handle this. Revenge is so much sweeter when it's claimed by the one who was wronged."

"I'm just saying…"

"This conversation is dead. It's my beef. I'll go about it how I see fit."

"Alright." Threat digressed, seeing he wasn't about to win the argument with his partner in crime. He didn't give a shit what Tiaz was talking about though, if he saw an opening to murder Ta'shauna, he was going to take it.

"Aye, you think that's them rolling up right here?" Tiaz asked, nodding at a black Suburban truck with pitch black tints that was driving up. He and Threat slid down in their seats trying not to be seen.

Threat glanced at the digital clock in the dashboard. It was 9 o'clock at night. The time he was told that Majestic's carriers would arrive to pick up his trap. "Yeah, that's most definitely them."

Threat and Tiaz watched as the two carriers un-boarded the Suburban. The twosome took a quick scan of the block before entering the yard of a modest home. One of them knocked on the door of the stash house in a coded pattern while the other kept an eye on the street. The eyeslot opened then closed. A moment later they were granted access to the domain. As soon as they walked into the spot, Threat and Tiaz slid on their black shades and pulled the black bandanas up over the lower halves of their faces. Threat pulled a Tec-9 from underneath his seat while Tiaz racked the shotgun that lay on his lap.

Click! Clack!

He hopped out of the car and hunched over. Threat got out of the car on his side so he wouldn't be seen if the carriers happened to come out before they took their places. Stooped over, the duo moved to take their places unseen in the darkness of the night. Tiaz got behind a Honda Tercel and held his weapon up at his shoulders. Threat took up space beside the vehicle the transporters arrived in. Squatting low, he gripped his Tec with both hands and waited for the men to re-emerge.

The carriers emerged from the house and one of them was carrying a duffle bag. They both had their guns held at their sides and were moving strategically, like a couple of Brink truck guards. Their necks were on swivels as they moved about surveying the avenue. This was the routine every time they picked up the money. The ten years they'd worked for Majestic they'd never had anyone try to rob them, but that didn't make them slouch or break their routine. They were on point with it at all times because if something were to happen to their boss's loot it would be their asses.

A Pinto drove by as the men were en route to their truck. Its headlights illuminated the street and casted Threat's shadow, revealing where he was hiding on the side of the SUV. The men frowned. The one holding the bag gripped its straps tighter. The other lifted his gun and let it bark just as Threat was rising to his feet, birthing sparks off the Suburban and the gate.

Threat ducked back down on the side of the vehicle, avoiding the fire of the raging gun. Tiaz shot to his feet and pulled the trigger of his shotgun, it recoiled and let go of a round of pellets. The blast took the cat holding the bag off of his feet. He fell on his back with his legs going up in the air. His face registered an intensity of pain that couldn't have been imagined. After dispatching the cat holding the duffle bag, Tiaz ducked back down behind the Honda.

The transporter that was busting his gun spared a glance at his fallen partner. It was a mistake he would pay for. A thunderous boom came from his left throwing him to the ground and causing him to drop his weapon. Clenching his jaws from the excruciation of his wound, he went to pick up his gun.A bullet went through his cheek, tearing through flesh and shattering the bone in the left side of his face. His head fell slack against the ground. He lay there with his eyes staring off into their corners with his lips apart. *Dead!*

Threat lowered his Tec after taking out his target.

He heard heavy breathing and hurried footsteps coming from his left. When he looked he saw the cat carrying the duffle bag running toward the house. Tiaz braced his shotgun against his shoulder and pull its trigger. The man crashed to the ground along with the bag, causing a few of the stacks to fly into the air. When he went to retrieve the money the door of the stash house flung open and two niggaz with choppas emerged. They cut loose with them thangs, keeping Tiaz and Threat at bay. One of them grabbed the bag of money while the other continued to let his choppa do what it do.

Police car sirens wailed as they hastily approached.

Tiaz and Threat met at the side of the Suburban, breathing heavily as they talked.

"Let's get the fuck outta here! This shit is botched!" Tiaz told his right-hand.

"Fuck that! I'm not going nowhere without some of that money!" Threat replied.

The niggaz with the choppaz retreated back inside of the stash house, slamming the door hard, causing paint chips to sprinkle the porch.

Tiaz hopped into the car and resurrected its engine while Threat picked up the stacks of money that was lost. He stuffed the money in all of his pockets and darted back to the car. Before he could pull his leg all of the way inside, Tiaz was already burning rubber pulling off.

***

Threat sat at the living room table counting the money from the botched robbery. Once he finished, he lay back in his chair and took a pull from his cigarette.

"Well, how much do we have?" Tiaz asked from the arm of the couch. He had his arms folded to his chest and was watching Threat count the money as he impatiently tapped his foot.

Threat blew out a gust of smoke. "Twenty grand."

"Fuck! We nearly got our dicks shot off for twenty funky ass bands."

"Relax. I got other licks lined up for us. I can't say they'll be as sweet, but they'll be worth our while, feel me?" Threat said, garnering a nod from his right-hand.

"What chu gon' tell ya man?" Tiaz asked.

"The truth. Shit got fucked up and we didn't end up with jack."

"Homie ain't gon' be tryna hear that."

"He either hears that or hears this." Threat held up his banger then sat it back down on the table. He dumped Tiaz' half of the money into a brown paper bag and handed it over to him. "Be ready, nigga. We're about to take this whole city for everything its worth." He swore, opening the door to let him out of the house.

"…And split it all down the middle." Tiaz dapped up Threat.

"Sho' ya right."

When Tiaz pulled into the driveway of Chevy's house he saw Te'Qui and Baby Wicked outside slap boxing. He hopped out of the car and came around watching the show as he neared the house. Baby Wicked had a longer reach, so naturally he had the upper hand. But surprisingly, little Te'Qui was holding his own. Tiaz smiled like a proud father watching the youngster defend himself. When he'd first met Te'Qui, he took him as a softy, but he could see now the boy had an edge to him.

Once the boys were finished slap boxing, they were breathing heavily and smiling. They slapped hands and gave each other props.

"What's up, Tiaz?" Te'Qui greeted.

"What up, Te'Qui?" Tiaz replied.

"What that shit two, O.G?" Baby Wicked slapped hands with Tiaz after he'd slapped hands with Te'Qui.

"What are y'all young niggaz up to?" Tiaz asked.

"We're about to take it to the store." Baby Wicked answered. "You want something?"

"Yeah, get me a bag of Doritos and a lemon Snapple." Tiaz reached into the brown paper bag and pulled out a hundred dollar bill, which he handed to Te'Qui. "Y'all can split the change."

"Thanks, man." Te'Qui said.

"Good looking out." Baby Wicked gave Tiaz dap.

Baby Wicked picked up his Huffy bike and Te'Qui hopped on the handle bars. Together they rode off onto the sidewalk and down the block.

When Tiaz came into the house there wasn't a soul in the living room. He grabbed a Heineken from out of the refrigerator and plopped down on the couch. He turned the flat-screen on and flipped through the channels until he came across a rerun of Breaking Bad. He watched the show while taking swigs from the cold bottle of beer.

Kantrell emerged from out of the hallway with a tear streaked face. She was startled when she saw Tiaz sitting on the couch. She quickly turned her head and wiped her eyes with the back of her hand. Tiaz sat up where he was perched and sat his beer down on the coffee table.

"Yo are you alright?" He questioned concerned, approaching her.

She sniffled and wiped her eyes with the sleeve of her blouse.

"I'm okay," she answered. "I got jacked for my ride a couple blocks from here."

"Are you straight?" The lines of his forehead deepened as he touched her arm.

"I'll be fine," she said.

"You call The Boys?"

"Nah, I don't fuck with The Ones."

"Me either. I just thought that maybe…"

"No. Never." She shook her head. "My daddy would turn over in his grave if he knew I'd gon' seeking out *the man* for help."

"Yo old man was a street cat?" he asked, garnering a nod from her. "Well, listen, you want me to call you a cab to take you home?"

"My dude is 'pose to be coming by to get me. Oh, my God," she held up her trembling hands and horror came across her face. "I'm so traumatized by that shit." Her terrified eyes met his. "Can—can you hold me, please."

"I don't think that's a…" Before he could finish his protest, she threw herself into him. Pressing her face against his chest and hugging him, sobbing into his shirt. He exhaled and wrapped his arms around her hesitantly. Resting his chin at the top of her head, he closed his eyes and inhaled the sweet scent of the shampoo expelling from her hair. Feeling her body up against his and becoming engulfed in the moment, he felt his fuck organ extend in his Dickies. She felt him and pressed herself against him. His eyelids peeled apart and he held her at arm's length.

"What? What's the matter?" She wanted to know, looking as if she was innocent but she knew exactly what the fuck she was doing.

"We can't."

"We can't what?" She pulled him close by the collar of his shirt, kissing him so hard that it felt like her lips were going to burst. He tried to pull back but she held fast, locking lips with him again. She then shoved him back onto the couch.

"Wait, what chu doing, girl?" His forehead furrowed and his nose wrinkled as he watched her slither down his torso, stopping at his zipper.

"What's it look like?" She smiled seductively, sliding her tongue across her top row of teeth as she unbuckled his leather belt and unzipping his Dickies. She kept her eyes locked with him as she reached inside of the open zipper and pulled his meat from its prison. She spat on it twice and grasped it, sliding her hand up and down it, anticipating it growing stiff. "Mmmm."

Tiaz wanted badly to grab her and make her stop but his hands wouldn't do what his mind commanded them. All he could do was watch that evil smile spread across her shiny glossed lips before she worked his Instrument of Love.

Before he knew it her lips peeled apart, showcasing the web of saliva inside of her mouth. He could feel the 97 degrees of heat that escaped her grill before she took in all of him. The temperature and wetness was the perfect marriage to bring him to his full potential.

"Ohhh, sssss, this shit ain't right Kantrell, it ain't right." He whispered as his eyes hooded and his breathing became labored, feeling her chin hit his sack as she glided her mouth to and from his member. He listened to the symphony that was her slurping and sucking. He felt his dick grow even harder. His blood had surged through it and it felt as solid as a brick of gold.

Her jaws sounded like a suction cup as it released him. She continued to jerk his fuck oragan as she stared him dead in his eyes, and teasingly licked his head. "I know, but it feels sooooo good, don't it?"

"Suck it, suck that black mothafucka." He squirmed around eager to feel her get retarded on that dick again. He licked his lips and bit down at the corner of the bottom one.

"Tell me to. Demand that I do, baby. Treat me like the lil' freak nasty bitch that I am." She let a hot avalanche of saliva slide off of her tongue and coat the head of him like wet cement, sliding her grip up and down his length.

"Ahhhh, shit," he croaked, throwing his head back and squeezing his eyelids closed. Suddenly he pulled himself together as he remembered what type of nigga he was. He flipped on the switch that was the bossed up gangsta and instantly he made an appearance.

"Suck my dick, bitch, I don't wanna hear nothing but chu sucking and swallowing this mothafucka!"

"That's what I'm talking a..." That last word died in her throat as he shoved her head down, filling that third hole in her face.

Tears ran from the corners of her eyes as she gagged on his meat. His eyes narrowed into slits. His nostrils contracted and expanded, while he tightened his jaws. He grunted loud and hard seeing his Sex Pistol engorged.

He got a kick at how she kept her eyes on him the entire time. That shit turned him on. "Yeah, yeah, yeah, suck it, suck it, sssss, awww." Dick still in her mouth he slowly rose to his feet with his hand pressed to the back of her head. She stared up at his face as he raped her drooling mouth, grinding and pumping that mothafucka as it it were that thang between her legs. His mouth quivered.

He went to pull out and she grabbed him by the wrists, pinning his arms to the sides of his legs. She bobbed up and down his shit, causing slobber to spill and hang like loose extension cords. He tilted his head back letting her see underneath his chin. His knees buckled and the muscles in his face flexed, he was about to blow.

"Aghhhh! Gaahhh!' His head shot down and he stared dead in her mothafucking eyes as he unleashed all of that creamy lather down her throat. She continued to suck him up. When he reached to stop her, she scowled and smacked his hand away. He staggered back and fell back on the couch with her still necking him, holding his meat about the shaft as she tried to suck every last drop out of him. He lay there like he was dead as she went on gobbling him up. When she let him loose, she showed him his unborn children cupped in her tongue and swallowed them as if they were cough syrup.

"Chevy isn't to know about this." Tiaz panted out of breath.

"She won't. Long as you fuck me and feed me I'll keep quiet."

Tiaz paused as he strained to hear what appeared to be the conversation of two nearing.

"Nigga, put that on something," Te'Qui said.

"Blood, that's on Lil' Face. Rest in peace," Baby Wicked replied.

"Oh, shit." Tiaz panicked, hearing the boys approaching. Hurriedly, he zipped up his Dickies and buckled his belt. Kantrell sat up on the couch, propping her hand against her head and acting as if she'd been watching TV the entire time. Tiaz cleared his throat and took a deep breath before opening the door. Te'Qui handed him his bag of items from the store then headed into his bedroom. Once the boys had left the room, a horn honked from outside. Tiaz pulled the curtains back to take a look and saw a silver Yukon Denali idling at the curb.

"Is there a silver truck out there?" Kantrell inquired, turning around on the couch.

"Yep."

"That's my ride." She hopped up from couch and grabbed her purse. She gave Tiaz a tender peck on the lips and cracked a slight smile. Grabbing his wrist, she turned his hand palm up and scribbled down her number. She then closed all of his fingers except the middle one before she sucked on it slow and nasty, keeping her eyes locked with his. She spun around, adjusting the purse on her shoulder and walking out of the door. He watched her ample ass shift from left to right as she sauntered off. He felt bad that he'd let her swallow his kids being that he was suppose to be with Chevy but he was a dog. It was in his nature so what was he supposed to do?

Kantrell walked out of the house pulling a tube of M.A.C lip gloss from her purse. She removed the cap and spread it across her succulent lips, mashing them together. En route to the SUV that awaited her, her mind wondered.

This bitch Chevy got her a good nigga but not for long 'cause I'ma 'bout to snatch this one up. I know the shit is kind of foul but hey why should she be the only one happy? Shit, I wanna get my back blown out and cup cake too. Besides, losing one more nigga ain't gon' hurt her. She'll bounce back. She did with Faison and Azule so one more ain't gone hurt her. Hell, she should be used to it by now. If not, fuck it, it's every bitch for herself in this cold world, straight like that.

Kantrell pulled open the door of the beast and climbed inside, slamming the door shut behind her.

"You okay?" He asked from behind the wheel, turning down the volume of Meek Mill's *Big Daddy*.

"I'll be alright, just a lil' shaken up, is all."

"Bitch ass niggaz got my baby shook. Don't trip 'cause both of dem faggots gettin' it." He swore as he pulled off. "That's on everything I love."

"Whateva, nigga, take me home." She blew hard and she rolled her eyes.

"Fuck is yo problem?" He asked with a hard face, looking her up and down.

Suddenly, a smile apprehended her face and she looked to him. "Nothing, baby, gimmie a kiss."

When he stopped at the light, he leaned closer and kissed her thirstily. Kantrell pressed her hand against the back of his head, mashing his mouth against hers. She was as dirty as they came, kissing that mothafucka with Tiaz' sperm residue marinating her tongue.

That wasn't the half of it either. See, she didn't really get jacked for her ride. Nah, she parked it a few blocks down and walked to Chevy's house. Her plan to suck off Tiaz was premeditated. She knew once he got a shot of her head that it would be hard for him to stay away from her. She knew she was shiesty but she didn't give a fuck. She wanted Chevy's man and she would have him. By any means necessary.

Chapter 13

When Tiaz awoke the next morning his dick was so hard that he was surprised he hadn't punctured a hole in the mattress. His manhood was as hard as a police man's nightstick. He had sex on his mind and was ready to give Chevy's pussy a good stroking. Without taking his face out of the pillow, he went to play with her pussy but his hand fell flat on top of the cool sheets. His eyelids peeled open and that's when he noticed she was gone.

Tiaz rolled over on his back. He looked down and saw his hardness protruding in his boxer briefs. He stared up at the ceiling for a while then closed his eyes, remembering how good Kantrell's head game was. He knew he'd already fucked up by letting her suck his dick, because he'd been unfaithful to Chevy. As bad as he wanted to he knew it wouldn't be right for him to taste the sweet nectar that was her sex. He wouldn't just be fucking around with some random hood rat; he'd be boning his lady's bestfriend, a woman that had been a sister to her. If he fucked her and Chevy found out the news would destroy her. He already knew that the girl's ex-fiancé had stepped out on her with another chick. She'd told him in a letter she'd written him. The letter expressed the hurt that she felt. He understood where she was coming from because Ta'shauna had stepped out on him with her son's father and left him to rot in prison. Ta'shauna's abandonment of him crushed him like an empty soda can. He understood the heartache that came with infidelity too well. And he didn't want to hurt Chevy, but the temptation of the flesh was a mothafucka.

Tiaz looked to his right and found a buttondown, tie, and slacks hanging on the wall beside the window. Beneath the clothes, on the floor, was a pair of black leather crocodile skin shoes polished to a shine. He sat up in bed, stretching and yawning. He slipped on some sweatpants, a wifebeater and some corduroy house shoes. He turned to head out of the door and something caught the corner of his eye. He stepped to the nightstand and found a couple of past due utility bills. He placed the bills on the nightstand exactly how he'd found them and went to his secret stash before leaving the bedroom.

Chevy was sitting at the kitchen table going ham on her laptop, writing what she hoped would become an urban classic and sipping a cup of black coffee. A smoldering Newport was wedged between her fingers as she punched the keys on the keyboard. Beside her on the table was an ashtray littered with cigarette butts. Her eyes were focused on the screen. She looked like a mad scientist hard at work on a serum that could prove to be quite valuable to mankind. She was so wrapped up in her craft she didn't notice when Tiaz entered the kitchen. It wasn't until he kissed her on the cheek and planted a brown paper bag beside her that she acknowledged his presence.

"Good morning." He greeted her as he kissed the back of her head and massaged her shoulders.

"Good morning, babe. What's this?" Chevy asked, taking a peek inside of the bag. When she peered inside of the bag she was in awe. She turned around in her seat and looked to Tiaz. "Baby, where did you get this money?"

"The homies gave it to me as a welcome home present," Tiaz said, sitting down to his plate of breakfast. He looked to Te'Qui. "What's cracking, lil' homie." He held out his fist and received dap.

"Nothing, going to work on this French toast," Te'Qui replied while eating.

"How much money is this?" Chevy looked through the brown paper bag.

"Something light, fifteen stacks."

"Oh, my God, fifteen stacks?" Her eyes widen and her jaw dropped. "That's light to you? You know how much over time I'd have to do to get fifteen grand?"

"Boo, that ain't nothing but lunch money to me. I told you how I used to get it."

A happy Chevy jumped to her feet and hurried over behind Tiaz, wrapping her arms around his neck.

Mauh! Mauh! Mauh! Mauh!

She kissed up the side of his face causing him to smile as he bit into a strip of crisp bacon.

"Ohhh, thank you, baby." She turned his face to her and kissed his lips. "I really need this; these bills are kicking my ass."

"You welcome, Love."

"Oh, yeah, I almost forgot," she snatched up the newspaper from where she was sitting. "I circled a few gigs for you to check out today." She pointed to the temporary job agencies she'd circled with a red ink pen in the paper. "I've already ironed something for you to wear." She stretched and yawned as he clutched the paper.

"Damn, Chev', your shit is kind of tainted." He spoke of her breath, fanning away the fumes.

"My bad, I've been up all night drinking coffee and smoking squares working on this story. Let me put this money up and brush my teeth." She grabbed the brown paper bag and kissed Tiaz again. "Thanks again, boo." She left her man and son at the table.

"Tiaz."

He looked and she was standing at the opening of the hallway.

"I'm so lucky to have met chu."

"If anyone's lucky it's me."

She blew him a kiss. He caught it and smacked it over his heart. She cracked a smile and dipped off down the corridor.

Tiaz pretended to be looking over the newspaper. He didn't have any plans of going on a job hunt. He was going to continue getting money by the means of his determination and his gun. Ever since he was old enough to piss straight he'd always gotten it how he lived and he'd keep on doing so until dirt was shoveled on top of his coffin.

Tiaz glanced at Te'Qui who was still eating his breakfast, then over his shoulder at the digital clock on the stove. "It's time for you to get dressed for school."

"Alright," Te'Qui rose to his feet and downed the last of his orange juice before heading off to his bedroom.

"If you want, I can drop you off." Tiaz shouted to him.

"Okay," Te'Qui said before disappearing into the hallway.

"Tiaz," Chevy called from the bathroom.

"Yeah, baby?" Tiaz answered back.

"You dropping Te'Qui off?"

Silence consumed the air as Chevy stood in the medicine cabinet mirror brushing her teeth. When she didn't get a reply from him she stopped her morning hygiene.

"Tiazzz!" she called out to him and waited for his reply.

"Yep." He said at her back, startling her as his strong hands gripped her hips.

She sighed with relief. "You scared the living shit outta me." She finished brushing her teeth and spat the white goo out into the sink.

"Can you take out the trash before you leave?"

"Sure thing, Lover." He said in between kissing up her neck as she washed her mouth out with Listerine. She then spat the green liquid out into the sink and turned off the faucet. She closed her eyes and a smile emerged on her beautiful face as he licked her neck and then nibbled on her earlobe.

"Not now babe, Te'Qui is still here." She told him as she felt his hands pulling at her pink Victoria Secret panties. She grabbed him by his wrists just as he'd slipped her drawers under her buttocks. She pulled them back up and turned around to him, kissing him tenderly.

"Come on now. Let a nigga get a quickie before he goes on this job hunt." Tiaz held Chevy close and cupped her ass.

"How about tonight?" She asked, caressing the side of his face.

"Tonight?" he looked disappointed.

"Uh huh, tonight once baby boy is asleep."

"Alright." He smacked her ass before he left the bathroom. Chevy watched him make his departure, thinking of how lucky she was to have him as a smile formed on her lips.

***

Tiaz dropped Te'Qui off at school and swung by Threat's house. He honked the horn twice and his homie came out, jogging across the front lawn in a black White Sox snapback and a crisp long sleeve black T-shirt. He hopped into the passenger seat and slammed the door closed. He turned to Tiaz, taking in his attire for the day. His forehead wrinkled.

"What?" Tiaz asked.

"What's up with your threads, nigga?" Threat asked as he buckled his seat belt.

"Oh," Tiaz looked down at what he was wearing. "You know a nigga gotta front like he's out here looking for a gig and shit. I'm rocking my work fit under these."

Threat chuckled and shook his head. "How long you gon' keep this shit up?"

"As long as I have to, Crim. Where we headed to first?"

"That nigga Limb's house, I've been calling that mothafucka but he hasn't been answering his phone. Swing by there so I can let this nigga know he's not getting shit."

Tiaz pulled into the driveway of Limb's house and Threat hopped out. He jogged up the steps and knocked on the door. He waited for a while but no one answered. He tried calling but Limb's cell went straight to voicemail. He peered in the window trying to see inside through the slight opening between the curtains, but he couldn't make anything out. He went into the back yard. Looking around, he saw the kitchen window was cracked open. He slid the window open and crawled inside.

Stepping his foot down onto the linoleum, he surveyed his surroundings.

Threat whipped his banger out from his waistline and jour-neyed into the living room. The living room had been ransacked just like the kitchen. He stood at the center of the living room calling out Limb's name. When he didn't respond, he crept up the steps with his banger held at his shoulder. He snuck down the hallway as stealthy as a burglar and kicked open the door of Limb's bedroom. Carefully, he entered the bedroom with his banger leading the way. He looked over the bedroom, which was also a mess and saw specs of blood on the headboard. Threat tucked his gun back on his waistline and hurried down the staircase, wiping whatever he touched with the sleeve of his black T-shirt.

When Threat emerged from the backyard, he saw Tiaz peel off a few dollars and hand them over to a skinny nigga in a Clippers jersey sitting on a miniature motorbike. He stuffed the money into his pocket and sped off down the street. On the back of the kid's jersey was his name DayDay.

"What did you find in there?" Tiaz asked Threat once he'd gotten back inside of the car.

"The place was turned upside down, there was shit everywhere. I went up to his bedroom and there was blood splatter on the headboard."

"What that lil' nigga just told me makes perfect sense, then."

"What did he say?" Threat inquired.

"That he saw a couple of cats leaving here with Limb and he didn't look like he wanted to go. He said he thinks they beat the shit out of him 'cause his face was swollen and he had blood on his shirt. He said when he drove by on his bike that Limb gave him a look like *please help me*. You think this has anything to do with that botched job from the other night?"

"I doubt it. That nigga Limb always has his hand in some shit. There isn't a cat in the city that doesn't want a piece of his ass. The only reason niggaz never touched him 'cause he was connected to Majestic. Somebody with some balls sent them goons over here to snatch Limb up. I'm telling you."

"I don't know, Threat. You don't think Majestic figured Limb had something to do with setting him up to get hit?" Tiaz asked.

"Man, hell nah. Any nigga could have sent them niggaz over here to pick his lanky ass up. That fool done fucked over too many people. If you gathered all the people he done screwed over in your yard and threw a rock, you'd hit someone every time. I'm telling you, don't wet that shit. Let's go see about getting this check." Threat laid his head back against the headrest as Tiaz resurrected the Caprice and pulled off.

***

Tiaz and Threat sat slumped in their seats watching the house they were supposed to hit. They'd been parked down the block and across the street observing their surroundings. Dollar signs flashed in their heads as they thought about the spoils that were inside of house. Every so often Tiaz found himself scratching his left palm, which was a good thing to him. When he was a little boy his grandma told him whenever his left palm itched, he had money coming to him. Needless to say he was excited about running up in that thang and making a nigga part with his shit.

"Fuck taking that broad so long to hit chu up," Tiaz exclaimed, scratching his left palm.

The message alert went off on Threat's cell and he glanced at the screen. "There she go." He smiled once he read the text. "Alright, she left the front door unlocked. It's show time." He pulled on gloves and a neoprene mask over the lower half of his face. He then chambered a round into the head of his banger.

Tiaz slid on dark shades and tied a blue bandana over the lower half of his face. Once he slipped his hands into a pair of black leather gloves, he removed his banger from the center console. Together they hopped out of the car and hustled up the block, keeping a constant watch for police cruisers and potential snitches.

***

Capone and Bleek sat on the sofa playing Madden. They ate from cartons of Chinese takeout and popped shit at one another whenever one of them scored a touchdown or interception from the other.

"The score is now 21-7. Call me pops 'cause I'm whopping that ass." Capone bragged and boasted after scoring another touchdown. He reached for the ashtray to retrieved his blunt and felt a pile of ashes. He frowned and looked to Bleek.

"Fuck you looking at, nigga?" Bleek asked off of Capone's expression.

"My nigga, if you gon' smoke it all up you could at least roll another one up. Damn." Capone cursed and sighed, agitated that all of his weed was gone.

"Nigga, don't look at me, I didn't do that shit." Bleek said seriously. "You better holla at Silk."

"I know that ain't my nigga Bleek over there snitching?" Silk said from where he sat at the living room table counting up the paper he'd gotten from his girls he managed. In addition to being the dope man, he was also a pimp. "Say it ain't so, homie. Say it ain't so." He took a pull from the roach end of a blunt and blew out a cloud.

"Ain't nobody snitching, I just don't feel like hearing this fool's mouth. Dude be bitching like a broad and shit." Bleek stated.

"Man, fuck you!" Capone waved him off. He then yelled out over his shoulder, "Yo' where Lexus ass at? I'm tryna get my dick sucked." He stuck his hand in his jeans, stroking his hardness.

"You got some money?" Silk questioned. "You the homie and all but chu gotta pay to play, cuz."

"I got chu faded, my nigga." Bleek held up a few wrinkled bills.

Silk nodded. "She's in the bathroom getting ready for this gig. Once she's ready, I'll have her take care of you then we gon' bounce."

"Cool," he smiled.

"Gimmie mine." Silk waved him over with the hand he held the roach in.

Bleek paused the game.

"Aww, come on, man." Capone complained.

"Shut up, nigga," Bleek went to rise from the couch and the door went flying open, as it was assaulted by a brute force.

Tiaz and Threat stormed inside waving their bangers around at the men present and barking orders. Silk attempted to reach for the .40 cal on the table beside the money, but Tiaz' menacing eyes and the threats he barked made him think twice.

"Reach, nigga! Gon' and reach so I can paint that wall behind you with your fucking brains!" The buff neck thug roared with his gun pointed at Silk's dome.

"Alright, man, chill, ain't nobody reaching for nothing." Silk raised his hands in surrender.

Tiaz narrowed his eyes as the man he was spazzing on before his face suddenly became familiar. The Mariner's S tattooed between his eyes took him to a place sometime ago. That's when he realized he was the one in the alley that night he and Threat had gotten caught up in enemy territory. He remembered him busting shots off in the air and ordering his homies to beat their asses inside of that alley nine years ago. When he recalled this, he saw the skinny crip smiling fiendishly as he pissed on him and Threat's faces. Tiaz' face balled up and his eyes flashed red with hatred. He looked over his shoulder at Bleek and Capone. They wore old nasty scars on the side of their faces. These were the same mothafuckaz whose faces he'd opened up with the broken glass bottle that very night.

"This them niggaz from the alley that night." He alerted Threat.

"What?" His eyes took a tour of all of the faces present in the room. He was in awe when he realized they were the same dudes. "Yeah, this is them." He nodded his head with a pair of unforgiving eyes.

"Awww, cuz, fuck y'all talking about?" Silk looked petrified. He genuinely didn't know what the two masked men were talking about. Tiaz yanked the bandana down from the lower half of his face, revealing his identity to the nigga. When he recognized his face, he felt his bowels shift.

"Oh, you wanna play stupid, bitch!" Tiaz marched over to him, grabbing him by the back of his neck hard. With all of his might, he slammed his face into the table, breaking his nose. When he pulled his head back, blood squirted all over the dead presidents, coating some of the bills red. Seeing he was barely conscious and moaning, he threw him to the floor and looked to Threat. "Tape his monkey ass up!" He pointed down at Silk with his banger. After he was done bounding Capone and Bleek with duct-tape, Threat rushed over and bound Silk's wrists and ankles as well.   "Yo, see if there are any garbage bags in the kitchen." Tiaz told his partner in crime.

Threat got a black garbage bag out of the kitchen and held it open beside the table. Using the hand he held his banger in, he swept all of the money off of the table into the bag.

"Alright, where the rest of the gwap at? The coke too 'cause I know you're holding."

"I ain't got nothing else, loc, that's it." Silk lied from where he lay bound on the floor.

Threat yanked his head back by his ponytail, drawing a shrill from him. He placed his banger by his ear and squeezed the trigger. The roar of the gun set off an eerie siren in his ear. His eyes bugged and the side of his face hit the carpet. "That's for lying to me."

"Freeze, mothafucka, don't move!" Threat heard Tiaz in his ear. Then there was a scream. He looked and Tiaz had his banger pointed at Lexus, who had her hands up in the air, trembling. "Is there anybody else in the house we don't know about?" He asked the stripper and she shook her head *no*. "Where is the rest of the money and yay at?"

Lexus looked at Silk and he shook his head.

"Fuck you looking at him for? You hear my nigga talking to you?" Threat asked.

She closed her eyes and swallowed hard. "There are two bricks inside of the couch cushions and about sixty bands in the safe in the master bedroom closet."

When she told Threat and Tiaz where the coke and money was stashed, Silk closed his eyes and shook his head. He then pounded his forehead into the carpet, hating he was about to be raped for all he had.

"Come up off that combo, homeboy." Tiaz pointed his head bussa at Silk.

"What?" Silk looked up at him like he'd lost his mothafucking mind, forehead creased with lines.

"You heard me, you beige mothafucka. Give me the combo to that safe."

"I ain't giving you shit, cuz, you got the wrong one. On the gang."

"That's on the gang, huh? Alright, Gangsta number one." Tiaz stormed over to him, grabbed him by the back of his neck and lifted his head up. Clenching his jaws so tight that they throbbed, he cracked him over the head with that steel, repeatedly.

Crack! Crackk! Whackkk! Bwackkkk!

"Arghhhh!" Silk balled his face so tight that he looked Asian, feeling the heavy blows against his skull. "Alright cuz, alright."

Tiaz let his face drop to the carpet and heard a thud. He stood erect gripping his blood stained gun and staring down at his handiwork. He'd cracked the pimp's head open to the white meat. The mixture of blood and white made his scalp resemble an apple that someone had taken a bite out of.

After Tiaz' display of savagery, Silk came up off of that combination to his safe. Once all of the money and drugs was bagged up and accounted for, Threat and Tiaz relieved the foursome of whatever jewelry and paper they had on them.

"Well, gentlemen, it's been real." Tiaz said, waving goodbye with a bag of goods slung over his shoulder.

Bloc!

The side of Lexus's face came apart when Threat sent a hot one through it. She made a loud thud when she hit the floor twitching as if her body was going through slight convulsions. The short killer stood over her with dangerous eyes, popping twice more into her thinking cap. *Lights out!*

"Thirsty ass bitch!" Threat spoke down on the corpse of his kill.

Bleek and Capone exchanged glances, trembling terribly as they were frightened for their lives.

"Ahh, shit, cuz, these niggaz 'bout ta kill us." Capone made an ugly face and tears accumulated in his eyes.

"Shut up, nigga!" Silk nudged him. "You sounding like a lil' ol' bitch, pull yo' mothafucking thong out cha ass! Be a fucking man!" He snarled.

Capone shut his mouth and silently whimpered, head and shoulders jerking.

Tiaz and Threat looked down upon him with pity. It was hard to believe those were the same niggaz that were popping all of that shit in the alley many moons ago.

"If y'all gon' kill us, cuz, gon' and handle yo' business." Silk glared up at Tiaz gritting his teeth. "Get the shit over with." He sucked his teeth and spat off to the side, ready to meet his demise.

Tiaz nodded to Threat. "Cash these niggaz out, Crim." Gunfire erupted and the living room was lit up by muzzle flashes. The noise was loud and disgruntled. When the firing ceased, smoke rose in the air and evaporated. For a time, the two men stood side by side taking in the mess they'd created.

"Come on, let's get out here." Threat nudged Tiaz and they made their exit.

Two hours later...

"I gotta job!" Tiaz came into the house, wearing a smile.

"Where at?" Chevy asked, giving him a hug.

"DHL," he lied. "It's data entree. I start tomorrow afternoon. The pay isn't much, but it's a start."

"Boo, I'm so happy for you." She gave him a kiss and a hug. "We've gotta go out to celebrate."

"Where is Te'Qui?"

"He's at Brice's house." She reported, staring into his eyes lovingly. "I was thinking you and I could paint the town red."

"I was thinking orange and blue." His lips curled at one end as he stared into her face.

"Which ever colors you want, my King."

"Alright then, Queen." He kissed her lips twice, then licked his own. "Mmmm, you taste like a peach." He commented on the flavor of her lip gloss after breaking their embrace.

"Those aren't the only lips that taste like a peach." She capped, causing a smile to blossom on his face.

"I hear that fly shit, boo, gon' with yo' bad self." He smacked her on the ass.

156

"Let me find something to wear and hop into the shower."

Once Chevy had gone into the bathroom, Tiaz opened the front door and grabbed the duffle bag that held his half of the money and bricks. He took a quick peer inside to make sure everything was accounted for and carried the bag off into the garage. He peeled the tape off of a box labeled *X-Mas* decorations and hid the two bricks inside. He then sealed the box back with the tape. He peeled the tape off of a box labeled *old books* and stashed his half of the money at the bottom of it. Once he'd sealed the box back with tape, he left the garage.

***

Faison sat in the center row inside of the home theater room of his home. After sucking on the end of the world's biggest blunt, he slightly parted his lips to allow the smoke to whip around inside of his mouth like the tentacles of an angry octopus before releasing it in a steady stream into the air. His left hand held tight to the chain that hung from around his neck and his thumb fondled it as he thought about his sister. Every moment of every day he thought about what he'd do to the bastard that had shot her and left her in a coma fighting for her life. He contemplated what he'd do when he finally caught up with the cock sucker. He didn't know whether he'd execute him and get it over with or strap him into a chair in the basement of an abandoned house and torture him hours upon hours until he begged for mercy in the form of a .40 caliber slug. The thought of finally getting Ta'shauna's shooter in his clutches made Faison's dick hard. He thought he felt himself about to cum hearing the man's horrified screams inside of his head as he tortured him mercilessly.

When Bone entered the theater, Faison didn't bother taking his focus off the big screen. He continued smoking his overgrown blunt and enjoying the 80s film that played. Bone stopped in the aisle for a moment watching Arnold bowl through an army of mobsters with a machinegun. He then approached Faison and sat down beside him, blowing hard before he delivered the bad news.

"Boss-man, it's as dry as the Sahara out there. Don't nobody know nothing. We put the muscle on cats and… "

"I'm not tryna hear any excuses, Bone. I pay you and Bird good money to handle my business out there, so I expect results. If y'all can't do the job then I'll find a couple of niggaz that can. Now, can you or can't you find the bitch made ass nigga that popped my baby sister?"

"Boss-man, I'm trying. It's just that…"

"It's a simple *yes or no* question, Bone." Faison interjected.

Bone blew hard and took a moment before replying. "Look, me and Bird are gonna…"

Faison closed his eyes and raised the hand he held the blunt in, silencing Bone. He was pissed off but he had love for the old school gangster, which was why he didn't pop fly out the mouth. "You know what, Bone. I don't want to see your face nor Bird's right now. Y'all niggaz take it home, fam. I'll call you when I need you. You're dismissed."

Bone glared at Faison and bit down on his bottom lip. He started to crack him in his jaw, but decided to let it slide. He didn't need nor did he want a beef with him. Bone stood to his feet and walked away. He stopped in the aisle for a moment and looked at Faison before continuing out of the theater.

Chapter 14

Meanwhile on the other side of the city in a seedy motel...

"Alright. We got fifty-five bands, four bricks of yay and two pounds of that Purple." Threat pointed to everything they'd come up on when they hit a dopeman's house earlier that night.

"Damn, Crim, you can smell this shit through the bag." Tiaz claimed after smelling the freezer bag the Kush was concealed in.

"That's how you know that's that killer. Roll up."

"Alright." Tiaz went about the task of rolling up while his road dawg divided the spoils. He was just about to take the first pull when he heard a knock at the door. He passed the blunt to Threat and picked his banger up from the coffee table. Approaching the door, he yelled out. "Who is it?"

"Semaj." The person on the other side of the door answered.

"It's Semaj. Put that shit in the bedroom."

Threat gathered everything up and took it into the bedroom.

Tiaz took a glance through the peephole. Once he confirmed it was Semaj, he opened the door and allowed him to enter the hotel room. When he closed and chained the door, Threat returned from the bedroom. He and Tiaz slapped hands with their inside man before he sat down on the couch. Threat took a couple of more puffs of the blunt before passing it back Semaj.

He took a couple of healthy draws before polluting the air, white smoke wafted around the living room as the crime partners listened to their guest.

"Smack's oldest boy plays basketball for UCLA, he's a big shot point guard. You've probably seen him in the papers or on the news, Julian Carr. Real cocky mothafucka, don't think his shit stank. Anyway, every Saturday night he parlays at this strip club in Hollywood called Sin City. Young nigga be in there popping bottles and throwing money in the air like it fell from out of the sky. Smack is over protective of the boy, he hired this big Mexican dude to be his personal bodyguard. That fat head fucka goes wherever the kid goes, so it'll be pretty tough to get to junior without him getting in the way." Semaj gave them the rundown.

"You gotta address on this clown?" Threat asked.

"Yeah, I gotta picture of him and the bodyguard, too." Semaj took the two pictures and a slip of paper with the address on it out of his breast pocket and passed them to Threat.

Threat looked over the pictures and passed them to Tiaz. "Shit should be a piece of cake."

"Like I said, man, your biggest problem will be the body-guard. From what I hear Butch is one mean motor scooter. Cock sucka is military trained, fam." Semaj took the blunt from Threat and took a few pulls.

"I'm not worried about none of that, a couple shots from the ratchet will break his big ass down like a key of dope." Threat held up his banger then laid it back down on the coffee table.

"Nah," Tiaz leaned over and sat the pictures on the coffee table. "We gotta keep things quiet so we won't draw attention. We'll go packing them thangs, but we'll also have a couple of tasers on us, too. I'll take care of the fat man and you'll take care of junior. Once I hit his big ass with that tasergun, he'll fold up like a lawn chair. While he's lying there pissing his pants, me and you would have been done tossed junior in the trunk and jetted out."

"That's a bet." Threat gave Tiaz dap. He looked to Semaj. "Yeah, fam, this is most definitely a go."

Smack was a big time heroine peddler out of the Bay Area. Rumor had it he was worth twenty million dollars. His money stretched as long as Rosecrans and he had an army of killers at his command. His resources were vast and unlimited, so if he wanted to get a nigga touched or make his wildest dreams come true, he could do so with just the snap of his fucking fingers. Needless to say, Threat and Tiaz were playing with fire when they came up with the idea of snatching his son and sitting on him for a ransom. But if things went how they had planned, they stood to come out on top two million dollars richer.If things went sour, they could find themselves in a hole in the desert wearing matching bullet holes on their foreheads. The job was risky, maybe even suicidal, but since they were teenagers the men had promised one another to either get rich or die trying.

Once Semaj left, Threat went to the bedroom and got Tiaz' proceeds from the caper they'd pulled earlier. He handed him two duffle bags, one for him and the other for the cat that had put them onto the lick.

"Yo, man, after I drop this nigga his shit off I'm headed to the house. You know Chevy barbequing and shit since it's the fourth of July. We're gonna have food and drinks, and you know I've got that Loud." He held up the duffle bag that held the pound of Purple Kush. "You should come through, Crimey."

"Nah, I think I'ma just relax and put something in the air."Threat told him. "Probably call Bianca over and freak off with her."

"If you change your mind, just pull up." Tiaz slapped hands with Threat.

"That's a bet. Hit me up and let me know you got in safe," Threat said to Tiaz as he prepared to close the door behind him.

"Alright," Tiaz replied, crossing the threshold into the hallway.

* * *

When Tiaz pulled up to the house Chevy and her family were out in the front yard. They stood around laughing and smiling as Savon and his homeboy danced around a firework that snapped, crackled and popped with bright colors. While Savon and his homeboy danced around the spitting firework, some of the children waved around their Sparklers. Hopping out of the car, Tiaz saw Te'Qui and Baby Wicked lighting firecrackers and Bottle Rockets. Tiaz spotted his girl and walked over kissing Chevy on the lips right before he told her he'd be right back.

"What's up?" He passed Kantrell on his way into the house.

"What's up, boo?" She cracked a smile, holding a Heineken at her lips.

"This dick." He smiled back.

"We gon' find out."

"Sho' ya right." He dipped off into the house where he stashed the duffle bag under the bed until he was able to get into the garage without so many eyes on him.

He then headed back outside and watched the firework show with Chevy and her family. Once all of the fireworks had been popped, everyone headed back inside of the house. They ate, drunk and talked amongst one another.

Tiaz went around the room chopping it up with different relatives of Chevy's, getting to know everyone. Every so often Tiaz would catch Kantrell staring at him. He couldn't wait to taste her goods again, since that day in the living room they'd been fucking on a regular basis. At first Tiaz felt guilty about stepping out on Chevy with her girl, but Kantrell had a shot of pussy that couldn't be faded. When she put that pussy on him he'd forgotten all about Chevy. The sex was so good he started hitting her off raw. While Kantrell was falling in love with Tiaz, he was falling in love with her sex.

Tiaz' cell vibrated with a text message and he glanced at the screen. It read: *I can't wait for you to blow my back out again.*

Tiaz looked up from the text to see Kantrell staring at him from across the room like she wanted to gobble him up. He smirked and put his cell phone back on his hip.

The sound of dice being rattled inside of someone's fist brought his attention over his shoulder. At the kitchen table was Savon, Te'Qui, Baby Wicked and a host of relatives. Tiaz loved a good crap game just as much as any hood nigga, so he couldn't miss out on the possibility of winning a few dollars. Tiaz was on fire as soon as the dice graced his palm. He was hitting sevens and elevens like they weren't shit. He was hot. You would have thought that the dice were loaded.

Once he finally crapped out, he decided to call it a night, especially since he was richer than he was when he started. While everyone else carried on gambling, Tiaz stood at the kitchen sink straightening out his money and counting it.

"Babe, can you take the trash out for me?" Chevy asked.

"Yeah, I got it." Tiaz continued to count his winnings.

"What chu got for momma?" Chevy asked over his shoulder. Tiaz gave her five hundred dollars of the twenty-five he won shooting craps. "Gimmie a kiss." He pecked her lips and she headed back over to her friends, stuffing the dead presidents into her bra.

Tiaz stuffed his grip into his pocket and grabbed the black garbage bag out of the trash can. He had his back to the street when he walked on the side of the house, so he didn't see the car stop behind him.

Suddenly, he stopped in his tracks. He didn't know why but he felt like someone was watching him. His face twisted into a frown and he slowly began to turn around to quiet the suspicion. As he did, the car began to roll off but once he fully turned around the car was already gone. He looked from left to right but he didn't see a soul. He shrugged and continued up the driveway. He opened the lid to a black trashcan and dumped the garbage bag inside of it. He went to turn around and was startled to find a grinning Kantrell behind him.

"Girl, you scared the hell outta me." Tiaz' heart thumped.

Kantrell giggled and grabbed the bulge in his Levi's. Her lips pressed against his and she forced him against the house, kissing him hard and sensually. Her hands moved in accord with her thoughts quickly unbuckling his belt and unzipping his jeans. She licked her palm down the middle with her long tongue. She then dipped her French tipped manicured hand into his Fruit of the Loom boxer briefs and stroked his thick worm until it stood erect.

A devilish smile stretched across Tiaz' face. "Oh, you won't some of this dick, huh?"

"Uh huh, mmmm," she nodded, eying him hungrily as she licked her top lip. Suddenly, she covered his mouth with hers and kissed him hard. Feeling his throbbing dick in her hand was her confirmation that he was down for the quick nut. He roughly threw her around so that her back would be facing him.

"Spread yo mothafucking legs." He kicked her legs apart roughly. "Now put cha hands against the side of the house, palms down, goddamn it, right now!" She did as he commanded, loving the authority in his delivery. Violently, he tugged her leggings and panties down. "Now toot cha ass up." He smacked her buttocks hard as fuck and she tooted that thang up, showing him the entrance to eternal happiness. "Fucking around with chu out here I'm end up getting caught, but this is what chu want, huh?" He looked around making sure no one was watching them. He looked up to the kitchen window and the music was blaring inside. *Good, they won't hear this bitch screaming,* he thought. "Is this what chu want, you fucking whore?" He reached around and grabbed her by the throat. Her nostrils flared and veins formed in her temples. She gagged when she spoke.

"Yes, yes, daddy, fuck me!" she said, breathing awkwardly.

"You want this dick bad, huh? Well, that's what I'ma give to ya." He stroked his meat vigorously until it reached its full potential, all the while keeping his head on a swivel for any witnesses to what was about to go down. *The coast was clear.*

"Ahh, put it in, put it in!" She gagged and wheezed from his hand clamping her throat. Tiaz licked the tips of his fingers and wet the head of his member. Grabbing his hardness, his slid the head of it up and down her moist slit, watching her juices trickle. Right after her pussy lips was swallowing all of him.

"Ssssssshit," Tiaz shut his eyes and threw his head back, his mouth hung slack. "Goddamn, this mothafucka off the hook!" He tucked his bottom lip into his mouth and spread her cheeks apart. He gripped that fat ass of hers and grunted as he laid into her, taking deep thrusts and pulling back and forth. The entire time he watched his meat reach into her depth and slide back out. Her cream lathered his dick and had it looking shampooed.

"Uh! Uh! Uh!" Kantrell's eyes were shut and a big smile was plastered across her face. He grasped her by her hair and yanked it back as he plowed into her, not giving a mad ass fuck if she enjoyed it or not.

"Haa! Haa! Haa! Haa!" A film of sweat dampened Tiaz' forehead as he punished Kantrell from behind, causing her ass to jiggle. Watching the ripple that went through her behind made his dick grow harder.

The buff neck thug could see the veins forming all around his endowment. Kantrell squeezed her internal muscles around his shaft. He released a soft moan when he felt her walls contracting around his stiffness. He then grasped her shoulders firmly and gave her a vicious pounding, tearing into her like a man possessed by a paranormal entity. She was making so much noise. He was glad the music was up loud inside of the house because if it wasn't for that then everyone would have surely heard her.

Tiaz was ramming Kantrell from the back as hard and as violently as he could. He wasn't making love to this woman, he was fucking her. Fucking her like she was some two bit whore off of Figueroa Avenue. He continued to plow into her until he felt a tingling in his loins. Quickly, he whipped his meat out of her and jerked it off toward the ground, his children tatting up the grass.

"Damn, boo, that hit the spot." She told him as she turned around, pulling her leggings back upon her.

"Yeah, that set a nigga straight." He admitted, stashing his meat back inside of his jeans and zipped them up. When he and Kantrell turned around to head back inside of the house, they found Te'Qui standing before them. The light post on the curb filled out his outlining making him look like a shape in the darkness. He'd been standing there but they didn't know for how long.

"Shit, he's gonna tell Chevy about us?" Kantrell worried.

Tiaz approached Te'Qui wearing a hard face and glaring down at him. The look the young man wore was one of uncertainty. He couldn't be too sure of what he'd seen. "What up, lil' gangsta?" Tiaz dapped him up.

"I was just coming to tell you that when you let me take over the craps for you I won a hundred and fifty dollars."

"You came up on you a lil' change, huh? What're you gon' blow it on?"

"I wanna buy me a gold chain, but I don't have nearly enough. Altogether I got $300 dollars with the money my dad gives me for my allowance. But the chain I want from the swap meet costs $800 dollars. I was thinking maybe you could give me the rest."

"What makes you think that I have $500 dollars to lay on you?"

"'Cause you put in work."

"Man, I only make $8.50 an hour at that punk ass job."

"I'm not some lil' stupid kid that doesn't know what's going on around him, so don't try to play me. I know you and your homeboy jack niggaz for grips."

Tiaz frowned, wondering how Te'Qui knew what he did for gwap. "What makes you think I'm out here knocking folks over?"

Te'Qui shrugged and said, "The streets talk. I don't really believe you work. You don't have a job, do you?"

"Nope." Tiaz gripped his shoulder. "Lil' homie, you're too smart for me. Street smarts and book smarts, that's a lethal combination.One of these days you and ya man Wicked are gonna have this city on smash. Listen, you keep what chu know about what I do to yourself, alright? And I promise I'ma show you a way to get money. You'll be able to buy that chain quicker than you think."

"How, kicking in doors with you and your homeboy?"

"Nah, you're too young for that, I've got something else in mind. I fucks with chu. You're my lil' nigga so I'ma put chu upon a hustle, alright?" He held out his fist.

"Alright." Te'Qui gave Tiaz dap and smiled. He couldn't wait to do whatever he had to do to get a gold chain. Inside of his head, he pictured himself trying different gold chains on at the Swap Meet.

"Come on, let's go in the house before your momma comes looking for us." He draped his arm over Te'Qui's shoulders and they made for the house.

"What do we tell Chevy if she asks what we were doing out here?" Kantrell whispered into Tiaz' ear as he walked off with Te'Qui.

"Just say we were out her blowing one." He whispered back.

Kantrell nodded in agreement.

"Te'Qui?" A voice called out in the night.

Te'Qui looked up and saw his father standing out by his truck. His young face lit up and he ran over to him, wrapping his arms around him.

Faison stared at Tiaz as he embraced his son. Tiaz stared Faison dead in his eyes. He'd never met him before but he'd heard enough about him to know he didn't like him. Faison broke the embrace from his son and popped the hatch of his Benz truck. He began pulling out different types of fireworks and sitting them on the curb. Seeing this, Kantrell ducked off into the house.

Moments later, Chevy and her entire family came outside. Savon stood with his goons, bangers at their sides in case any drama jumped off. They went to follow Chevy, but she said something to them that made them stay where they were on the porch. Tiaz fell in step behind Chevy, she tried to wave him back but he wasn't having it.

"Faison, what are you doing here?" Chevy asked.

"What chu mean what am I doing here? I came to pop fireworks with my son." Faison smiled and winked at his son, continuing to pull the fireworks out the hatch.

"Faison, I told you to call before you come by here, you can't just be popping up." Chevy scolded wearing a frown.

Faison and Chevy had agreed to set aside their differences for the sake of Te'Qui. They came to an understanding and had thought it would be in their child's best interest for them to continue co-parenting.

"I called you six times. I hit your cell and the house phone." Faison said.

"Faison, you did not call either of my phones." Chevy said, pulling her cell phone out of her pink hoodie. She checked the screen of her cell phone and she had six missed calls from Faison.

"See there, now say you're sorry," Faison said, closing the hatch of his truck.

"Please." Chevy shot him a *get the fuck out of here* look.

"Dad, you gotta lighter?" Te'Qui asked excitedly as he held a big rocket he was dying to set off. Baby Wicked was standing beside him and they both couldn't wait to light the rocket and see what it would do.

Faison reached into his pocket and pulled out a Zippo lighter. He handed the lighter to Te'Qui and he began to set the rocket up to light it.

"Who's the guard dog?" Faison asked of Tiaz.

"Tiaz, this is Faison, Te'Qui's father. Faison, this is my boyfriend Tiaz." Chevy made the introductions.

Tiaz extended his hand and Faison looked at it as if it was dripping piss. Faison then shook his hand, squeezing it as hard as he could. He was looking for him to wince in pain, but he kept a solemn face.

"'Sup?" Faison smiled fiendishly.

"Are you done?" Tiaz asked of him squeezing his hand.

Faison released his hand and wiped it on his shirt while staring him in the eyes. Chevy shook her head and rolled her eyes. "Chevy, I need to holla at chu," he looked back to Tiaz, "*in private.*"

"Babe, give us a minute, okay?" Chevy said to Tiaz. He nodded and kissed her hard and passionately, intentionally trying to get under her ex's skin. He then shot daggers at him before walking off.

Faison stepped to Chevy once Tiaz walked off. "How dare you bring some nigga around my son that I don't know shit about? He could be a fucking pedophile for all I know."

Chevy blew hard and gathered her wits before speaking. "You're right, Faison. You're absolutely right. I should have let chu meet Tiaz before I brought him around Te'Qui. You got that. I'm sorry. 'Cause had it been you bringing some bitch around my baby I hadn't met, Lord knows I would have been on your head. But chu can't blame me, though, especially with the way you've been acting lately."

"Regardless, Chevy, you should have made it so I met him."

"Once again I'm sorry, but that's the last time I'm apologizing. If you're expecting me to beg for your forgiveness, forget it. You've done worse. You and I both know that."

"Whatever, Chevy." Faison went to help his son light the big rocket.

Chevy watched Faison for a time, then she went back to join her family on the porch. While everyone went inside of the house, she and Tiaz stood out on the porch wrapped in one another's arms. They looked on as Te'Qui lit the end of the big rocket and watched it shoot into the air, exploding in beautiful bright colors.

Faison watched Chevy and her new man from a far seething inside, clenching and unclenching his fists.

This nigga's gotta go. He tryna snatch my family right from under my nose but I ain't having it. Not now not ever. I'm Te'Qui's father and I'm Chevy's man. Homie is either gon' see himself outta the picture or he gon' see his ass dead, straight like that.

Chapter 15
The next day

Tiaz lay in bed with the satin sheets partially covering his nakedness, smoking a cigarette and watching Chevy get dressed for work. They'd just finished having sex about twenty minutes ago. She had expected it to be a quickie, but the romp ended up lasting far longer than she'd expected. She was late for work so she didn't have time to shower like she'd planned.

She'd propped her leg upon the tub and cleaned where it counted with a wet, soapy washcloth. She hated half ass bathing, but it would have to do until she made it back home. Once she had gotten dressed and smoothed the wrinkles out of her uniform, she put on her Timex watch and stepped before the dresser mirror. She dipped her hand into a jar of Pro-style and rubbed the gel together in both hands before applying it to her hair. Once she was done, she brushed her hair back into a neat bun.

"Love, you look sexy than a mothafucka in that lil Rent-A-Cop uniform, make me wanna take 'em down one more time before you leave."

Chevy smiled as she slipped on her jacket. "Uh uh, I'm not fucking with chu, you already got me late for work as it is." She picked up the bag containing her laptop and her lunch bag. She leaned over beside the bed and kissed him before heading out of the bedroom. Once he heard the front door close, he saw Te'Qui come out of his bedroom. Tiaz watched him as he smoked his cigarette, he went into the living room and then he came into his mother's bedroom.

"My momma went to work?" Te'Qui asked Tiaz and he responded with a head nod. Te'Qui plopped down on the end of the bed. "Good, now show me that hustle that's gon' get me that chain." He rubbed his hands together greedily.

Tiaz grinned and mashed his cigarette out in an ashtray on the dresser. He rolled out of bed as naked as the day he was born. Te'Qui looked away not wanting to see his flaccid fuck stick. He picked his boxer briefs up from off the floor and stepped into them, one leg at a time. "Come on, I'ma show you how to get this money."

"Aye, you mind showing Wicked, too?"

"Yeah." Tiaz nodded. "I like Wicked, I fucks with the lil' homie."

"Cool." Te'Qui ran out of the room to retrieve his friend.

Fifteen minutes later...

Te'Qui and Baby Wicked sat at the kitchen table. The young knuckleheads' eyes were glued to their teacher as he stood before them with a brick of cocaine. Tiaz'eyes shifted back and forth from Te'Qui to Baby Wicked as he spoke, square dancing from his lips.

"This is a kilo of uncut cocaine. Y'all lil' niggaz know how hard it is to get a brick of uncut coke? Damn near impossible. Most of the shit out here has been stepped on so much that it ain't even coke anymore. Its bullshit, watered down." Tiaz sat the brick on the table and partially un-wrapped it. He then grabbed a butcher's knife out of the block of knives on the kitchen sink. "See, Hollywood will put chu under the impression that a kilo is already a powdered substance, but that's bullshit." He stabbed the butcher's knife into the white brick, cracking its surface. "Bricks of white are as hard as your mothafucking head. Some cats use grinders and shit to avoid the lumps and clumps in it. But me I use the handle of a knife. That's how my pops used to do it." He took the Joe from his lips and beat the exposed part of the brick down with the handle of the knife until it was a powder. Then he smoothed some of it out with the butcher's knife. "Yeah, see there? Shit is powdered, no lumps or none of that shit. I'ma start y'all off with an ounce. You've gotta crawl before you walk, feel me? Y'all slip on these gloves." He smacked a box of latex gloves on the kitchen table. "I'ma show y'all how to cook this shit up." While the boys busied themselves putting on latex gloves, Tiaz turned on one of the burners of the stove, twisting the dial so that the blue flames were at the height he was pleased with. Afterwards, he got a coffee pot and a box of bacon soda down from the cabinet. He sat them down at the kitchen table along with a couple Gemstar razors and a spoon. He then put the coke and the bacon soda into the coffee pot, adding the amount of water he desired.

"Y'all lil' niggaz paying attention?" he asked, watching the water fill the pot.

"Yeah." The juveniles answered in unison.

"Smooth." He replied, sitting the pot on the burner. "Now, we gon' let this shit boil for like five minutes." He adjusted the dial just a little bit and stepped back, watching the white mist manifest inside of the coffee pot. When it was time he grabbed the ice tray out of the refrigerator and picked up the coffee pot, dropping a few cubes inside of it. He rotated the pot counter clockwise as he added the cubes.

"Why are you putting ice cubes in it?" Te'Qui asked.

"To reduce the temperature, lil' nigga, pay attention," He told him as he held up the pot and motioned the youths over. "Now look, y'all see that cocaine in there? It's starting to form into a rock." He carried the pot over to the sink and added some cold ass water to it. Once the coke had frozen to a solid rock, he scooped it out and sat it down on a plate. After letting the crack cool off, he grabbed one of the Gemstar razors and showed the boys how to cut the shit up.

"Alright, B-Dubb, you give it a try." Tiaz told Baby Wicked as he stood beside Te'Qui. He watched the little nigga follow instructions until he had a small mishap.

"Slow yo' roll, homeboy," Tiaz snatched the cigarette from his mouth and turned to him. "You putting too much bacon soda in that shit. You gon' run the fiends off."

"My fault, OG."

"Don't wet it." He took the coffee pot from him. "Practice makes perfect."

It took a couple of tries but Te'Qui and Baby Wicked finally got the hang of cooking coke into crack. Afterwards, he showed them how to weigh it, chop it and bag it.

Tiaz didn't find anything wrong with having taught Te'Qui how to cook up drugs. The way he saw it he was teaching the youngling a trade. He could remember when he was around his age and his big homie had taught him some hustles. He was thankful back then because had it not been for him he would have starved out in those scandalous streets. He thought of it as him giving back to the community. He was providing a service at a very small fee. He was teaching the boy how to get it on his own so that he wouldn't have to ask a mothafucka for shit. Hell, should the day come where he and Chevy parted, he was sure that his surrogate son would use his lessons to take care of home. With that in mind he felt like he had did his good deed for the day.

"Fuck we gon' sling this shit at?" Baby Wicked asked Tiaz. He was sitting at the table beside Te'Qui chopping rocks from a tan crack cookie.

Tiaz shrugged. "Shit, this ain't my hood, I don't know."

"Where ever we hustle at it can't be in the 20s, if my uncle Savon catches me, he'll peel the skin off my ass." Te'Qui added his two cents as he bagged up rocks.

"I know where we can get money, its enemy turf but we'll be strapped up." Baby Wicked said.

"Man, I don't care, as long as it's nowhere around here." Te'Qui replied.

"Man, if y'all ever get knocked with this shit..."

"We already know, so don't worry. I'm notta snitch and Wicked ain't either." Te'Qui interjected.

"Alright," Tiaz rose to his feet, ruffling Te'Qui's head as he passed him.

***

Te'Qui rolled on the handlebars of Baby Wicked's Huffy as he peddled. The wind whipped through their hair and disturbed their clothes as they rode through the ghettos of The Bottomz. They went on tour through the 20s, the 30s and settled in the 40s. The 40 Avalon Gangsta Crips territory to be exact.

Baby Wicked brought his Huffy to a skidding halt. He dismounted his bike and Te'Qui hopped off the handlebars. Baby Wicked stashed his bike inside the yard of an abandoned house with boarded up windows and tall dead grass the color of hay. He came out of the yard and met back up with Te'Qui, surveying his surroundings. The youngsters knew that they were dead ass wrong for attempting to hustle on enemy turf, but the allure of the almighty dollar was just too strong.

"Alright," Baby Wicked began. "I got the strap, I'ma hold it down here. You post up across the street." He pointed across the street to the corner. "Don't worry, the fiends can smell a nigga with work on 'em, they'll come in droves tryna cop this shit. That paper will come flowing in like pouring springs. Trust me, this smoker by the name of Yuckmouth used to stand right there and hustle until he died of a circulatory overload; poor bastard." He shook his head in shame. He then checked the chamber of his chrome thang. Seeing that it was fully loaded, he closed it and tucked it in his waistline. "Gon', Blood, I got chu. Let's break the bank out here." He gave Te'Qui a complex handshake and ended it by snapping his fingers two times.

Te'Qui jogged across the street to the corner. He posted up keeping an eye out for crack heads and any possible threats. Besides the chirping of birds and cars passing by every so often, the block was particularly quiet. About an hour had passed and not a crack head had come through looking for a blast. He looked across the street at Baby Wicked and he shrugged. He looked up into the sky, closed his eyes and blew hard. He spat on the ground. The foot steps coming from his left brought his attention around. A haggard looking crack head wearing a beat up straw hat and worn sandals that displayed his yellowish toenails and ashy feet approached him. Straw hat tilted his head back and scratched his nappy chin hair.

"You holding, youngsta?" he asked.

"Dimes," Te'Qui told him.

"Gimmie three of them thangs," The old head passed him three wrinkled bills and he passed him three tan rocks wrapped in plastic. The man put the crack into his pocket and shuffled away.

Te'Qui looked at his homeboy.He grinned and gave him a nod. It seemed like after the first customer copped, the crack heads were coming back to back. He sold all of the rocks he had on him as well as the ones Baby Wicked had. The boys had to head back to the house to get some more work. They cooked, chopped, and bagged up the work at Te'Qui's house.

Two hours later...

It was 3 o'clock in the afternoon. The boys were posted back up on the block. The crack heads were coming like clockwork. Te'Qui had money stuffed inside of all of his pockets, even the small pocket above the big pocket of his jeans. With the first batch of rocks, he'd made Tiaz'cut of the profits, now it was him and his homeboy's turn to eat.

He had just sold a couple rocks to a husky, light skinned crack head missing four front teeth. The crack head walked away and he held up four fingers, signaling that he had four more rocks to get off. Baby Wicked smiled and nodded his head. He then pointed down the street. Te'Qui followed his finger and found a youthful looking cat that was bopping up the block, eating a bag of sunflower seeds. His head was hidden beneath a navy blue hoodie that was zipped up to his neck. The gold chain that hung down his chest held to a bust of Riley Freeman from The Boondocks cartoon. The chain swung from left to right with each step that the young man took. He moved forth with a waltz that oozed swagger and confidence.

Te'Qui frowned when the young man stopped before him. He could tell by the way he dressed and carried himself that he wasn't there to cop. It dawned on Te'Qui that if he wasn't a crack head then he had to be from Avalon Gangsta Crips, the gangsters' turf that he and his right-hand were hustling on. The young man took the time to finish eating his sunflower seeds before speaking.

"Y'all lil' niggaz know who's hood this is?" he asked calmly as he reached back into his bag of sunflower seeds. When Te'Qui didn't respond, he continued on, "Avalon's. This is our hood and ain't nobody getting money 'round here that ain't brethren. Y'all lil' niggaz are stepping on our toes, clogging up the mula pipe line. There's a steady flow of traffic that comes through here to cop and y'all are snatching them up before they even reach our trap. I'm here to tell you that y'all ain't hustling over here no more. As of this moment, this shit is shut down."

"Man, fuck outta here," Te'Qui waved him off. He turned his back on the young man and went about his business of waiting for the crack heads to come cop.

"Te'Qui, what's up?" Baby Wicked hollered from across the street.

"This funny ass dude talking 'bout we can't hustle over here no more." He hollered back. He spoke as if the young man wasn't behind him.

"Man, fuck that nigga." Baby Wicked's face twisted into anger, it had been a minute since he'd shot someone and here was his chance to break that spell. He was going to run up on the young man and if he popped some fly shit then he was going to lay him the fuck down.

The young man looked over to Baby Wicked who was jogging toward him from across the street. He noticed that the youngster had his hand hid behind his back. The young man shook his head in pity of the younger boys, saying, "Lil' dumb mothafuckaz." He whistled and a black Nissan Pathfinder bent the corner coming to a screeching halt before Baby Wicked, stopping him in his tracks. The baby face hoodlum went to lift his .38 and a MP-5 emerged from the backseat window. Clutching it was a bronze skinned man with evil eyes and a blue bandana covering the lower half of his face.

"Drop the gun lil' nigga before I blow your guts all over that fence behind you!" The bronze skinned man barked with authority. His husky voice and the sight of the powerful machine gun sent chills up Baby Wicked's spine. He swallowed hard and tossed the .38 special aside.

Te'Qui's heart quickened and he panicked. He didn't know what to do. Before he could come up with a resolve he felt the barrel of cold steel press against his dome. His eyes darted to their corners and found the young man behind a black revolver. He closed his eyes and swallowed hard, thinking that this would be his last day on earth.

"A hardhead makes a soft ass." The young man shook his head. "Y'all are young and don't know no better, so I'ma give y'all a pass. Stay the fuck from over here. I'm giving you a fair warning. You hear me?" Te'Qui nodded *yes*. "Good."

Crack!

The young man struck him across his dome with the pistol and he crumpled to the sidewalk. He gritted his teeth in pain and rubbed his aching head. The young man tucked his banger into his waistline and casually walked toward the Pathfinder, eating the sunflower seeds.

"I'm Maniac and that's the homie, Time Bomb." Bronze skin nodded to the young man who had just hopped into the backseat and slammed the door. "Y'all remember the names. If I see y'all punk asses down here again, I'ma come through and lay this whole fucking corner down. You got that?" Baby Wicked nodded *yes*. "Alright then." He pulled the MP-5 back into the Pathfinder and told the driver to pull off. As the Pathfinder drove off its passengers shouted out Avalon and threw their hood up out of the windows.

Baby Wicked picked his pistol up and ran over to his home-boy. He helped him up to his feet and examined him for wounds. "Are you alright, Blood?" he asked.

"I'll be okay." Te'Qui assured. "Bitch ass nigga hit me in the head with his strap."

"He didn't take the money and the work, did he?"

"Nah, I still got it all."

"Come on. Let's get back to the house." He draped his arm over his shoulders and ushered him across the street.

Chapter 16

Tiaz was sitting on the couch holding the telephone to his ear with his shoulder while preparing a blunt. He was dressed in a black beanie and camouflage army jacket. His feet were propped upon the coffee table and the flat-screen was on. Love and Hip Hop was on the screen, but he wasn't paying it any mind. His attention was focused on the conversation at hand.

"Yeah, man, I casted the line and some mothafucka bit, took the bait right off the hook. Fifteen cents, it's all profit, Crim. It's all profit so it's a win, win situation. Feel me? Nah, do your thang, I'ma have this broad roll me out there." He licked the blunt closed and sealed it shut by sweeping the flame of his Zippo lighter back and forth across it. Once he was done, he tucked the Zippo lighter into his jacket pocket and took a few pulls from the blunt. Its tip glowed ember each time he sucked on the end of it.

Tiaz was talking about the four kilos of coke that he had left from a caper he and Threat pulled. He'd been sitting on them for a minute looking to find someone that would take them off of his hands. When he couldn't find someone to cop the keys from him, he put the word out to his homies that he was offering a finder's fee for anyone that could find him a buyer.

About an hour ago he'd gotten a call from one of his homie's saying that they'd found a buyer. He shot him the buyer's phone number and he hit the cat's line. They agreed to meet up at a discreet location with one other person to make the exchange.

Tiaz was well aware of how Kantrell's father had taught her how to defend herself with her fists and firearms. Since Threat had other business he had to attend to that day, he enlisted her on the drop he was to make that night. Tiaz would feel comfortable with her watching his back in case shit popped off. While he was in prison he'd heard stories about the hit man known as Casper. His murder game was official and his work would have his name on the tongues of everyone in the underworld. Once thought as a myth, the assassin known as Casper would now forever be remembered as a legend.

"But anyway, nigga, I'ma get back with chu once I'm on my way back from this drop. Alright, peace." He hung up the telephone and went on to smoke his blunt, watching Love and HipHop.

Hearing keys at the front door, he looked over his shoulder at the door. He pulled his banger close and placed his finger on the trigger. The front door opened and Te'Qui and Baby Wicked came inside. Baby Wicked followed him into the kitchen and filled a Ziploc bag full of ice. Te'Qui sat down at the table rubbing the lump that had formed on the side of his head. When he was handed the Ziploc bag of ice, he held it to the knot on the side of his head.

"Fuck happened to y'all?" Tiaz frowned, coming from around the couch.

Baby Wicked looked to Te'Qui and he shook his head. "Te'Qui, fell off the handlebars of my bike and bumped his head."

"Oh, okay," Tiaz nodded. He then snapped his fingers and flexed them.

Te'Qui reached into his pocket and pulled out a handful of money. He plucked out a few bills and handed them to Tiaz. Tiaz' cell phone's alert went off and he checked his messages. He then put the cell phone back on his hip and looked back up. "I'm outta here. You young niggaz stay up." He dapped the young niggaz up.

Once he was gone, Te'Qui emptied his pockets out on the kitchen table and began counting the money he'd made from the day's hustling. Baby Wicked sat down in the chair beside him to help him count. Once the count was done, they realized that they only had enough money for one chain.

"What do you think we should do now?" Te'Qui asked.

"We get back out there and get the rest of the money for another chain." Baby Wicked told him.

"You heard what them niggaz said, they're gon' body us the next time they catch us out there." Te'Qui lay back in his chair, holding the ice bag to his head.

"Fuck them. Yeah, they caught me slipping, but next time I'm thumping on any nigga that step to us that ain't looking to cop." Baby Wicked assured him. "Besides, if one of us gotta chain, then the other should have one, too. We homies, we should shine together. All we need is $400 dollars mo' and we can call it quits. Look, I'ma 'bout to go to the house, you good?" Te'Qui nodded and slapped hands with his homie before he left.

***

He sat up in bed half naked smoking the roach end of a blunt as his eyes watched her curiously. Her clothes and shoes were strewn on the floor and bed. She'd been rummaging through the drawers trying to find the right thing to wear that day. She settled on a pair of black skinny jeans and a T-shirt.

"Uh! Uh! Uh!" Kantrell jumped around trying to fit that big old booty of hers into the jeans. She fell back onto the bed. Holding her legs up and pulling on the loops, she finally managed to get herself in them. She bounced back upon her feet and buttoned the jeans, zipping them up. She then slipped on her socks and grabbed her Nike Dunks.

"Where are you goin'?" he asked.

"Out?" She responded simply.

"I know that. Where?"

She rolled her eyes as she laced up her sneakers. "Who are you? My P.O?"

"Fuck you think you talkin' to?"

She looked over her shoulder. "Yo ass!" She went to lace up her other sneaker. He snatched the roach from out of his mouth and yanked her head back, drawing a howl of pain from her lips. She grimaced and yanked away violently, leaving strands of hair between his fingers. He looked to the hair in his palm and she felt the back of her scalp, wincing. She looked to her hand and it was bloody.

"Mothafucka, no you didn't!" She looked at him like *I can't believe you did that shit.*

"Yes, I did." He mashed what was left of the L out in the ashtray. Jumping to his feet, he hastily approached her asshole naked and dick swinging. He cracked his marred knuckles about to beat the brakes off of that ass. "You gon' learn today, bitch!"

"Yo' ass is gon' learn, nucca." She pulled open the top drawer and drew her piece, a nickel plated .32. He raised his fist to knock fire from her and she pointed that little fucka right between his eyes.

"Fuck you gon' do with that?" He grumbled.

"This..."

Pow!

"Arghhh!"

She shot over his left shoulder, knicking his earlobe. He doubled over frowning and holding his ear, hearing the weird siren blaring in his head.

"March cho' punk ass up outta my spot or the next one giving you a disectomy." She lowered the small pistol at his family jewels. He looked up at her with clenched jaws, holding his ear. Veins were at his temples and his face was rose pedal red, he wanted to kill that bitch, but she had him in a bad way.

He went to pick up his jeans and she shot at his foot causing him to jump back. "What the fuck, man?" He hollered.

"Nah, leave as you are."

"What?"

"*What?*" She mocked him, clutching the weapon with both hands. "You heard me, waltz yo monkey ass outta here, just like that."

"You gotta be shittin' me." His brows mushed together.

- "Am I?" She looked him dead in his eyes, unflinching. From that look he knew that she wouldn't hesitate to send him to a place where evil dewelled for all of eternity.

He twisted his lips and turned around. She escorted him to the front at gunpoint, opening the door.

"You ain't gon' get away with this shit, bitch." He glared at her as he crossed the threshold, the blinding white light of the sun swallowing him. She slammed the door and locked it. *Fuck him,* she thought as she went back to getting dressed.

***

Tiaz coasted Kantrell's silver droptop Beemer up the freeway, while she played the passenger seat. Kantrell listened to 2pac's *Me and my Girlfriend* as she rolled a blunt.

Her hair flowed in the air as the wind combed through it. Her long legs stretched out and rested on the windowsill, leaving her manicured feet to feel the cool breeze outside. Kantrell put fire to the end of the blunt and took a few drags. She blew smoke into the air and leaned over to Tiaz, putting the blunt between his lips. He took a couple of pulls from the L. He was in the middle of blowing the smoke from between his lips when Kantrell turned him to face her. She covered his mouth with hers and kissed him sensually. She then pulled away and blew the smoke that he had trapped in his mouth out of hers. She kissed him once more on the lips and turned around in her seat, continuing to smoke the blunt.

Tiaz glanced at the mixed beauty as he drove up the freeway. She'd been begging him to kick Chevy to the curb and let her be his number one. She claimed to have mad love for him and would hold him down no matter what. Kantrell wanted to be his *Ride or die bitch* at any cost, even if it meant losing Chevy's friendship.

She was hung up on Tiaz and getting dicked down every now and again wasn't enough for her. She wanted to be the one he camehome to, the one he confided in, the one he called wifey. She wanted to be able to call him her man and for it to really be true.

Kantrell told Tiaz with her he could be who he really was. He didn't have to front like he was going to work every day when he was really kicking in nigga's doors. She didn't care that he was out there thugging just as long as he was hers.

Tiaz thought what Kantrell was saying sounded damn good, but he already had a rider on his team. Chevy had been there for him while he was locked up and when he had touched down. She ironed his clothes, cooked, cleaned, encouraged him to follow his dreams, rubbed his back and fucked him unconscious. Chevy treated him as if he was royalty. She truly knew how to make a man feel like a man. The only problem was she wouldn't be down to be his thug misses. There was no way that she'd support his lifestyle. She told him that she made Te'Qui's father quit the game before she agreed to marry him. So there was no way she was going to allow him to do his thing and still be with her.

Kantrell on the other hand was down with whatever. He told her his getdown and what he was about. She went with whatever he wanted to do and didn't ask any questions. She was a soldier no doubt, but he had to question her loyalty. How devoted to him could she be if she was willing to step out with her best friend's man?

Tiaz knew he was wrong for fucking around with Kantrell as well, but he reasoned it was different because he was a man. A man was expected to fuck around with an abundance of women. He believed it was in a man's nature to have more than one woman, so it was okay if he got himself a little something on the side just as long as he took care of home.

Tiaz wasn't for sure if he was going to put Kantrell down on the team just yet. He had to feel her out and see where her head was. For now he was going to use her as a pawn on the chessboard that was his life. If she proved to be worthy, then maybe he'd consider her request.

Tiaz exited the freeway and pulled over to the side of the road. He turned the stereo down and turned to Kantrell. "Listen, for all I know I could be walking into a setup. I don't know this nigga from a hole in the wall. He could be looking to pop me and take this work. Some real gangsta shit could go down once we get in here. I need to know that you're about this life. You say you wanna be my *ride or die* well, this is your time to show me something, feel me?"

"I told you I got chu, boo. I don't even know why you're tripping. I'm that bitch you need on your team, down to ride to the very end, just like Pac said."

Tiaz placed his hand over Kantrell's left breast and felt for her heart beat. The pace of her love muscle was calm and steady. She wasn't scared. She was really with it like she'd claimed.

Tiaz popped the trunk and removed something wrapped in a sheet. He hopped back behind the wheel and handed Kantrell the thing that was wrapped in the sheet. Tiaz pulled away from the curb and back into traffic. Kantrell removed the sheet from the object it was concealing and revealed an AK-47. She checked the banana clip to make sure it was full then smacked it back into the weapon, cocking the hammer on it. The choppa was cocked, locked and ready and so was she.

Night had staked its claim over the streets when Tiaz drove into the deserted underground parking garage of the Hawthorne Mall. The ground of the garage was covered in loose trash and splinters of wood. The shopping center was empty and had been abandoned for the past fourteen years. It was the perfect place to make an illegal transaction. There weren't any eyes or surveillance cameras around to witness the exchange.

Tiaz turned the Beemer around and parked at the center of the parking garage. He executed the engine and headlights then lay back in the seat. He pulled his banger from under the driver seat, chambered a round into its head and tucked it into his waistline. He then picked the duffle bag up from the floor of the backseat and brought it up front. He unzipped the duffle bag and made sure the bricks were still inside then zipped it back up.

"Is that them?" Kantrell nodded toward the windshield at a Buick Regal that had just rolled into the underground parking garage.

"Yeah, I think so." Tiaz flashed the headlights twice so that the Buick Regal would know where to come. As the Buick Regal approached, he hopped out of the car toting the duffle bag. He stood out in front of the Beemer. The Buick Regal stopped a few feet away and its headlights cut off.

For a time everything was quiet and still. All that could be heard was the night's traffic and an airplane flying above. Kantrell sat up in her seat and gripped the AK-47, ready to be the cause of someone's death if a threat was posed. She chewed on bubble gum and watched the Buick Regal closely through her designer shades.

The driver side door of the Buick Regal opened and Bone stepped out wearing a bulletproof vest. He walked to the back passenger door and pulled it ajar. A Versace loafer stepped out, a jeweled hand grasped the door and a husky body pulled its self into view. Bone closed the door and the husky man advanced in Tiaz' direction. Each step the husky man took toward the muscle bound thug exposed more of his facial features until his identity was revealed. Seeing Faison made Tiaz' face contort into a mask of hatred. His hand slowly moved toward the banger on his waistline.

"This doesn't have to get bloody unless you insist." Faison spoke with a calm voice.

Tiaz calmed down and dropped his hand to his side. He cleared his throat before he spoke. "What the fuck do you want?" he asked.

"What I want is for you to stay away from my family. They're mine." Faison scowled. "Pack your things and crawl back into whatever hole in the ground you crawled out of."

"And if I don't?" Tiaz asked.

"Then I'm going to put chu and everyone you love into the fucking ground!" Faison barked like an old angry dog.

"You may as well get used to me, homie, 'cause I'ma continue to be a father to your boy and I'ma keep dropping this seven inch bone off in your baby momma, feel me?" Tiaz grabbed the bulge in his jeans and smiled wickedly.

"Feel this!" Faison whipped out his banger and pointed it at his forehead. At the same time Tiaz whipped out his and pointed it at Faison's forehead.

Kantrell drew a bead on Bone with the AK-47 and Bone drew a bead on her with his banger. Tiaz glanced down at his chest and saw a red dot at the center of it. He looked up and saw that it came from Bird. He was standing in the sunroof of the Buick aiming an M-16 equipped with an infrared laser and scope. The youngster had the assault rifle trained on Tiaz' heart and was ready to give the trigger a squeeze.

"Drop your strap!" Faison ordered. "You're out gunned!"

"I'm not dropping shit. We can all be some dead mothafuckaz tonight!" Tiaz shot back.

Faison could see in his eyes that he was serious about dying at that moment. He didn't see any fear in him or hear an unsteady voice when he spoke. Fasion was willing to do whatever he had to do to get rid of the brazen goon, but he didn't want to sacrifice himself in the process. The plan was to make him a memory so that he could get back with his family. He couldn't get back with his family if he was dead. Faison took his banger from Tiaz' forehead and placed its hammer back in place. Once he'd fallen back, the red dot disappeared from the thug's chest and Bone lowered his gun to his side. Tiaz lowered his banger to his side and signaled for Kantrell to lower hers.

"Alright, kamikaze, you win this one." Faison told him. "Tonight relish in your victory, but know this, I will have my woman and my son back, whether it's over your dead body or another's. That's a promise." He swore.

Tiaz leaned forth and whispered into Faison's ear. "I'll try to remember that while your bitch slobs on the end of my dick tonight." He stood erect and smiled fiendishly at Faison who mad dogged him. He looked from the drug dealer to his henchmen. "You gentlemen have a nice night," He waved his middle finger. Tiaz hopped back into the Beemer and pulled off under the watchful eyes of Faison and his henchmen.

"All of this over some pussy? Chevy must have some bomb between them thighs." Kantrell exclaimed. She snuggled back into the seat and put fire to the other half of the blunt. She took a few pulls and expelled smoke from her mouth. "You think he noticed it was me back there? The last thing I want him to do is run back and tell Chevy."

"I don't think so. He would have said something, then." Tiaz assured.

"Cool," she nodded.

"On another note, you handled your business out there, kid. I'm proud of you."

"I told you I'd do the damn thang."

Tiaz nodded. "That's what's up. Well, the night is still young and we're still holding these bricks. I'm tryna come up. Are you down?" He held out his fist.

"I got cho back." Kantrell dapped him up.

Chapter 17

Juvie rolled through the streets in his Dodge Charger R/T. He pulled to a red stoplight and hung his diamond flooded Audemar out of the window.The illumination of the light post bounced off the face of the expensive watch and casted a pretty rainbow.

The red light turned green and he drove on. One hand steered his vehicle while the other held the lighter that lit the blunt dangling from between his full, black lips. He took a few more pulls from the blunt and then blew out a roar of white smoke. After two more pulls, he passed the blunt off to Threat who was sitting in the passenger seat watching the streets pass him by in colorful blurs.

"So, how do you like working for Don Juan?" he asked.

Threat nodded as he brought the blunt to his lips. He took a pull from the blunt and expelled smoke. "It's cool, real cool.A nigga eating. I got my own spot, my own whip, jeweled out." He separated the iced out bust of Martin Luther King that hung from his neck and the iced out name tag that spelled out *Threat* in cursive.

"Don says you're an official nigga. I used to hear all about how you and ya boy Tiaz was busting fools heads when I was in middle school."

"That's what's up." Threat passed the blunt back and brushed the ashes from off his Trukfit shirt. Murder was a touchy subject and he for damn sure wasn't about to discuss the dirt he'd done in the trenches. Fuck did he look like?

"Yo man, I'ma stop at this deli up here and get me something to eat. I'm as hungry as a hostage."

Threat glanced at the digital clock in the dashboard to see if they had enough time to stop to get something eat. It was 7:43 PM. They didn't have to make the exchange until 8:30 so it was all good.

"Cool. I'm kinda hungry myself."

"Here we go." Juvie acknowledged the deli through the windshield. He pulled over and executed the engine. He and Threat hopped out of the truck and headed for the deli.

When they stepped into the establishment, the bell hanging over the door rang. The short young man standing behind the counter in a hairnet and apron lifted his head from the Don Diva magazine he was reading and tossed it onto the seat of a chair.

"What's cracking, Juvie?" The young man slapped hands with him when he approached the counter. He greeted Threat and slapped hands with him, too.

"I can't call it, homie." Juvie replied as he and Threat looked over the fine slices of cold cuts and cheeses that were behind the glass. "Hook us up with a couple of sandwiches, Lil' Stan. I'll have my usual and get my man here whatever he wants."

"Alright," Lil' Stan replied, slipping his hands into plastic gloves. He made Juvie's usual and prepared the sandwich that Threat desired. He placed the sandwiches into separate bags along with a can of soda and a bag of potato chips.

When Threat went to reach for his bag, Lil' Stan stuck a gun into face. The face the youngster mustered made the short killer throw his hands up in the air.

"What is this all about?" Threat frowned.

"You're about to find out?" Juvie approached with a gun at the back of his head. He'd just locked the door and turned the *open* sign over to the *we're closed* side.

"Follow me, there's something I wanna show you." Lil' Stanmotioned for him to follow along with his gun. He opened the door and walked into the back room, followed by Threat and Juvie. Juvie came in behind them and locked the door.

Threat's mind was temporarily taken off of the cold steel pointed at his face when he saw the sight suspended before him. Jaquez was chained to the ceiling butt naked with a gag in his mouth. His body was covered with cuts and bruises and his face was so swollen that you'd have thought he was bitten by a poisonous snake. From the looks of him, Threat could tell that someone had put in over time beating the living shit out of him.

"Fuck is this?" Threat looked to Juvie who was eating his hero sandwich.

He ignored him and approached Jaquez. He walked around him as he took bites out of his sandwich, eying him with an expression of disgust. Jaquez' head turned as far as it could as he tried to follow Juvie, in fear of what he might do to him next. Jaquez' arms and legs trembled and he pissed on the floor, expanding the puddle of yellow fluid below him.

"A snake's punishment! Dirty mothafucka!" In a rage, he threw the hero sandwich at Jaquez' head and it came apart, scattering lettuce, tomatoes, turkey and cheese everywhere.

The side door came swinging open. A moment later Don Juan came out gripping a machete and kicking a battered Boxy out through the door. Boxy's husky, naked body came crashing onto the floor. His mouth was gagged and his wrists were bound with ducttape. His face as well as his entire upper body was bloody and covered with cuts.

"Young niggaz was tryna rob me, Threat, him and Boxy." Don Juan finally spoke. "All of the shit that I've done for these niggaz. Putting clothes on their backs, food in their bellies, raising them as if I was the cat that skeeted them inside of their mommas. Can you believe these bitch ass niggaz? When I caught wind of the shit, the first thing I thought was that chu put 'em up to it. But bitch boy here," he smacked Jaquez' ass, "said you didn't have anything to do with it. I mean, you can't blame me for thinking so, the idea wasn't too farfetched. You do have a history of sticking cats up. You and I have been homies for a long time, Threat, but I give every man a reasonable doubt. You can't put shit past a nigga. *Trust no man* is what I always say. I'm sure you'd agree." He spat on Boxy and approached Jaquez. "Do you have anything to say before I send you to The Most High?" He pulled the gag down from Jaquez' mouth and listened to what he had to say.

"It wasn't me, man! It was Boxy!" Jaquez told him. "He came up with the plan to rob you. He made me…"

A punch to the gut knocked the wind out of Jaquez and caused him to grimace. "I ain't even tryna hear that bullshit, bruh. You're a grown ass man, can't nobody get chu do shit you don't want to do. I know you, Jaquez. You do whatever Boxy tells you to do! You'd probably suck his dick if he suggested it. You're a weak ass nigga, Crim, and it just cost you your life."

In one last desperate attempt, Jaquez screamed at the top of his lungs. "Pleeeeease, somebody help me!"

Another punch to the gut silenced him and caused his head to drop in pain. Don Juan placed his hand over Jaquez' mouth, muffling any more attempts at screaming. Jaquez' eyes bugged as the machete came into play.

The light in the ceiling bounced off the blade and caused it to twinkle. Don Juan drove the machete through the bottom of Jaquez' chin and it came out through the top of his skull. His eyes crossed and came undone once he gave his last breath. Don Juan pulled his machete out of his head and removed his hand from his mouth. Jaquez' head hung and his chin touched his chest, sending a red river spilling down his torso.

As Don Juan approached Boxy he brought his naked body to its knees. Boxy stared Don Juan dead in his eyes. He wasn't afraid to die. "You got heart, my young nigga, that's what I always liked about chu. You could have been my number two, but all that potential is going to waste." He planted his sneaker on Boxy's shoulder and gripped the machete with both hands. Using all of his might, he brought the machete down, burying it deep into his thick skull. When the machete met Boxy's head, it made a *thock* sound.

Specs of blood hit Don Juan's Miskeen T-shirt, but he didn't pay it any mind. With two strong tugs he was able to free the machete from the youngster's head. Once he'd recovered it, he hacked away at his hide until he was bloody and exhausted. When he was done he stabbed the machete into his chest and looked to Threat, wiping his face with the inside of his shirt. "Gon' and bounce, my nigga. I'll get up with chu later. Juvie, give 'em his piece back."

He gave Threat his banger back and he tucked it into his waistline. He opened the door and was about to go through it when Don Juan called him back, prompting him to turn around. "You and that nigga Tiaz lay off of my people. If you wanna rob niggaz cool, do your thang. But my customers are off limits." Threat didn't say a word, he continued out of the room. Though he didn't reply to what he'd been told, the hustler knew he'd gotten the message loud and clear.

A few hours later...

"Don Juan has been on to us, he knows we've been hitting his buyers and the cats he's connected with." Threat spoke from the kitchen table where he was focused on cleaning his banger.

"How do you think he found out?" Tiaz asked from where he sat on the kitchen sink.

"Shit, I don't know, probably been having someone follow us.Hard to say," Threat answered.

"I take it this means you're not tryna go through with this whole ransom thing." Tiaz looked at him like *nigga, you better not say yes.*

"What?" Threat shot his brother from another a funny look. "I don't give a fuck what Don Juan talking about. This is how I'm eating. That mothafucka is not paying my bills.To hell with him. Shit, if these cats we hitting can get got, then his prettyass can, too. Nigga play Superman and get the Kryptonite." He pointed the unloaded banger at Tiaz then went back to cleaning it. "Feel me?"

The buff neck thug laughed. "That's my goon.That's the Threat that I know. Fuck all of these niggaz, if they aren't with us than they're against us. And if they're against us, then they're meeting gunfire."

"You mothafucking right." Threat agreed.

Tranay Adams

Chapter 18
The next night

A black Mercedes Benz pulled in front of a night club. The vallet, a young brother in a red vest, came to the driver side and opened the door. Threat stepped out of the whip, one crocodile skin Stacy Adams shoe at a time. When he pulled himself into view, he was decked out in an apple-jack and a navy blue sweater vest, which he wore over a button-down and tie. On his wrist was a gold Michael Kors watch. It was simple, yet classy. Smoothly and with a flick of his wrist, he slipped the vallet the crisp folded $50 dollar bill in his palm.

Threat went around to the passenger side door and pulled it ajar. He held out his mitt and a feminine hand grasped it. Threat pulled the hand into him and a thick vixen stepped her red and silver spiked Christian Louboutin heel onto the curb. She brought herself into plain sight and the people standing on line turned their heads in awe. Her eyes were hidden behind black shades and her thick lips were covered by flaming red lipstick. Bianca's chunky frame was hugged by a red jumpsuit with silver spiked shoulders and a silver chain that stretched across her huge melon breasts. She held a matching handbag in her hand.

Tiaz hopped out of the backseat and walked around to the sidewalk to open the door for Chevy. He kept it gangster in a white blazer, which he wore over a white OBEY T-shirt with an image of a gray tiger on it, white Levi's and a pair of low-top gray All-Star Chuck Taylor Converse. Stepping upon the curb, Tiaz opened the door for his lady and stood aside.

All eyes were on Chevy when she emerged from the backseat of the luxury vehicle. Her hair was pulled back in a bun and her shapely figure filled out an off white Christian Dior dress with the back out. On her feet were gladiator sandals of the same designer. Diamond looped earrings graced her earlobes and three white gold and diamond bangles decorated her wrists. She took Tiaz under his arm and they assembled with Threat and Bianca.

A few feet down from the entrance of the club sat a sixty-five year old man who looked every bit of his age. He wore a porkpie hat, shades and a short sleeve black button-down shirt with beige stripes on both sides. On his lap sat a guitar that he played with expertise as he sung the lyrics to a song about heroin.

He told a tale about how heroin had pimped him and took him for everything he had. And she'd left him alone with an aching belly and empty pockets. An open guitar case sat at the old man's feet. Inside there were bills of all denominations and even a few coins.

As the old man wailed his guitar and crooned, Chevy pulled out a few dollars and dropped them into his guitar case. The old man finished his song and the last wails of his guitar. He got applause from Chevy and the people standing in line to get into the club. He held his hat slightly above his head, smiled and thanked Chevy for the money she'd dropped into his guitar case.

Tiaz, Threat and the girls continued toward the entrance of the club. They bypassed the people standing in line, drawing stares and whispers. They stopped before a pale skinned bouncer with a thin goatee. He was a tall man with a wrestler's physique dressed in a black turtleneck and matching blazer. His demeanor came off as *fuck with me and get your ass stomped out.*

"Are you folks on the guest list?" The bouncer asked, looking over the clipboard.

"Yeah," Threat answered.

"Name?"

"Benjamin Franklin." He sat a $100 dollar bill on the clipboard.

"Right this way, Mr. Franklin." The bouncer stuffed the $100 dollar bill into his pocket with a grateful smile, unhooking the velvet rope. He stepped aside and allowed the quartet to enter.

As soon as the quartet crossed the threshold into the club the first thing they noticed was the violet scenery and the roar of Bobby Shmurda's *Hot Nigga.* The dance floor was packed with men and women dancing provocatively and grinding on one another. Tiaz nodded his head to the music as he and Threat lead their women to a vacant booth. As soon as they stashed themselves into the booth they were approached by a hostess with a bubbly personality and banging body. She took their orders and returned promptly with their drinks. Threat dropped a $100 dollar bill onto the hostess' tray. She beamed and thanked him before sauntered off, swinging her big old ass from left to right.

"This mothafucka is live tonight." Threat said to Tiaz as he looked over the atmosphere of the club.

"Yeah, this mothafucka is turned up." Tiaz nodded and sipped his drink.

Chevy oozed out from the booth. She sat his drink down and grabbed his hands, trying to pull him to his feet. "Come on, Gangsta number one, come dance with me."

"Uh uh," Tiaz shook his head. "I can't dance to save my life. A nigga got two left feet, girl."

"Come on, tough guy, come boogie with me," she cooed.

"Nah, go on," Tiaz waved her off. "I'll watch you." He picked up his drink and took a sip. Chevy pouted her lips and made a face like a sad baby.

"Come on, Chev'. I'll cut up the floor with you." Bianca took Chevy by the hand and brought her out on the floor. Threat and Tiaz looked on as the girls danced out on the floor. They sipped their respective drinks and talked amongst one another.

"Man, that mothafucka Bianca is thick as shit." Tiaz commented on Threat's girl as he observed her dancing with Chevy. "Sexy lil' Spanish bitch. You never did have a problem busting yourself a bad piece of ass. I don't give a fuck if you was in a Platinum Fubu jersey and some Knobetta jeans, you was gon' pull yourself a dime."

"You're tipping your hat to me, but Chevy is one of the baddest pieces I done seen you with in a minute. And her homegirl, what's her name? Kantrell?" Tiaz nodded *yes*. "Crim, I'd drink that ho's bath water with a straw. Mmmhmmm." He shook his head, thinking of how fine Kantrell was.

"You're a fool, man." Tiaz chuckled as he nudged him.

"What? Lil' momma could get it. If you weren't my nigga, of course. It ain't my place, but I gotta say, you're sticking your head in a lion's mouth dipping your dick into old girl. From what chu tell me, Chevy's a mean motor scooter. She's not like a lotta these bitches that talk that shit but not gon' do too much but sic The Boys on you. Chevy on the other hand, she'll really put a hole in a nigga. You said she shot her son's father, what chu think she'll do once she finds out you've been playing hide the salami with her best friend?"

"I'll never have to worry about that, my friend." Tiaz smiled slyly and sipped his drink.

"Why is that?" Threat asked curiously.

"'Cause I'm never gon' get caught, Pimp Suit." He crunched on the ice and motioned for the hostess.

"Play on, playa." Threat dapped up him.

Tiaz felt his cell phone vibrate and removed it from his hip. He glanced at the screen and smiled. Kantrell had just sent him a picture message of herself naked in Lil' Kim's infamous pose.

She'd been sending him naked picture messages since they were on the way to the club and Chevy had almost caught him sneaking peeks at them. When she asked who he was texting, he told her that it was a buddy of his from work trying to set up a date for them to hang out. He didn't think Chevy quite believed him, but she dropped it so he didn't give it a second thought. Tiaz smiled and licked his lips as he texted Kantrell back.

I'ma give dat pussy a blk eye da nxt time I c u.

"Oh, so you can text your lil' friend from work but chu can't dance with wifey?" Chevy smiled and took a sip of her Patron silver margarita. The sound of her voice startled him. He hastily put his cell back on his hip.

"Nah, Love, you know it's not like that. A nigga just not tryna embarrass himself."

"Look," Threat tapped Tiaz and nodded to the dance floor.

The trio turned around and Bianca was grinding upon an older man. Her jumpsuit was rolled up so high that you could see her salmon colored Victoria Secret panties. The cat she was grinding on had one hand on her shoulder and the other held behind his back. It almost looked like they were fucking.

Any other man would have been jealous to see his lady rubbing her ass against some stranger's package but Threat was oddly turned on. He got aroused at the idea of watching Bianca getting banged out by another man. The thought of it made his dick as hard as Chinese arithmetic. He'd tried to get Tiaz to do it but he wasn't feeling it. Tiaz thought if he was to do it that Threat would hate hisself later for having gone through with it. But Threat even went so far as to offer Tiaz money, but still the hulking thug wouldn't break.

Chevy sat on Tiaz' lap sipping her drink through a straw and watching Bianca and the older man. "Uh uh, they're doing way too much out there." She voiced her opinion.

"Pops may as well whip it out and fuck her on the dance floor."Tiaz commented.

"Threat, you alright with your girl out there like that?" Chevy asked.

Threat kept his eyes on Bianca and the older man as he sipped his drink. "Sis, baby girl can do whatever she wants. I ain't got no papers on that pussy, feel me?"

"Hey, if you like it then I love it." Chevy replied. Feeling Tiaz' cell vibrate, she turned to him. "Damn, can't chu tell your coworker that you're out with your girl tryna have a good time?"

"My bad, boo. I promise, no more interruptions tonight." He turned his cell on silent then placed it back on his hip. "There, you happy?"

"Yes," she smiled.

"Gimmie some lip." Tiaz told her. They kissed three times then continued watching the show on the dance floor. The older man was now laying on the floor with his hands behind his head, looking at Bianca's ass as she grinded into him, cowgirl style while looking back at him.

The hostess brought Tiaz back his drink. He took a sip and continued to watch Bianca and the older man. Once the song finished, Bianca got to her feet and pulled the older man to his.

Bianca returned back to their table, sat on Threat's lap and patted her sweaty forehead dry with a couple of napkins.

"I'm parched." Bianca picked up her drink and took a sip. She felt something hard press against her ass and smiled. She looked back at Threat. "Is all that for momma?"

"Uh huh," Threat grinned and locked lips with Bianca.

The older man approached wearing a charming smile. He was a mahogany toned brother with a salt and pepper goatee. You could tell by his appearance that when he was a youth he was a handsome lad, but old age and street life had caught up to him. The man wore a purple fedora and a tailor-made suit. Over it he donned a cape like a pimp out of a 70s exploitation flick. On his feet were black Mauri shoes and they were shining like buffed hospital floors.

He stopped before Chevy and Tiaz. He removed his fedora exposing his finger-waved hair and patted the beads of sweat from his forehead with his handkerchief. He put the fedora back on his head and slipped the handkerchief back into his suit jacket's breast pocket.

"Hello, Ms. Lady, would you like to dance?" he asked Chevy.

Before Chevy could open her mouth Tiaz spoke up for her, "Nah, she's good, homie. She's chilling with her man right now."

"Brotha, I believe I was talking to the lady." The older man acknowledged Tiaz for the first time.

"And I believe I was talking to you." Tiaz clenched his teeth, exposing the skeletal bone structure of his jaws. Though he was displaying hostility, the older man was still boasting that charming smile of his. It was as if he didn't even acknowledge the mean mug he was projecting.

"How about it, Ms. Lady?" The older man addressed Chevy once again.

Tiaz made to get up but Chevy leaned all of her weight back against him. She grabbed the back of his neck and kissed him, their tongues dancing in one another's mouths. They kissed on the lips one last time then she looked to the older man. "Like my boo said, I'm chilling with him right now." The older man tipped his fedora and wandered off into the sea of people out on the dance floor. "That old man was weird." She sipped her drink.

"You set that old nigga right, Love." Tiaz kissed her on her neck.

"That's right, I know who this pussy belongs to." Chevy stated proudly.

"Is that so? Well, tatt my name on it so I know it's real." He told her as he kissed on her neck. Chevy laughed and tilted her neck to the side where he was kissing her.

After a couple of more drinks Chevy was finally able to get Tiaz to come out onto the dance floor with her. She, Tiaz, Threat and Bianca had a ball dancing the night away. Although Tiaz was having fun, he couldn't help but notice that the older man Bianca had been dancing with was watching them while savoring his glass of dark liquor.

The older man played the corner of the club along with two henchmen that Tiaz hadn't taken notice of until now. He couldn't quite make out what they looked like due to them being hidden within the confines of the shadows. When the deejay announced the last song, Tiaz looked over his shoulder and saw that the older man and his henchmen had vanished.

The quartet made their way outside before the last song was over so they wouldn't be caught up in the wave of club goers leaving. As soon as they stepped foot outside, Tiaz and Threat were called by the old man who'd been playing the guitar when they first arrived at the club.

"Say, you two brothas wouldn't happen to be Tiaz and Threat, now would ya?" The old man asked as he took pulls from the cigarette wedged between his fingers.

"Who wants to know?" Threat and Tiaz turned around with scowls plastered on their mugs.

"That's confirmation enough." The old man said to no one in particular. He dropped the cigarette on the ground and mashed it out under the heel of his dress shoe. He sat up in his chair, gripping the guitar and clearing his throat. He swallowed then began to sing a song about the Grim Reaper coming to claim the souls of two men who were ignorant of his presence.

Tiaz, Threat and the girls watched the old man as he performed the ballad. The old man finished the last few bars of the song.

"He wears a hood over his head/a scythe with a blade 'bout as long as your leg/ it's too late to scream 'cause you're already dead/ what's understood doesn't have to be said/ here he comes/ here he cuhhhhhhmes/here he comes/ here he cuhhhhhhmes/ death awaits..."

While the old man continued his crooning, Tiaz and Threat's heads darted around. They were on high alert, looking all around for any threat to their lives.The old man brushed his thumb and index finger across the strings of his guitar one last time, finishing the song. He then removed his hat and wiped the sweat from his forehead with the back of his hand.

"Who told you to play that song for us?" Threat scowled.

"A smooth talking dude in a snazzy purple suit described how you two brothas looked and gave me your names." The old man went on to tell them. "He asked me did I have any dark songs I could play. I told 'em I sure do. I sung some of the lyrics to that there original piece I just serenaded you young men with and he liked it. Man paid me a $100 dollars and told me to sing it to you."

Threat and Tiaz exchanged glances, realizing who the old man was talking about.

"What was his name? Did he tell you who he was?" Tiaz asked.

The old man lit up the cigarette he removed from his pocket, took a couple puffs then blew out a roar of smoke. Shaking his head *no*, he replied, "Afraid not, gentlemen. The fella dropped a yard on me, described you two and told me to sing that song to you when you came outta this here establishment." He motioned toward the club with the hand he held the cigarette in.

"Majestic?" Bianca said, remembering the name. Threat and Tiaz turned around to her. "While we were dancing he told me his name was Majestic."

The sound of a horn being honked startled everyone and caused them to turn to the street. A limousine was there. Its windows were tinted so dark that you couldn't peer inside. The backseat window slowly rolled down and exposed the face of the man hidden inside.

It was Majestic, and he was smiling sinisterly. Instantly his face morphed into a frown and he squared his jaws, moving to point something out of the window. Tiaz and Threat's eyes bugged and their mouths dropped open. They were frozen with terror and all they could do was wait for the shot that would end one of their lives.

***

Baby Wicked stood before the nightstand mirror practicing drawing his .38 special from his waistline. He'd pull the pistol from his waistline and point it at the mirror. He did this several times, trying to shorten the draw time with every try. He wanted to be swift on the draw when Maniac and Time Bomb came back around. He had to be ready when that beef came his way. He was dealing with killers who were in a league of their own. They'd murdered more men than he could count on the fingers of both of his hands. They'd perfected the art of murder, while he wasn't even a novice. So he had to be on point when the drama jumped off again. He and Te'Qui's lives depended on it.

"How long are you going to keep that up?" Te'Qui asked as he broke down Kush buds upon a Source magazine.

"'Til I'm the fastest gun on the east," Baby Wicked answered. "You need to practice too, since we're going to be trading places back and forth while we're out there."

"I will." Te'Qui sprinkled the Kush inside of the blunt and licked it closed.

"Moms know that you're spending the night?"

"Yeah, she went out to some club with Tiaz and his homie, Threat," he replied, taking a pull from the blunt.

"Here, nigga, you try it." Baby Wicked passed him the .38 and took the blunt from him. He watched Te'Qui practice his drawing while he smoked on the blunt.

They had to be ready for the Avalon's this time, their lives would be at stake.

***

The hospital room was dimly lit. The only sound that could be heard was the TV of the neighboring patient and the machines that kept Ta'shauna Reed alive. With a bullet to the skull the doctors had written her off as a goner but miraculously she survived what should have been a fatal wound. Now she was in a fight, not one you could face with your fists, but one you would with your spirit and determination. After her surgery, the doctor said that it was out of his hands and it was all up to her now. If her will was strong enough, then she could come out of her coma and make a full recovery. If it wasn't then The Reeds would be making funeral arrangements.

When Threat had shot her in the head that day he believed that was the end of her. So for her to survive the fatal blast, shocked him. Now he had to rely on her not making it post surgery, but then there was another thing he wasn't counting on, though. Her will to survive being stronger than her willingness to die.

If Ta'shauna wasn't anything else she was a fighter. She'd been chunking them all of her life. So it wasn't nothing for her to knuckle up and throw down for hers, but this was different. This was the greatest fight of her life against an opponent she didn't see coming. It didn't matter, though, because there wasn't any way in hell she was going out without a fight.

Beep! Beep! Beep!

The heart monitor made its noise as a zig zag green line ran continuously across the screen. There was a stillness and then calmness inside of the room. And then a miracle happened. Ta'shauna's right-hand twitched.

***

Kantrell came down the staircase wearing a crooked grin and looking at her cell phone's screen. She was looking through the naughty pictures that she'd been sending Tiaz that night. After making herself a sandwich and pouring a glass of Ginger ale, she plopped down on the couch and turned on the flat-screen. She picked up the remote control and turned on the Blu-Ray player, activating the movie she was going to watch that night: A Good Day to Die Hard.

She bit into her sandwich just as the previews for other movies began to play, the blue glow of the television flashing across her face.

Meanwhile...

He parked the G-ride around the corner from her house and killed the engine. He placed a neoprene on the lower half of his face and pulled the drawstrings of his hood, closing it around his head. His gloved hand dipped beneath the driver seat and came back up clutching a chrome .45 with a black silencer.

Once he made sure it was locked and loaded, he hopped out of the stolen car and crept up the driveway of the house next door. He hopped the back gate of the house and landed into the backyard of Kantrell's crib. He moved as stealthy as a thief, tip toeing up the steps of the back porch.

Tucking his weapon into the small of his back, he pulled out the pins he'd need to pick the lock. Having gotten the door open, he snuck into the house smiling sinisterly as he withdrew the gun from around his back. When he emerged into the kitchen's doorway he could see the back of Kantrell's head as she watched TV. The living room was dark and the illumination of the television outlined her head.

Yeah, bitch, I told you, you weren't getting away with that shit, he thought as he lifted his weapon to deliver the kill shot.

To Be Continued...
Bury Me A G II
Marked for Death

Submission Guideline

Submit the first three chapters of your completed manuscript to ldpsubmissions@gmail.com, subject line: Your book's title. The manuscript must be in a .doc file and sent as an attachment. Document should be in Times New Roman, double spaced and in size 12 font. Also, provide your synopsis and full contact information. If sending multiple submissions, they must each be in a separate email.

Have a story but no way to send it electronically? You can still submit to LDP/Ca$h Presents. Send in the first three chapters, written or typed, of your completed manuscript to:

LDP: Submissions Dept

Po Box 870494

Mesquite, Tx 75187

DO NOT send original manuscript. Must be a duplicate.

Provide your synopsis and a cover letter containing your full contact information.

Thanks for considering LDP and Ca$h Presents.

Coming Soon from Lock Down Publications/Ca$h Presents

BOW DOWN TO MY GANGSTA

By **Ca$h**

TORN BETWEEN TWO

By **Coffee**

BLOOD STAINS OF A SHOTTA **III**

By **Jamaica**

STEADY MOBBIN **III**

By **Marcellus Allen**

BLOOD OF A BOSS **V**

By **Askari**

LOYAL TO THE GAME **IV**

LIFE OF SIN II

By **T.J. & Jelissa**

Bury Me A G

A DOPEBOY'S PRAYER **II**

By **Eddie "Wolf" Lee**

IF LOVING YOU IS WRONG... **III**

LOVE ME EVEN WHEN IT HURTS **II**

By **Jelissa**

TRUE SAVAGE **VII**

By **Chris Green**

BLAST FOR ME **III**

A BRONX TALE III

DUFFLE BAG CARTEL

By **Ghost**

ADDICTIED TO THE DRAMA **III**

By **Jamila Mathis**

LIPSTICK KILLAH **III**

WHAT BAD BITCHES DO **III**

KILL ZONE **II**

By **Aryanna**

THE COST OF LOYALTY **II**

Tranay Adams

By **Kweli**

SHE FELL IN LOVE WITH A REAL ONE **II**

By **Tamara Butler**

RENEGADE BOYS **III**

By **Meesha**

CORRUPTED BY A GANGSTA **IV**

By **Destiny Skai**

A GANGSTER'S CODE **III**

By **J-Blunt**

KING OF NEW YORK IV

RISE TO POWER II

By **T.J. Edwards**

GORILLAS IN THE BAY II

De'Kari

THE STREETS ARE CALLING II

Duquie Wilson

KINGPIN KILLAZ III

Hood Rich

STEADY MOBBIN' **III**

Marcellus Allen

SINS OF A HUSTLA II

ASAD

CASH MONEY HOES

Nicole Goosby

TRIGGADALE II

Elijah R. Freeman

MARRIED TO A BOSS 2...

By Destiny Skai & Chris Green

Available Now

RESTRAINING ORDER **I & II**

By **CA$H & Coffee**

LOVE KNOWS NO BOUNDARIES **I II & III**

By **Coffee**

RAISED AS A GOON I, II, III & IV

Tranay Adams

BRED BY THE SLUMS I, II, III

BLAST FOR ME I & II

ROTTEN TO THE CORE I III

A BRONX TALE I, II

By **Ghost**

LAY IT DOWN **I & II**

LAST OF A DYING BREED

BLOOD STAINS OF A SHOTTA I & II

By **Jamaica**

LOYAL TO THE GAME

LOYAL TO THE GAME II

LOYAL TO THE GAME III

LIFE OF SIN

By **TJ & Jelissa**

BLOODY COMMAS I & II

SKI MASK CARTEL I II & III

KING OF NEW YORK I II,III

RISE TO POWER

By **T.J. Edwards**

IF LOVING HIM IS WRONG…I & II

LOVE ME EVEN WHEN IT HURTS

By **Jelissa**

WHEN THE STREETS CLAP BACK I & II III

By **Jibril Williams**

A DISTINGUISHED THUG STOLE MY HEART I II & III

LOVE SHOULDN'T HURT I II III

RENEGADE BOYS I & II

By **Meesha**

A GANGSTER'S CODE I & II

By **J-Blunt**

PUSH IT TO THE LIMIT

By **Bre' Hayes**

BLOOD OF A BOSS **I, II, III & IV**

By **Askari**

THE STREETS BLEED MURDER **I, II & III**

Tranay Adams

THE HEART OF A GANGSTA I II& III

By **Jerry Jackson**

CUM FOR ME

CUM FOR ME 2

CUM FOR ME 3

CUM FOR ME 4

An **LDP Erotica Collaboration**

BRIDE OF A HUSTLA **I II & II**

THE FETTI GIRLS **I, II& III**

CORRUPTED BY A GANGSTA I, II & III

By **Destiny Skai**

WHEN A GOOD GIRL GOES BAD

By **Adrienne**

A GANGSTER'S REVENGE **I II III & IV**

THE BOSS MAN'S DAUGHTERS

THE BOSS MAN'S DAUGHTERS II

THE BOSSMAN'S DAUGHTERS III

THE BOSSMAN'S DAUGHTERS IV

Bury Me A G

THE BOSS MAN'S DAUGHTERS **V**

A SAVAGE LOVE **I & II**

BAE BELONGS TO ME

A HUSTLER'S DECEIT I, II

WHAT BAD BITCHES DO I, II

By **Aryanna**

A KINGPIN'S AMBITON

A KINGPIN'S AMBITION **II**

I MURDER FOR THE DOUGH

By **Ambitious**

TRUE SAVAGE

TRUE SAVAGE II

TRUE SAVAGE **III**

TRUE SAVAGE **IV**

TRUE SAVAGE **V**

TRUE SAVAGE **VI**

By **Chris Green**

A DOPEBOY'S PRAYER

Tranay Adams

By **Eddie "Wolf" Lee**

THE KING CARTEL **I, II & III**

By **Frank Gresham**

THESE NIGGAS AIN'T LOYAL **I, II & III**

By **Nikki Tee**

GANGSTA SHYT **I II &III**

By **CATO**

THE ULTIMATE BETRAYAL

By **Phoenix**

BOSS'N UP **I , II & III**

By **Royal Nicole**

I LOVE YOU TO DEATH

By Destiny J

I RIDE FOR MY HITTA

I STILL RIDE FOR MY HITTA

By **Misty Holt**

LOVE & CHASIN' PAPER

By **Qay Crockett**

TO DIE IN VAIN

SINS OF A HUSTLA

By **ASAD**

BROOKLYN HUSTLAZ

By **Boogsy Morina**

BROOKLYN ON LOCK I & II

By **Sonovia**

GANGSTA CITY

By **Teddy Duke**

A DRUG KING AND HIS DIAMOND I & II III

A DOPEMAN'S RICHES

HER MAN, MINE'S TOO I, II

By Nicole Goosby

TRAPHOUSE KING **I II & III**

KINGPIN KILLAZ

By **Hood Rich**

LIPSTICK KILLAH **I, II**

CRIME OF PASSION I & II

Tranay Adams

By **Mimi**

STEADY MOBBN' **I, II**

By **Marcellus Allen**

WHO SHOT YA **I, II**

Renta

GORILLAZ IN THE BAY

DE'KARI

TRIGGADALE

Elijah R. Freeman

GOD BLESS THE TRAPPERS I, II, III

THESE SCANDALOUS STREETS I, II, III

FEAR MY GANGSTA I, II, III

THESE STREETS DON'T LOVE NOBODY I, II

Tranay Adams

THE STREETS ARE CALLING

Duquie Wilson

MARRIED TO A BOSS…

By **Destiny Skai & Chris Green**

Bury Me A G

Tranay Adams

BOOKS BY LDP'S CEO, CA$H

TRUST IN NO MAN

TRUST IN NO MAN 2

TRUST IN NO MAN 3

BONDED BY BLOOD

SHORTY GOT A THUG

THUGS CRY

THUGS CRY 2

THUGS CRY 3

TRUST NO BITCH

TRUST NO BITCH 2

TRUST NO BITCH 3

TIL MY CASKET DROPS

RESTRAINING ORDER

RESTRAINING ORDER 2

IN LOVE WITH A CONVICT

Tranay Adams

<u>Coming Soon</u>

BONDED BY BLOOD 2

BOW DOWN TO MY GANGSTA

Bury Me A G